LATIN AMER
4405 EAST-
BETHESDA, M

Coronation

Coronation

JOSÉ DONOSO

Translated from the Spanish
by JOCASTA GOODWIN

NEW YORK

ALFRED A. KNOPF

1965

L. C. *catalog card number: 64-11416*

THIS IS A BORZOI BOOK,
PUBLISHED BY ALFRED A. KNOPF, INC.

FIRST AMERICAN EDITION

Originally published in Spanish by Editorial Nascimento, Santiago, Chile, in 1957 as *Coronación*

FOR

Carmen Orrego Montes

PART ONE

The Gift

1 🜚 Rosario stood holding the door open while the boy leaned his bicycle against the steps leading up from the garden to the kitchen. He went in, panting under the weight of his basket, which was crammed with bottles, jars, packets of noodles and vegetables. He dumped the load on the marble-topped table, emptied it methodically, and then stood staring into the steam rising from a pot on the stove. Rosario guessed that something must have gone wrong, for he had dropped the jerky, flustered movements which always reminded her of a little black darting beetle. Possibly he wanted to ask a favor, or was about to confide some secret to her. The cook, who was normally dour and unbending, liked him best of all the delivery boys from the Fornino Emporium. He was the only one who seemed to respect the ties between herself and the store. Although she had been a widow for years now, nothing flattered Rosario more than to have her connection with that prestigious institution recognized. Her late husband, Fructuoso Arenas, had worked there before marrying her and taking a job as gardener with Misiá Elisa Grey de Abalos.

"What's the matter, Angel?"

Angel stared glumly around the vast kitchen, his eyes lingering over the fleet of bottles and pans drawn up in immaculate array along the shelves.

"Don Segundo is after me," he said.

"You must have been making trouble again, Angel . . ."

"It's not that, Señora Rosario. Anyway, the other boys stir things up just as much as I do. He's just got it in for me. And the only reason is that I'm Mario's friend. You know Mario—he's that big ox with a gold watch."

"Yes, I know him, and what I know I don't like. He's a bad character, that one, not a shred of respect for anyone. But why should Segundo be after you then? You should be more careful . . ."

"Well, it's because they caught him with a package the other day which should have been delivered to the old lady in 213. I *told* Mario not to take it, I don't go for that kind of thing, but anyway, they caught him and now Don Segundo wants to throw him out for stealing . . . and me too, because I'm his friend."

Angel's voice trailed off to a despondent murmur. Suddenly he glanced up at Rosario, blinking as if to fight back the tears.

"Why don't *you* speak to Don Segundo?" he asked her. "They think a lot of you at the Emporium. I just don't know what my old lady will do if I get thrown out of the place . . ."

Rosario's answer was prompt and decisive.

"All right, then. Segundo will have to listen to what I say. After all, it was only through my Fructuoso he got that job at the Emporium in the first place."

Angel's spirits seemed revived by this. He shook back the lock of black hair that had fallen over his forehead. They arranged that he should come back in a day or two to find out the outcome of Rosario's interview with Don Segundo. He said goodbye and then bounded lightheartedly down the

steps to get his bicycle, which he wheeled along the gravel
path, giving Don Andrés Abalos a quick nod as he passed
close by where he was lying stretched out in a ramshackle
wicker garden chair. Then he pushed open the wrought-iron
gate and cycled off down the street.

Don Andrés had been sitting in the green shade of the
lime tree for more than a quarter of an hour, trying to rouse
himself sufficiently to open the newspaper that lay folded
across his knees. The necessity of making some kind of
reply to the boy's greeting, even if only a slight nod, prevented him from lapsing into complete lethargy. He yawned
and stretched his arms and long legs encased in the neat
gray trousers appropriate to a man of his age and position.
A sound almost like a purr came from his throat. It was
as if his whole body were creaking with pleasant drowsiness.
He felt tugging at his consciousness a faint, barely perceptible impulse to unfold those virgin pages, with their
fragrance of printer's ink, but contentedly allowed it to sub-
side and did not move. It was that glass of wine to which
he had succumbed after dessert which was responsible.
Rosario's puddings were so delectable, such apparently in-
substantial confections, that it was all too easy to let oneself
be tempted into eating dish after dish. And then of course
one would want a glass of wine to round off the meal, and
the upshot of it all was that even the slightest physical
exertion proved unthinkable for at least an hour afterwards.

Fortunately no exertion was required of him as he lay
becalmed in this island of scented shade with its faint
susurrus of tiny sounds—the flight of insects and the almost imperceptible rustling of young leaves and tender new
shoots. He need only leave open the smallest chink in his
senses to be inundated with the radiance of the atmosphere
and the light which spangled his brightly polished shoes as
it streamed down through the branches. At that hour the

temperature was precisely right in his grandmother's quiet garden.

Of course the house and its occupants were old and forgotten now, but owing perhaps to that glass of wine he had drunk or the warmth of the sun against the front of the house, Don Andrés found no difficulty in dispelling such melancholy reflections. The house where Misiá Elisa Grey de Abalos lived with her two elderly maids, Lourdes and Rosario, was a sort of chalet decorated with ornamental balconies, wooden cutouts, and little flights of steps. It stood in a large damp garden, and there was a palm tree on either side of the front entrance. A third story was hidden from sight by an improbable-looking conglomeration of gables and little crenelated turrets and decorative carvings in profusion. The house had one serious defect—its site had been so ineptly chosen that it only got a few hours of sunshine each day. The sun rose behind it in the morning and the long shadow of a nearby hill lay across it by early afternoon. Once upon a time the front of the house would have been painted every year on or around the eighteenth of September, like the roses, white below and red at the tips. But there were scarcely any rosebushes left now, and everything was growing old and neglected. Two or three cats were in the habit of sunning themselves around the stone urn at the foot of the steps, but they could no longer sharpen their claws on the cactus in it because the plant had withered long ago, withered or rotted or been eaten by worms. Chickens were always invading the garden, and one would see them pecking and clucking their way along the shell-strewn paths whose dwarf-box borders had been kept so neatly clipped while Fructuoso was alive. But Fructuoso had died a good fifteen years ago, and since then, out of consideration for his widow perhaps, no one had gotten around to hiring another gardener. What was the use? The years had slipped away and now it no longer seemed worth bothering about. It was ten years or more since Misiá Elisa had last left her room, and these days she hardly ever got out of bed, even on the only occasions when she received visitors—her birthday and her saint's day. Not that she had many visitors nowadays, even on these important occasions. In fact, except for Dr. Gros, the nonagenarian's personal physician, and a few old ladies who dropped in uninvited with their sticks and cameos, the only people who came into the house were the delivery boys who brought the groceries by bicycle from the Fornino Emporium.

Don Andrés told himself that he really must pull himself together and unfold his newspaper. The nearest he got to it, though, was smoothing his bald patch with both hands and then clasping them over the small paunch which years of sedentary life had deposited below his waistline. Lourdes often tried to console him for the unfortunate distribution of these excess pounds by assuring him that corpulence was a mark of beauty. Looking at the tiny maid's unnatural girth, however, Don Andrés was not convinced.

His comfortable financial situation, which exacted nothing more arduous from him than signing a few odd papers from time to time, had preserved him from ever having to work for a living, and his reclusive, bookish temperament had, with an equally slight expenditure of effort on his part, protected him from all the more squalid vicissitudes of everyday life. Except for this modest paunch of his, which bespoke a fondness for the pleasures of the table, his fifty-odd years had dealt kindly with him. Perched on a neck that was still firmly muscled beneath a little loose skin, his face kept all its former clarity of outline. His high-bridged nose and impressively sculpted chin remained untouched by time, and there was a humorous gleam in the faded blue eyes behind his glasses. There might not be many pleasures in

his life, but those there were, chosen with all the freedom
which his temperament and situation allowed him, were by
no means negligible. They consisted of studying French
history, adding to his collection of walking sticks, and keeping up to date on the events that shaped the country's
internal politics, the last of which provided endless discussions at the Union Club with the few and, alas, un-
deniably tedious friends who remained to him.

Don Andrés could not remember his grandmother's house
without Lourdes and Rosario. Of the two he liked Lourdes
best. He always felt that Rosario, for all her inimitable
desserts, was much too much the alchemist, with little time
or patience for anything but delving into mysterious secrets
in the laboratory of her spotless kitchen. Moreover, it was
Rosario who ordered the weekly groceries from the Emporium, and this link with the outside world and with her
conjugal past only added to her steadily increasing sense of
importance, to which the severe line of her upper lip and
aggressive virago's moustache bore witness.

Since Lourdes had never had any contact with the outside world to speak of and her position in the household
was neither taxing nor well defined, the Abalos family
had gradually come to absorb all her interest. She was a
mine of information about distant relations, dates of birth,
who had married whom, when, where, and why. As Andrés
often found it impossible to maintain even a semblance of
composure in his dealings with his grandmother, he tended
to spend a good part of the one afternoon a week he reserved for these visits chatting to Lourdes. Lourdes, with
the officious, slightly impertinent familiarity of an old re-
tainer, never failed to scold him for not having married or
admonish him for leading what, in a bachelor of his means
and independence, could only be a licentious existence.
Andrés always blushed. He had been blushing like this for

years, too embarrassed to do more than remonstrate gently.

"You must be out of your mind, Lourdes. Whatever put such thoughts into your head?"

But Lourdes would only shake her head sadly, not believing a word.

Lourdes took a month's vacation each summer and spent it at the house of her brother-in-law, who was a tenant farmer on a large estate in the vineyard country. But the forty-odd years she had spent working for Misiá Elisa had accustomed her to big-city life, even though she never left the house, and she soon began to feel homesick for the pampered urban ways of Santiago. Also, she invariably wore herself out sharing in the work of the farm in spite of her relatives' protests. And then the miserable cottage they lived in got her down. Thus her month's vacation rarely lasted more than two or three weeks.

· So it had been no surprise to anyone when a telegram had arrived from Lourdes a few days before, announcing her intention of returning that very afternoon. Although Don Andrés had already paid his grandmother his weekly visit, he returned to welcome Lourdes back. He looked at his watch. Allowing for the time it took to get to the house by taxi from the station, there were at most five minutes to go before she arrived.

He gave a sigh of relief. Lourdes would soon be back, and what was more, she was bringing a girl with her to look after Misiá Elisa. The old lady's nurses did not last long as a rule; they usually left in a fury, shaken and humiliated by the unpleasant shocks this apparently harmless patient held in store for them. The last incumbent had thrown up the job after only two months, just a week before Lourdes set off on her annual vacation. This alarming development meant that her vacation had acquired a specific purpose, to remind her brother-in-law of his wife's promise on her death-

bed that her youngest daughter, Estela, was to be left in
her care. Now that Estela was seventeen, Lourdes felt justi-
fied in making use of her in this emergency. Misiá Elisa
would not be so alarming once the girl arrived on the scene.
At any rate for a while, till she, like all the rest, left in despair, letting the burden of responsibility for his grandmother
fall back on his shoulders—which were beginning to weary
of it.

All the same, Don Andrés could not deny that the one
afternoon a week he spent with the invalid in the big damp
house had come to mean a lot to him and brought him something of value which he did not find in his usual way of life.
It was almost as if he felt grateful to this one surviving
relative for causing him genuine anxiety and an inordinate
distress and suffering. The old woman was an absurd,
immensely precarious link between himself and the emotional
facts of life. She was the only link he had. Until she died
he would not be forced to face up to the fact of his utter
solitude. One good thing about Misiá Elisa's long illness
was that it had helped him learn to contemplate that day,
which could not be far off, with only mild distress.

At precisely the moment when Andrés finally decided to
open his newspaper, in the hope that it would help banish
these unpleasant thoughts from his mind, a taxi stopped
outside in the street and Lourdes got out, followed by a
girl who could be none other than Estela. They came into
the garden laden with bundles, baskets, packages, and
flowers.

"How well you look, Lourdes!" Don Andrés cried as they
came near. "Absolutely blooming! Why, you don't look a
day over fifteen!"

"Oh, Don Andrés! How my back aches from all that
sitting—I'm getting too old for jogging about . . ."

The two women put their things down on the ground.

Estela lingered behind her aunt, almost as if trying to hide. It was five in the afternoon. The shadow cast by the nearby hill was stealing across the garden and had almost reached the spot where they were standing.

"Come," Lourdes spoke to her niece. "I want to present you to Don Andrés."

Estela greeted him briefly and unsmilingly, scarcely raising her eyes from her large, new shoes. She addressed him as *patrón*. *Patrón*! That really was the limit, he thought, in this day and age and in a civilized country! And the irony of it was, his cronies at the club thought him a shade too democratic, if anything, a fact he was inordinately proud of.

The girl's appearance was not prepossessing, he decided. Still, after a closer look, he came to the conclusion that it would be silly to expect more of a little peasant girl. She was strong, well built, and a curious warm, opaque coppery shade all over, which extended without shading or highlights over her full lips, rather high cheekbones, roughened hands, and downcast lids whose thick lashes hid dark, slanting, glistening hollows. Don Andrés noticed that the backs of her hands were the same coppery shade, but the palms were several shades lighter, and pinkish, almost as if they were more naked than the rest of her body. A shiver of distaste ran up his spine. Still, the poor girl's appearance would be enormously improved in a maid's white apron. Perhaps, in her own way, she might even be passably pretty.

"Can you read?"

"Yes, *patrón*."

"Of course she can! You can't beat country people," Lourdes answered, beaming till her eyes dwindled to two delighted spots behind the glasses which constantly slid down her tiny nose.

Don Andrés went through the prescribed questions to

prove to himself as much as to Estela that he was no less
human and no less concerned for his employees' welfare for
being *patrón* here. Would she be happy in Santiago? Would
she find it hard to get used to city life? Wouldn't she miss
her family and friends? He hoped she would stay a long
time and be happy looking after the invalid. When he
informed her what her salary would be, the girl's face
remained impassive, but somewhere in that hermetic counte-
nance he thought he detected the ghost of a smile.

"Take her inside and get her settled," Andrés said.

Lourdes set off in the direction of the kitchen, followed
by her niece laden with baskets and bundles.

Andrés unfolded his paper with a sigh of contentment.
It was a great relief to know that the proper person to care
for his grandmother had at last been found. Someone to
whom he need not explain the tragic situation—because to
do so would only bewilder her. He sensed in this girl all the
traditional capacity of a peasant for dumb endurance, the
unquestioning submission to the realities of a situation, however harsh. Because of this, she would not suffer as the other
nurses had. Estela was too primitive a being, her ego was
still quite amorphous. But she would benefit from innumerable advantages, simple country girl that she was. Yes, she
was uniquely suited to the job, infinitely more so than all the
other women, including nuns, who had tried their hands at
it without success in the past few years.

Rosario and Lourdes were the only people who could put
up with Misiá Elisa, and even they avoided going into her
room more than they had to during one of her bad spells.
Strictly speaking, they were no longer servants, for Grandfather Abalos had left them both handsome legacies on
condition that they remain with his wife till her death. This
stipulation had proved unnecessary, as things turned out:
both of them would have stayed on anyway, legacy or no

legacy. Their whole world consisted of the corpse of a
family, and its traditions, represented by Misiá Elisa.

Perhaps having someone young near her might help to
alleviate his grandmother's anguish, that smoldering hate,
that diabolical force which drove her to spit obscene, gutter insults at everyone. Luckily the poor woman was not
always in such a state. There were spans of hours, days,
even weeks when the manic frenzy and exaltation were
replaced by serenity and peace.

But these intervals of calm seemed a pitiful consolation
when Andrés thought of his grandmother as she had once
been. She had been so gracious then, so quiet and so clever.
The whole house breathed serenity in those days; everything she touched seemed to take on new significance and
harmony. And she had been so beautiful! Her Anglo-Saxon
blood showed in the fairness of her skin and hair, in the
almost excessive refinement of her features, and also in a
certain suggestion of a captive bird, which became more and
more accentuated with the years until at last senility obliter-
ated all traces of individuality from her face, leaving only
the ridge of an arrogant nose and a certain peculiar fixity in
her mad, staring eyes.

The affliction from which she suffered had crept up on
her over the years, so many years that his memories of
a perfect, irreproachable grandmother went far back to
Andrés's early youth. He had been seventeen when he first
noticed, on that now crumbling stone bench, a symptom of
the malady that was finally to destroy her reason.

Andrés remembered that particular spring as one of the
most prodigal and radiant he had ever known. The light
had seemed almost palpable as it streamed through the
acacias and lime trees and lay in green clusters about the
lawn. Grandfather Ramón, stout and florid, had just finished
setting up his camera and tripod near a tangle of shrubs

that had recently burst into bloom, hoping to make use of
the last hour of sunshine, before the garden was shadowed
by the neighboring hill, to photograph his wife. His grandfather's moustaches curved like handlebars on a bicycle,
and he wore an alpaca jacket and a straw boater. Andrés
had parted his hair carefully in the middle, and Lourdes had
placed a yellow rose in his buttonhole.

"Ready!" Don Ramón called out. "Now run and find Elisa
and tell her we are waiting for her!"

His grandfather's voice, usually sonorous and majestic,
as became an eminent lawyer and parliamentarian, betrayed
a spark of enthusiasm. Photography was his latest craze. He
kept putting on and taking off his pince-nez, which hung
from a cord around his neck. He plunged under the camera's
black hood and pulled its snout in and out as if it were an
accordion, advised at every step in this operation by Andrés.
Finally the boy made his way to the verandah where his
grandmother was waiting, rocking herself to and fro in her
Viennese bentwood chair in the midst of a veritable jungle
of ferns, dwarf palms, begonias, and great pots planted
with thickets of bamboo. When she saw her grandson coming, she smiled and put up her parasol, and she said:

"Are we ready, then? Shall we go?"

⸮ If his grandfather's passion was taking photographs, his
grandmother's was posing for them. Whenever Don Ramón
announced a photographic session, his wife would spend the
whole afternoon trying on clothes, each outfit more dazzling
than the last, in order to select the one which best set off
her beauty. As time passed, her vanity was becoming
puerile.

Grandfather stood waiting for them beside the camera,
fanning himself with his straw boater. His wife took her
seat on the stone bench—carved to look like twisted tree
trunks—and the full skirt of her lilac dress billowed out

around her as she bent forward from the waist, with both hands resting on the handle of her parasol.

"In profile, Elisa, yes, that's good. But don't let the brim of your hat shadow your face. Yes, now, that's it!" Don Ramón exclaimed. He set his pince-nez on his nose, took off his boater and handed it to Andrés, and plunged his head under the black hood. "Now don't move, my dear . . . Click! There!"

He straightened up and asked Andrés for his hat. He always took great care not to let his bald patch catch the sun. While he changed the plate, he remarked:

"That ought to turn out very well! The light is just right, and I like that pose. I'll have it developed, and next week we can see it in the stereoscope. It's a pity you decided on that hat, though. There's something peculiar about it . . . it seems too small, or as if half the feathers were missing."

At this, Misiá Elisa rose suddenly, her face tense, and ran toward the house. Andrés followed her to the verandah, where she had collapsed into the rocking chair, flinging her hat on the floor.

"What's the matter, Grandma? Don't you feel well?"

She sighed and covered her face with her hands.

"Can I get you something?"

"No, thank you, dear. Go, go help Ramón."

"No. Something's wrong . . ."

There was a short but ominous silence. Then, turning her blue gaze on Andrés, she cried:

"All they ever think about is humiliating me! I can't imagine what they get out of it . . ."

She might have been talking to herself. A strange expression had come into her eyes, a look at once intense and remote.

"Humiliating you?" Andrés asked, puzzled.

"Do you really suppose Ramón isn't in league with those sluts? I know just what's going on, don't think I miss anything . . ."

"But what sluts, Grandma?"

"Oh, then you're in with them too! I would never have thought it of you! Your poor parents, may God keep them, could not have loved you more than I do. And you a monster, too! I don't understand why they've all changed toward me, especially Ramón. What have I done to him? I could forgive him anything, anything. But the way he went on about the feathers . . . that was too cruel!"

"Feathers? What feathers? What's wrong with you, Grandma? You must be out of your mind!"

Misiá Elisa jumped to her feet and pierced Andrés with a look of intense hatred.

"Bastard! You, too?" she cried.

Then she swept into the house and slammed the door. Andrés ran to tell his grandfather what had happened. The old gentleman was stowing away his photographic apparatus in tin boxes painted black inside. He told his grandson not to worry, not to let a trivial incident like that upset him. It was all part of the morbid fancies women indulged in at a certain age, when they realized they would not always be . . . well, young and lovely. This brought on all sorts of absurd scenes on the slightest of pretexts, or sometimes on no pretext at all. But they soon passed. The most disquieting thing about the whole business, really, was that afterwards Elisa would have absolutely no recollection of what she had said or done until weeks or months later, when she made another scene.

"What about the feathers, then?"

Smoothing his moustache thoughtfully, Don Ramón led his grandson to a bench, where they sat down in the shadow of the hill.

"Not long ago your grandmother got it into her head that Lourdes and Rosario, who as you know are angels of virtue, both of them, were stealing the ostrich feathers off her French hats to decorate their own for their days off. You've seen them. As if they ever wear anything more elaborate than a shawl to go out."

Andrés could not believe his ears. Don Ramón explained that he had gone into the whole matter very thoroughly, taking great care not to hurt the maids' feelings, of course, and he had finally convinced himself that these accusations of his wife's were simply fantasies. But that was not all. Elisa had gradually become convinced that both women were leading lives of scandalous immorality and she invented incidents and details to corroborate their viciousness. Finally, one evening, she had insulted them openly, calling them whores and thieves. It had taken all his powers of persuasion to pacify the poor creatures and staunch their torrents of tears. Elisa, however, still maintained that they were stealing from her, her feathers especially. And then, quite innocently, he had to go and mention those feathers! His wife was always losing things, he added, things of no particular value or importance—combs, for instance, or gloves, or handkerchiefs—and then she would blame Lourdes and Rosario for stealing them. Still, fortunately these incidents occurred only once in a while.

His grandfather's explanation astounded Andrés, who had noticed nothing. He decided to keep his eyes open in the future and watch for symptoms. This proved all too easy: it was during the following year that everything that had lain hidden under apparent harmony finally erupted into the open. The house was no longer peaceful. Each time there was a scene, it was worse than before. Misiá Elisa's vocabulary, which had never alluded to even the basic needs of the human body except in French, and then as if by accident, suddenly became obscene, virulent, desperate. Her husband racked his brains, wondering where she could have learned such words. But it was not just her vocabulary that had changed. Her imagination defiled everything it touched on, and she charged the whole world with disgusting immorality and the most abominable sexual excesses. It was as if Misiá Elisa's field of vision had been obscured by a cloud of filth which prevented things from growing straight, depriving them of light and air and poisoning everything natural and simple at the roots. Since Lourdes and Rosario had the most to do with her, it was on them that she vented most of her venom. She persisted in accusing them, among other things, of stealing everything she had. She almost died of anguish when she discovered that one of the tortoise-shell pins she used to fasten her noticeably graying blonde chignon was missing.

At first the maids, at each new outburst, threatened to give notice. But every time Don Ramón's persuasive tongue would smooth things over and make light of the incidents, and the women would eventually be persuaded to stay. They were particularly grateful to Don Ramón and his grandson for venturing to defend them: this only made the scenes and outrages worse, and in no time the mistress was accusing them of loving the servants more than they loved her.

Ten years or so later, it became evident that Misiá Elisa's illness was grave. The house, once filled with the quiet murmur of voices, footsteps muffled by thick carpets, doors closed softly, now reechoed with the shrieks of Misiá Elisita (as the servants still called her), and her hysterical berating of everyone around her, particularly her husband. She found wounding and humiliating intentions in his most trivial remarks, and hounded him relentlessly night and day.

Andrés once listened horrified while his grandmother attacked her husband because, she said, he was sorry he had

married her. She accused him of despising her because her
parents were foreigners. He did not realize that she came
of a much more distinguished and aristocratic stock than he
did. Her family, she claimed, was related to all the crowned
heads in Europe.

"This obsession with her blue blood is appalling," Don
Ramón confided to his grandson. "It's the most intolerable
of all her claims simply because it's so ridiculous. The odd
thing is, she never once mentioned it before: it must go
back to some secret grievance she has been nursing all her
life, which only comes to light now that her self-control has
broken down. What can have given her this ludicrous
mania for grandees and titles? Her father was a fairly
wealthy English businessman in Valparaíso, a sound, respectable gentleman and a well-known clubman, but there
was never any talk about family trees. And even if there
was, it can only have been old wives' tales. When I married
her it seemed the most natural thing in the world. No one
criticized the match or looked down on her or said that I
had made a bad marriage, as Elisa now claims they all did.
And as for this talk, talk, talk all day long about her connections with kings and dukes and princes and heaven
knows what else! And reading me every tidbit she can find
about European royalty in those magazines she makes me
get her . . . it's absurd! She talks about nothing else but
these idiocies now! She's driving me mad too . . ."

"Is my grandma mad?"

"Cerebral arteriosclerosis, according to the doctors. It
started very early. She is still more manic than lunatic,
but it will go on getting worse. Everything she has kept
hidden all these years, out of fear or shame or insecurity,
erupts into her life once the conscious censor is relaxed,
and peoples it with these fantasmal presences . . ."

Don Ramón's parliamentary rhetoric had always im-

pressed Andrés, as if the clarity of his grandfather's mind
were shoring up a world that threatened to fall apart. But
as the years passed, Andrés came to realize that this
lucidity was not invulnerable. In fact, it was so fragile that
in the clash with his wife's madness his reason was the first
to give. Don Ramón Abalos, whose character and conduct
had always been universally respected, as had his exceptionally acute intelligence, was slowly deteriorating. He
grew gloomy and irritable, and spent more and more of his
time at the club. This in itself was enough to expose him
to the most appalling scenes and quarrels. He paid very
little attention to his appearance, and none at all to his profession. Oddly enough, when Lourdes and Rosario discovered that Don Ramón was keeping a mistress, their
attitude toward him changed completely. They scarcely even
spoke to him. Secretly they blamed him for being the cause
of poor Misiá Elisita's illness.

Don Ramón died when his wife was almost sixty. Toward
the end, the poor old man had been reduced to a mere
shadow. He would fly into a rage at the slightest provoca-
tion, he often did not return home for weeks on end, and
when he did he would retreat behind some book which
he propped on the lectern of his armchair in the library and
did not even pretend to read.

Those who had not been on intimate terms with Don
Ramón knew so little about his widow's mental state that
when she suggested traveling in Europe for several months,
the doctors made no objection. Their one stipulation was
that she should take a companion with her. The companion
returned to Chile after only a few months, in a fury, leaving
Misiá Elisa to continue by herself.

Andrés, meanwhile, had taken advantage of this interlude
to establish his independence. It was impossible to go on
living in his grandmother's house. He had a right to lead

his own life, a man's life, and find new friends and surroundings. He took a bachelor apartment, which he filled
with books, his collection of walking sticks, and the quiet
life he led. When his grandmother returned to Chile, there
were bitter quarrels about his move: she accused him of
selfishness. Andrés was often on the verge of giving in to
her, but he finally overcame the stirrings of compassion,
which would have destroyed him in the end.

Misiá Elisa's condition grew worse with time. She no
longer shrieked and screamed. Instead, she hissed out
monstrous insults at everyone, even the shadows that glided
across her bedroom walls. She had not left her bedroom once
since her seventieth birthday, and she was now almost
permanently bedridden.

Sometimes, as one of the boys from the Fornino Emporium bicycled up to the house, he would catch sight of
the old woman's white face between the curtains of one of
the second-floor windows, staring out into the light and air.
She did not seem to notice the passage of time, or the birds,
which hung motionless as though cast in metal among the
leafy branches of the trees she had herself planted over half
a century before.

2   It was clear that only she, Rosario Candia,
widow of Arenas, could get this affair straightened out. She
was not going to stand by while that monster Segundo, who
owed his present position to Fructuoso anyway, gave poor
Angel the sack for no better reason than that he liked
throwing his weight around. It was no good them thinking

they could pull the wool over her eyes. After all, she had
known the Forninos in the days when they were nobodies
and their store was just a little place on the corner like
hundreds of others, where Don Narciso chatted away in his
incomprehensible jargon to all the maid servants in the dis-
trict, just as if he were one of them, and his wife was kept
busy shooing off the cats who dozed on the cool piles of
lettuce in the summer heat. Now that one of Don Narciso's
nephews had modernized the place and made it into an important and flourishing business, Segundo, of course, felt
he had a right to look down on absolutely everyone. That
was why he wanted to get rid of Angel—oh no, he didn't
fool her! Well, she would bring him to his senses, and he
wouldn't be able to brush *her* off! It was true that none of
the Forninos greeted her or shook hands with her when she
went shopping at the Emporium nowadays, but that was
because Segundo was the only person there who knew who
she was. But Segundo Garcia needn't fool himself; she
wasn't afraid of him . . .

Rosario had not been out of the house once since Lourdes
left on her vacation a month before, and she was beginning
to feel the urge to make a little trip to the Emporium. She
took off her apron and picked up her purse, just in case.
She always thought of the just-in-case side of things, unlike
Lourdes, who was always caught unprepared. She had been
like that all her life, poor thing!

A tall, broad-shouldered figure, the cook marched toward
the little square in front of the Emporium. Several people
greeted her, the adults respectfully and the children a little
fearfully. And not without reason. She had a long horse-
face, dark and furrowed like old unvarnished wood. Her
only concession to personal adornment was the knot of hair
coiled at the nape of her neck.

In the old days, when Rosario and Fructuoso were newlyweds, they had often invited Segundo to dinner at the Abalos house. Sometimes they would stay up till two in the warm kitchen, with its smell of spices and condiments and exotic aromatic tisanes, talking over recent events at the Emporium and everything that happened in the Abalos and the Fornino households. Although Lourdes rarely went to the Emporium, she began to take a great interest in it and everything about it. She asked all sorts of detailed questions about the merchandise and the Fornino family's connections, and it was soon apparent that she was disposed to marry Segundo. But, as they were both timid, the subject was never brought up between them. Rosario was of the opinion that Segundo did not speak to Lourdes because he was a pig, as Misiá Elisita said all men were. Anyway, it soon became clear that whatever Segundo's more serious plans might be, they did not include Lourdes. After Rosario's husband died, the only dealings they had with him was the weekly telephone call to order the groceries.

Rosario was crossing the square when she caught sight of Angel and Mario sitting quietly on a bench behind some shrubs, eating grapes, which they fished out of a newspaper cone. Mario, who was sturdy and long-limbed, was sprawled out with his arms along the back of the bench, looking as if he did not have a care in the world. He had a bush of chestnut hair, one lock of which hung loose over his forehead.

"They chucked us out, Señora Rosario, they chucked us out," Mario said when he saw her.

"What are you doing here then?"

Angel hung his head, shamefaced and frowning.

"How can I go home like this? My old lady wasn't able to go out washing this week, and now I'm out of a job . . ."

"What's the difference, man, what's the difference?" Mario said. "This . . . coward here has been sitting around like this all morning, refusing to budge. I keep telling him we ought to try to pick up a bite of something around here somewhere . . . fill our bellies at least. . . . Come on, don't be a fool . . . let's go . . ."

As he talked, the sun danced in his brown eyes.

"Let him think if he wants to, and stop being so nasty," Rosario snapped. "Instead of trying to help, all you do is make things worse for him. It's because of you they threw him out, isn't it. You're the thief. . . ."

At this, Mario jumped to his feet, his eyes no longer sunny.

"Me? I'm the thief?"

Rosario was about to repeat her remark when Angel interrupted hastily and apprehensively.

"Please go away now, Señora Rosario, please . . ."

"Oh, no, you're not getting off so easily," Mario said. "What have you been saying about me, you little bastard?" The shadows in the depth of his eyes were sharp and menacing.

"Nothing . . ." Angel answered weakly.

"That you are a thief, and you'd better watch out," Rosario interrupted.

Mario gave Angel a furious punch, which almost knocked him off the bench.

"Me? *I'm* a thief? You miserable little shit! Who was it who never delivered the extra package that went with the order from 213, eh? Tell me . . . who gave it to me to hide so that when I was caught and I wouldn't tell who had taken it, they chucked me out, eh? Eh? Tell me . . ."

He was standing now. He had square shoulders and firm, narrow thighs. He was about to grab Angel and hit him when Rosario took hold of his sweater and stopped him.

"Now, now, look here . . . he's smaller than you are, don't hit him, don't be a coward . . ."

"So I'm a thief, am I?" Mario growled at Angel. "They may have pinched me all right, but it isn't me who's a thief, it's *you*! I never stole anything. Leave me alone, Señora," he turned to Rosario, who was hitting him with her purse. "Leave me alone! I'm not going to hurt this creep. I'm not a thief, and I've never been one. You're the thief, get that? And now get moving if you don't want me to knock the piss out of you . . . Come on, get moving . . . beat it!"

Angel stood up. He put his hands in his pockets and hurried off, looking as if he would like to break into a run but was afraid to. Still furious, Mario watched him till he vanished around the corner. Then he sat down. He seemed to have forgotten that Rosario was still standing there. He started muttering to himself and twisting the gold watch around on his wrist.

"It's my fault, I suppose . . . but he shouldn't go around saying things like that . . . it's all a man's got, his reputation . . ."

Rosario shot him a surprised glance, as if she were seeing him for the first time.

"Why . . . that's just what my poor Fructuoso used to say!"

How mistaken she had been about Mario! He was a fine boy, polite and everything. And he had the same views as Fructuoso! That Angel was as worthless as a dead fly. How disillusioning though. . . . She was too good-hearted, that was the trouble, it misled her sometimes. Now she really must hurry and tell Segundo what had really happened. She would make him take the poor boy back . . . even if it meant dragging old Don Narciso out of his grave to do it!

". . . and then like a fool I wouldn't tell Don Segundo anything, and got thrown out as a reward for behaving like a man!" Mario murmured. "We'll see if someone doesn't let him down, though! He's such a cry-baby, that Angel, he gets out of trouble by making a scene and crying! The rest of us have troubles too, but we don't go around beefing about them all the time! And to think I took him to the movies when he couldn't raise the cash. . . . I was broke too, but a friend of mine takes the tickets in the balcony at the Baquedano and he let us in . . ."

He was talking away wildly, as if working the poison out of his system. As he talked, his anger seemed to cool. Soon he was back in the same indolent, sprawling attitude Rosario had first found him in and the light was beginning to sparkle again in the depths of his tawny eyes.

"Listen, Mario, I'm going straight over to tell Segundo what really did happen. He's a friend of mine, and they always listen to me in the Emporium. Come around to the house tomorrow evening, and I'll tell you what happened."

She raced off without saying goodbye, full of excitement. Mario watched her go, picking at the few grapes left on his bunch. Suddenly, as though he had just remembered something, the light died out of his eyes again.

"You really think they'll listen to an old bag like you?" A look of misery darkened his face.

"*Thief!*" he said.

As he heard himself saying the word, he screwed up his eyes so hard that his young face became a map of wrinkles. It was as if he thought he could eradicate the stain of the word this way. Then he let his muscles slacken again, his face took on the vacant expression and his body the relaxed position of a few moments before.

Mario spent the afternoon wandering along the streets and through the public gardens. He felt that if one more thing went wrong—he didn't know what exactly—all his efforts to fight back the tears and depression might collapse. When the chill of the autumn evening fell on the streets and his stomach began to burn with hunger, he set off in the direction of home.

Dora, his brother René's wife, was peeling potatoes. She had a scarf tied around her face. She threw the potatoes one by one into the pot, which was slowly coming to the boil over the weak primus flame. Mario moved a pile of scraps of material—striped, checked, and plaid—laid a half-finished, green polka-dot rabbit on top of the pile, and sat down and began leafing through a picture magazine.

"This filthy tooth is hurting worse," Dora mumbled.

"What's wrong?"

"Well, it was hurting again, see, and so I gave it a good yank because I thought that would stop the pain, and out it came. But it's cold in here . . . and I keep having to go from the fire to call the children in . . ."

It was often cold there. The two rooms at the end of a dark, narrow passage, where René, Dora, Mario, and the two children lived, were built of badly joined wooden planks. Dora had papered over the cracks with old newspapers, but the children soon hit on the game of slitting them through with their nails or the edge of a peso just along the cracks, and since the door did not shut properly, the place was always whistling with drafts. Also, the floor was partly bare earth, and the whole structure backed into an unplastered tile and cement wall.

"That shitty primus doesn't give out any heat anyway," Mario murmured. Without looking up from his magazine, he wound his scarf around his chest. "Trust you to start pulling teeth in this weather. Now you've only got the two front ones left!"

"And two lower molars. What difference does it make if there's one less?"

Mario remembered that when Dora and René first went together she had such pretty teeth that a little snot-nose like him had fallen in love with her and used to cry with embarrassment if he were ever left alone with her. But that was years ago; René's wife looked like a hag now. Her thin greasy hair was pushed back behind her ears, where it hung down lankily. Her face looked as if someone had thrown a limp rag over a wire mask twisted into the shape of her features as they had once been, and the rag still hung there, a grotesque travesty of her former face.

"I had such pretty teeth too, when I was a little girl! And so many of them! I seemed to have more than the other girls in the factory. Like my poor dear mom, who had all her teeth till God took her."

Dora had started, and once she got going, there was no stopping her. Mario looked sideways at her and tried to concentrate on his magazine. Only the jokes and little anecdotes could take his mind off his worries; if he listened to Dora, pretty soon he wouldn't be able to fight down his depression at having lost his job and being called a thief.

"My mom used to sing to the guitar so beautifully! That's why I started to learn. But it's years since I last sang. . . . René used to like it, but not anymore. They all used to send for mom to come and sing at the weddings and christenings, from all the houses in the neighborhood, and she used to take us with her and they gave us something of everything. My mom was plump, really plump, like I used to be, and when she sang her cheeks went pink and she laughed a lot to show off her teeth. That's why we were so popular in the neighborhood. They called us the singer's kids. When my mom sang, the gold filling between her two front teeth used to sparkle. When I was a little kid, what I wanted most was to look like her, and they all said I had a mouth like hers, so I used to keep poking a little stick between my front teeth to make a hole so I could get a gold filling."

"Oh, shit, stop it, will you! That's *enough*! Stop raving like a nut! Can't you see I'm reading?" Mario shouted.

He reached for the green-dotted rabbit Dora was making to sell, and his fingers tightened around it as if to strangle it.

"Let go my rabbit . . . let go my rabbit, I tell you, you lousy bastard! Look at me . . ."

Mario averted his eyes from Dora's face. He stared at the other unfinished toys in the room: a red-checked donkey straddling the head of the iron cot, a yellow chicken wrapped in a clean piece of paper which had been stuck in with the jars of food on the shelf. Then he looked back at his magazine.

But Dora had run across to him. "Look at me, I said," she shrieked. "Just take a look, you bastard! Who made me look like this, eh? Who made me like this so a miserable little creep like you thinks he can tell me to shut up? Look!" she screamed, pulling off the scarf and thrusting her face close to Mario's. She opened her huge mouth. Mario closed his eyes to shut it all out, especially the sight of the hole, where the badly extracted tooth had left the gum still bleeding.

"Wasn't it from bringing you up, eh? Eh? And having more and more kids, God only knows why? Oh yes, we were going to live in style when we first got married! We would be here just for a while, René said, till he got the little house he had been promised. And who do you suppose promised it to him? His pool-playing friends, and those people at the pawnshop where he says he works? Sure! Who else? Does he think I'm crazy enough to believe him? I let him get around me and gave up a good job at the factory, jerk that I was! Sure, they're going to give him a house! Who is, I'd like to know? The Benevolent Society for Up-and-coming Thieves?"

Mario buried his head in his arms. He hated to hear René called a thief . . . it seemed to bring the worst menace of all nearer. He squeezed his eyes shut till he could see spots, stars, green-checked rabbits and red-striped chickens. Then he didn't have to think what Dora was shrieking about.

Dora soon quieted down. She always did. She wiped her hands on her apron, sat down on an empty sugar crate beside a bundle of toy-animal parts—ears, paws, tails, and headless bodies—and started sorting the pieces and cleaning them. After a moment Mario said:

"Listen, I've been thrown out. Don't tell René or he'll beat me . . ."

Dora shook her head sadly.

"All right, kid. Why did they fire you?"

"Old Don Segundo's up to his tricks again. That old man's so sly . . ."

Dora was behind Mario. She couldn't see him sitting there with his eyes all screwed up, not reading at all. When he screwed up his eyes, instead of seeing stars and colors, he saw the words THIEF, THIEF, THIEF written in fiery letters before him. Dora knotted the scarf around her face again. The two loose ends hanging on top of her head made her look like a caricature of the rabbit she was covering in green-spotted cotton.

Suddenly Mario asked: "Listen, are you sure René's a thief?"

He brought this out very slowly, as though he were afraid of hearing it spoken aloud. It was the first time he had ever dared ask this question, though he had often had to fight to defend his brother's reputation in the neighborhood. Not that he loved or admired René. But somehow, while he was defending him with his fists, hitting out and getting hit in return, he seemed to be defending himself, not from a bad reputation so much as from a great danger, from vague but malevolent voices, a chill that threatened to envelop him and make the life he knew intolerable.

Dora said: "How should I know? He never tells me anything, hardly even speaks to me, you know that. Sometimes he leaves stuff under the cot in that case he had when he was a peddler. But he never lets me see what it is. He says it's stuff he buys here and there to resell at a profit."

Outside in the dark, narrow passage the neighbor's children set up a fiendish shrieking as they played with a yapping dog. Mario watched Dora, humming as she sewed. She stitched away deftly and eagerly as if she expected to find a solution to all her problems in this making and selling of stuffed toys. She finished covering the rabbit in its green-spotted skin. Then she selected two matching buttons from a tin box and with a few deft stitches fixed them into place for eyes. Then she held the animal at arm's length to admire it. It was the best rabbit she had ever made.

"Listen, you loved René, didn't you?" Mario asked.

Dora got up. She went over to the stove to stir the soup. Then silently she peeled an onion and dropped the skin on the floor beside the potato peel. When she had put the cover back on the pot, she said:

"Of course."

The children's game outside had ceased, and the whole uproarious gang rushed out into the street with the dog barking behind them, barking and barking till finally both shouting and barking receded into the distance. Everything was quiet again.

"Of course," Dora repeated, more quietly.

The back of Mario's neck felt cold. He wound his muffler around his neck again.

"If I had a little more money, just a little bit more, I could do something. But that pig René wastes what little he earns God knows how, God knows who with. If I had just a little more money, if he'd only give me enough to buy bread and beans with, I *know* I could get him to like me again. Do you think it's fun sharing a bed with a man who's always telling you you're skinny and smell of onions and haven't got any teeth? What can I do about it . . . I haven't got a rag to my back. If I had some money, I'd get one of those long shawls they're wearing now, a red one with a long fringe, and I'd get some teeth. I'm sure if I had some teeth René would look at me again. I'm sure of it! But you can't expect him to take me anywhere when I look like a scarecrow. It wouldn't cost him much, just a little bit each month. The woman at the bakery has a cousin who's studying at the Dental School and she says she could fix me up. I used to think I'd get something from these toys, but I feel so low these days I don't seem to find time to make them . . . I feel all weak, it's odd . . . I guess I'm growing old. He'll give the money to other women, though, and buy them all drinks so they'll think he's marvelous . . ."

She stopped for breath. This seemed to give her new strength as air filled her lungs, and she grew angry all over again.

"I'll make him buy me some teeth! Yes, I'll *make* him. I saw a lawyer's sign in Sierra Bella Street. I'll make him get me a whole set, every single tooth!"

"Why don't you shut up?" Mario roared.

He jumped up and ran out of the room, slamming the door, and then went into the long, freezing alley and wept.

3   When Andrés arrived at his grandmother's house that morning, Rosario and Lourdes were both in the kitchen listening to a serial on the radio while they plucked a chicken. Lourdes signed to him to keep quiet for a minute, for the episode was just ending.

". . . then the young count went across to where lovely

Corina was reclining on a divan by the window, pale amid her furs. In the soft light of a May evening their eyes met, and with this look they both knew that all their past sorrows, all the vile plots that had been laid to keep them tragically apart for so many years, had been expunged in a moment. From this time on there could only be truth between them . . ."

The last words were spoken to the accompaniment of sobbing violins, which lingered on for some time after. Lourdes switched off the radio and dropped the chicken into a bucket.

"Poor little thing! What poor Corina went through!"

"How is my grandmother, Lourdes?"

"Very well, very well indeed. You really ought to listen to this serial, Don Andrés. It's so beautiful and so sad, and Corina's father is so wicked you wouldn't believe it! If you listened to more nice plays like this, you would fall in love and get married, you would learn how to love . . ."

"Always the same old nonsense! Now, tell me, is there any news?"

"News? Isn't it news to you that I can be sitting here quietly, listening to the serial at eleven in the morning? You can't imagine how good the señora has been! She's no trouble at all—I think she's fallen in love with Estela. Would you believe it, we haven't had a single scene all week? The child seems to have bewitched her, though how, I can't think—when she's with us she just sits there looking as if she wouldn't say boo to anyone—doesn't she, Rosario? All Misiá Elisita can talk about is what a good, innocent girl Estela is. She's promised to teach her all kinds of things, embroidery even, I think. Just think, it's twenty years since the señora last threaded a needle. But you know how she is —she thinks things which happened ages ago happened just yesterday. Lord knows what else she'll teach her!"

Andrés noticed a green-spotted cotton rabbit on the kitchen table.

"What's that funny-looking thing?" he asked.

"A present I was given for doing someone a favor," Rosario answered.

"The things people think of! A rabbit with green spots . . . !"

"It *is* hideous," Rosario agreed, "but it's the thought that counts."

"It isn't sewn very well," Lourdes added. "It must be home-made."

Seeing that Rosario was getting ready to tell him the whole story of how she had gotten the toy, Andrés went out, leaving them to finish plucking the chicken.

Lourdes remarked: "I think the young count must look a little like Don Andresito . . ."

"A count with glasses? Counts don't wear glasses."

"Yes, that's true!"

"Well, the chicken's done! You'd better go out while I cut the head off. I know you don't like seeing me do it."

Lourdes went out through the kitchen door, and Rosario put the chicken on the marble-topped table and struck the head off with a great blow of her knife. Then she made a slit between the legs, plunged in her hand and drew out a fistful of entrails which left a bloody smear on the table.

"All right, you can come back," Rosario called.

Lourdes came in. She had always been tiny, and she had grown so fat over the years that now when she walked she looked more as if she were being slowly wheeled along. Slowly, because she was well over seventy and her varicose veins prevented her from being too active. But this had not lessened her appetite for life. Her cheeks, on which the high blood pressure of her youth had traced maps of red veins, shook with frequent laughter and incessant friendly chatter.

And the sight of a loaf of corn bread or a warm, fragrant meat pie would instantly make her forget Dr. Gros's solemn warnings about her health.

While Rosario finished scrubbing her hands, Lourdes took the plucked bird, pulled out one last feather, and put the chicken in the pot.

"Is the doctor coming Saturday?" Rosario asked.

"What a silly question! You know he always comes, saint's days, birthdays, and all. But I wonder if he'll bring his wife this year. Remember what happened last year? All that food spread out, and no one to eat it. What I couldn't understand is why there were so few leftovers. I'll tell you one thing, though—I saw the doctor's wife stuffing herself! And, you know, she had the nerve to come to me after and ask me to wrap up some leftovers to take back to the children! If it had been him, I wouldn't have minded. But I don't go for her. She thinks a little too much of herself. The doctor is such a nice gentleman, so kind—always was, too, ever since he first came here to play with Don Andresito when they were little boys. Her family, you see . . . well, they're nice people, of course . . . but I have an idea there's something funny somewhere, her father or grandfather, I think. How many people came last time? Six, was it?"

"There won't be as many as that for the birthday party."

"They get fewer and fewer every time. People are so ungrateful. They forget about the poor señora—good, kind lady that she is . . ."

"A lot of them have died . . ."

"That's true. Don Dionisio last year, he was so religious . . ."

"And Señora Matilde . . ."

"Yes, that's true. She passed on, too. And she was much younger than the señora, poor thing. We shouldn't expect many people then . . ."

"Not many at all . . ."

"Remember what it was like in the old days?"

"Of course!"

"They used to be splendid, the señora's parties, all those people and a wonderful great banquet and her in the middle of it all dressed like a queen! All she needed was the crown . . ."

"Mmm, that was before Don Ramón made her so unhappy."

"Yes, the poor thing. What she's been through! How old is she now, ninety-four?"

"Every bit of it. She always says she's ninety to make herself seem younger."

"Poor woman . . ."

"It's a long time . . ."

"Mmm . . ."

Andrés meanwhile had gone upstairs as slowly as if his feet were sticking to the red carpet at each step. Going up to see his grandmother was always a gamble. Sometimes she would be as gentle and sweet as the grandmother in a fairy story, but there were other occasions when she raged like a wild animal, lashing out at anyone who came within reach. He felt more than usually apprehensive today, probably because of that attack of indigestion which had kept him awake most of the night. But the moment he entered the room and found the curtains drawn back and the place flooded with light he felt certain that today, at least, everything was going to be all right. Instead of receding as patches of deeper darkness into the gloom around them, the bed, the chest of drawers, and the huge wardrobe showed up clearly in the bright light which detailed the molding of the feet, followed the curve of the brass handles, and pointed up the different grain of walnut and mahogany. In a sea of family photographs and chromolithographs of saints, the

faces stood out individually, some impressive behind
whiskers, others tenderly in the shadow of a lace mantilla
or a faded shawl. The wallpaper's enormous floral pattern,
which merged into the shadow of the walls once the sun had
passed, was brilliantly distinct at this hour when everything was luminous and bright.

Misiá Elisa de Abalos's bed was a great vessel of dark,
shining wood. The old woman was sitting up in it, white
against the sheets, holding a mirror in a shaking hand. It
seemed incredible that those eyes, under their mothy,
crumpled lids, should be capable of fastening on her re-
flection in the tiny oval mirror. She held a pair of tweezers
in her other hand and she was carefully plucking the hairs
out of her chin. Estela, wearing a stiffly starched white
uniform, was sitting by the bed on a stool.

"Good morning, Grandma. How are you feeling today?"

"So old and so ugly, child! I can't imagine why I've grown
all these hairs—I never had any before. They say a corpse's
hair goes on growing after it's dead . . . I suppose that's
what is happening to me."

It was this easy familiarity with the idea of death that
Andrés found most distressing in his grandmother. Her
chatter about death and dying offended him more than any
of the obscene words often heard from her lips. It aroused
an obscure, deep sense of disquiet within him. Disquiet it
was, however, and nothing more. He did not believe that
one should let oneself be swayed or governed by irrational
fears. This was the mark of a sensibility run wild, without
shape or direction—of an unbalanced mind, in short. Andrés
prided himself particularly on his own excellently balanced
mind, and on the harmonious, orderly state of his emotions.
Everyone had to die, that was unquestionably true. But
somewhere deep down in Andrés, in some far, childish
corner of his being—relic perhaps of the religious beliefs he

had finally discarded at the end of adolescence—there persisted a fierce, ineradicable conviction, fed by his most secret, inadmissible fears, that he himself would never die, that death was for everyone else, but not, in some way, for himself. Andrés, who was normally so perspicacious in analyzing his own feelings and sensations, shrank from examining this absurd, half-formulated belief too closely lest he destroy it altogether. Meanwhile, he would tell himself that life and death were ebb and flow, day and night, the one corollary to the other. What was the point of going beyond that?

Hearing his grandmother discuss death as if it were the most natural thing in the world was like raising the lid halfway on a multitude of potential horrors. He had to resist the temptation to peer under the lid, look firmly the other way, if necessary run away from that voice which kept brutally insisting that he face up to something he already knew he would have to face up to one day. But not yet. Fifty-three was not really old, particularly for a man of his excellent health. He made a point of getting Dr. Carlos Gros to give him a thorough check-up at least four times a year.

"Well?"

"Fit as a boy."

"What about these curious attacks of indigestion then . . . ?"

"Well, if you gorge yourself, what can you expect? You ought to be more careful."

"So I'm not quite so fit then, after all . . .?"

"For heaven's sake, man, there's nothing whatever the matter with you! You're carrying on like a fussy old bachelor."

For a time the satisfaction of finding himself in excellent health would still that obstinate flicker of terror. Besides,

there were so many pleasant things to occupy one's time
with, and keep such thoughts at bay—things like that still
uncut volume of General Caulincourt's memoirs lying on
his bedside table, waiting to be read; like those long, lei-
surely strolls through the streets and public gardens, observing and meditating; like that immensely rare Chinese
walking-stick he had heard about, said to belong to an
impoverished gentlewoman in the Avenida Recoleta whom
he proposed to lay siege to quite mercilessly. All this was
enough, more than enough!

". . . and this modern music! It's infernal!" Misiá Elisa
was saying. "And sinful. A good girl like you, Estela,
shouldn't go and hear that sort of music. You should have
heard the music we used to have! Now that really was
lovely! And the dances! You had to know all the steps, and
move gracefully as well. It wasn't all hops and skips like it
is now. The quadrilles and the lancers . . . you don't know
how to do the lancers? I'll show you tomorrow when I get
up, just wait and see! I remember when we lived in the
Cerro Alegre, in Valparaíso, my father used to take us to
hear the Philharmonic. It was always a very elegant occasion, and all the best people went. The ladies wore their
jewels and their prettiest décolleté gowns, and all the
gentlemen were in dress shirts. It was really splendid! A
friend of my father's used to accompany us, another English-
man, what they call a 'sportsman.' He had told my father
that he wished to marry me, which was the way things were
done in those days, and very proper, too. I knew this. I
don't know how I knew, because neither of them ever said
anything to me about it, but you know what girls are like!
I adored dancing with him. He was the best dancer in
Valparaíso, and everyone was mad to dance with him, but
he always chose me. And then, ninny that I was, I had to
go and fall head over heels in love with your grandfather

Ramón, who was very solemn and never went to balls. The gentleman I was telling you about was called George Lang. I wonder what became of him. He must be married now, and have a big family . . . I'd like to see him again . . ."

"But Don Jorge Lang was your father's friend and the same age as he was! And his grandchildren are all older than me. How could he possibly still be alive?"

"That's got nothing to do with it. He wore the most elegant gloves you ever saw! They should have buried him with his gloves on! Hee, hee, hee! Poor George Lang! Whatever happens, you must call him up and tell him I'm absolutely furious with him for not coming to see me . . ."

The old woman went on reminiscing happily. While she chatted away, Andrés noticed that Estela, who had been sitting quietly listening with her hands folded in her lap, had unclasped them and let them fall apart. Andrés quickly averted his eyes from those suddenly exposed palms. For some reason the sight made him feel embarrassed, as though he had surprised the girl in some intimate action. The slight variation in color from the opaque, coppery shade of the backs of her hands to the soft, crumpled, probably moist pink of those disturbingly naked palms suggested something instinctive, almost feral, lying in wait for him, something inadmissible in his highly civilized world, or in this room, where the only obtrusive thing was the nearness of death.

Andrés dispelled this curious sensation without much difficulty. A lifetime of simply avoiding anything that might distress him came in useful now. A negative policy, certainly, as he would be the first to admit, but the fact remained that he had never done anyone any harm in his pursuit of the ideal, a modest ideal perhaps, but still an appreciably greater achievement than most people could lay claim to.

It was amusing to watch Estela's face, and Andrés liked being amused. It was diverting, for instance, to see how her normally expressionless face awakened and came to life as it mirrored the old woman's expressions and followed her into the times and places her aged voice conjured up. Looking at those round, marveling eyes and parted lips, Andrés was unable to guess how much of his grandmother's monologue the girl understood; not all of it, certainly; perhaps very little indeed. Observing Estela's innocent amazement, however, Andrés found himself hoping that this transparently ingenuous peasant girl might bring a little peace at last into the old woman's life. Not so much by performing her duties efficiently as by the gift of her enthralled interest in the dead world of Misiá Elisa's past. As she thought about this world and pictured it to herself, correctly or not, Estela rejuvenated it, and himself along with it. Assuming, of course, that the poor girl was capable of thought and imagination . . .

Misiá Elisita went on talking. Her eyes, normally cloudy and lusterless, were lit by sparks of intelligence. Andrés reflected that his grandmother had not been as lucid as this for years. He suddenly pictured the house as it had been in his youth, cheerful, brimming with the unobtrusive routine that is the very stuff of life. Suddenly it seemed as if not just light and air but all the scents of the garden, and even the sound of birds rustling the branches, were wafting in through the open windows. Estela's youth and freshness no longer seemed incongruous.

The idea of returning to live in his grandmother's house, both to enjoy the peace and tranquillity apparent everywhere today, and to be closer to the old woman, crossed Andrés's mind.

Then he remembered the last time he had yielded to the temptation to spend the night there. Misiá Elisa had been gravely ill at the time, with a bout of pneumonia that seemed likely to prove fatal. Reluctant to abandon her on the verge, as he thought, of extinction, he let Lourdes make up a bed for him in the room he had had as a boy, which was directly above his grandmother's. In the end, the old woman's hold on life proved so tenacious that she finally rallied, in the teeth of medical opinion, and her body was quickly healed, but her mind remained sick.

On the last night of his stay, Andrés had gone up to his room late. He had a book with him, a book he was particularly fond of, which he had read many times with undiminished enjoyment and admiration. He switched off all the lights except the one by his bed. Then he settled himself comfortably within the pool of light cast by the lamp in the darkness of the big, low-ceilinged room, and opened the favorite book. Before he could begin reading, however, he became aware of something out there in the surrounding darkness, beyond the handsome objects which the light threw into rich relief—his grandmother's monogram embroidered on the sheets, his own fingers supporting the finely bound book. The darkness seemed alive, animated by some kind of presence, possibly no more substantial than a sound. He stared at the curtains hanging white and still, perfectly still, in front of the windows. Yes, it was a sound, a sort of purring. Andrés shut his volume of Saint-Simon and listened.

What was it?

Of course! It must be his grandmother talking to herself in the room below. Having identified the source of the noise, Andrés opened his book once again, confident that his faint feeling of disquiet had been appeased. But he found that he could not read; the noise seemed to have attached itself to his eardrums. He shut the book again,

thoroughly depressed. Now his wandering attention fastened
on the monologue ascending from the room below, which
was making everything around him vibrate minutely. The
noise swelled and Andrés irritably tried to make out what
his grandmother was saying. But the meaning was lost as
her monologue filtered up through the floorboards, leaving
only the husks of words, which ran together into this
maddening purring sound. Andrés returned to his book. But
though his eyes read on, his mind stayed closed to the
sense of what was written on the pages. His attention was
still riveted on the sound from below. All that the words
conveyed was their emotional coloring—violence, cunning,
anger, despair. Reading was impossible. He turned off the
light, deciding to get some sleep at least. But the purring
sound grew louder in the darkness, and so did the faint
vibration of everything in the room, till even the pillow
Andrés pulled over his head to muffle the noise seemed to
be affected. Suddenly the noise stopped. Feverishly, Andrés
tried to make use of the respite to get some sleep. But it was
hopeless. Almost immediately the old woman began her
meaningless recitation again.

Andrés got no sleep at all that night. He was sweating
all over, on his bald head and on his neck and even on his
hands, which were usually dry-skinned. He got up several
times. But it was no use. The reality of his grandmother's
insanity had been driven deep into his mind, expelling any
other thoughts or feelings and throwing him completely off
balance.

The memory of that night armored him against any
temptation to repeat the experience. He was much better off
as he was, in his own apartment, which held no mysteries
and was both exceedingly comfortable and very much his
own, the perfect setting for his self-contained bachelor ex-

istence, with its strict routine. Whereas this house, where the very woodwork was permeated with the sick woman's voice, represented a serious threat to Andrés's mental equilibrium.

4   The man pulled down his mask and switched on the electric current. Instantly there was a loud explosion, and both he and the knot of curious onlookers standing at a prudent distance from the wrought-iron grille that was being soldered turned blue all over. Some of them moved back a little as the dark jet of flame spurted out. A small boy, whose mother had told him he would be blinded if he looked at the light, did not dare do more than gaze at its reflected glare on the chest of this demi-god or demon who wielded such dangerous power.

"Never seen this before?" Mario asked, leaning non-chalantly against his bicycle.

"No," answered Estela.

They had been watching the masked man for some time. At first Estela had been afraid to look, but by alternately teasing and encouraging, Mario had finally persuaded her to go a little closer. Only then, and as if making a great effort, did she look up and see the blue flame and its reflected glare, which was brighter than daylight itself, on the trees and people and on Mario's face, which could not conceal his pride at being the first to introduce her to such a marvel. Estela smiled imperceptibly, her pleasure only just strong enough to curve her mouth into a ghost of a smile. She struck Mario as being greatly enlivened by this first spark of gaiety he had noticed in her. Once she stopped being so solemn, she seemed alive and vibrant, not like she

had been when he first met her a week before in the kitchen
of Misiá Elisa's house. But these country girls! They really
must be green if something as corny as a soldering torch
left them standing open-mouthed!

"Does it scare you?"

"Yes . . ."

The remarkable simplicity with which she admitted to
being afraid made Mario laugh. He laughed softly at first.
But then, seeing Estela's look of bewilderment, he began
roaring with laughter without quite knowing why, his head
thrown back and the blue flame lighting up his throat and
the little creases around his eyes. As she watched him,
Estela began to laugh too, her own rising mirth keeping
pace with his. They laughed till their eyes streamed with
tears and they both felt quite weak.

"I bet you've never been to a movie," Mario said. When
he said the word *movie*, the girl's face flooded with sudden
joy as if he had at last uttered the magic word she yearned
to hear. At home, in the country, her sister-in-law had often
described the picture her husband had once taken her to
see in the village . . . it was all in color, she said, and
actresses with hair like golden clouds talked and even sang,
but without appearing to be really there at all . . .

"No."

"But you'd like to?"

"I asked my aunt Lourdes to take me just the other day,
but she wouldn't."

"I bet she said it was a sin. Those old bags always think
it's a sin, just because it's dark in there . . ."

"Dark? But how can you see the actors if it's dark?"

"Hey!" he began, laughing again. "I . . ."

But both the answer and the laughter broke off abruptly
as he realized that he had in fact no idea how one did see
in a darkened theater. The girl stood there waiting for an

explanation. Mario felt cornered. He would have to think
of something fast if he wanted to emerge from this impasse
with honor.

"Come to the movies with me Saturday night and see if
I'm not right."

Estela shivered. By the light of another blue flash Mario
saw the girl's features close up once more: her eyelids
dropped again; the last trace of amusement vanished and
was replaced by a look of intense solemnity; her high cheekbones and tight-shut lips flushed bright pink. Then Mario
flushed too, as though some shameful weakness of his had
been found out, and moved a little away from the girl.

"We'll go on Saturday then? Hell, why not?" he repeated,
very slowly. He made a great show of scraping the mud off
his bicycle wheel while he talked her into accepting the
invitation, against his better judgment—he knew his friends
would laugh at him if they saw him with this little country
mouse who didn't even wear make-up. He didn't find her
at all pretty. The chicks he usually dated were snappy
dressers who told jokes and knew the names of all the actors.
He even had one girl friend who spoke a little English. . . .

"But they won't let me . . ."

"Oh, come on, that doesn't matter! I bet the old girls go
to bed early. You can come out later on . . ."

"But I'm supposed to be looking after the señora then."

"What's the point of all this looking after her? I bet she's
asleep by eight and doesn't wake up again all night."

"She does sleep heavily, that's true. I sleep in the room
next door. Sometimes she says things in the night, and talks
to herself, but she never seems to wake up. I wake up sometimes and think I hear her calling, but she never is. She
sleeps right through the night."

"What difference will it make, then, if you go out?"

"No, no, I can't. I have to look after the señora."

Mario was about to go on trying to persuade her when he suddenly fell silent, astonished at himself. What was he pleading with this little country girl for, anyway? He already had as many girls as he could cope with, lively, wise-cracking girls, too. He liked free-and-easy girls, dating one, then another, lots of laughs, making remarks aloud in the balcony so all the people sitting around him started laughing too. Mario was the leader of them all, down at the Condor Club, and his sallies and escapades were notorious. They called him the Big Hummingbird because he was always flitting from flower to flower. There was a Little Hummingbird too, Washington Troncoso. But he, Mario, was the more popular of the two. In the evenings, after their regular football game, played with a ball made of a wad of crumpled paper tied with string, Mario would stand around on a street corner with his friends, hands in their pockets and cigarettes dangling from their lips. The women who went past would be greeted with complimentary sallies, or at the very least admiring whistles from the boys, especially Mario. Sometimes he would follow one of them and, as he was attractive and lively, women usually took to him. Later at the club, his greatly expanded and embellished account of the adventure would leave the others' eyes shining with admiration.

But if they saw him with this country kid! He knew that it would only take one false step to bring his reputation crashing down, and no one seeing him with a frightened little thing like Estela would ever believe that he took her out for the one reason a real man takes a woman out. When that man is nineteen, that is, and has not the slightest intention of giving up his freedom, even if he could afford to do so.

"It must be beautiful . . ." he heard Estela say, very softly and as if to herself.

Then Mario suddenly saw her irradiated with light, as
if she stood right in the heart of that fierce, blue, dangerous
flame. She had come much closer to him, as if placing herself in his protection. She was so little and dark! The bright
reflected light and the faint stirring of the air revealed an
almost imperceptible trace of down on the curve of her
cheek. Mario looked away, frowning. For some reason, his
snappy backtalk and the seductive technique of a backstreet
Don Juan seemed inappropriate with Estela, and this left
him at a loss, awkward. He glanced at his watch.

"Hell, I'm late. Don Segundo will flay me alive. I'd
better get moving. See you Saturday then, Estela. I'll be
waiting for you on the corner at nine-thirty. Nine-thirty,
eh? Don't let me down . . ."

And he leaped on his bicycle and pedaled off without a
backward glance.

That night, at dinner, Estela let fall one or two hints that
she would like to go to the movies. Lourdes immediately set
out to convince Estela, armed with both moral and economic
reasons, that she ought not to go. Estela was quickly convinced, but this in no way altered her desire to go. At home
she was expected to be so submissive, obeying other people's
injunctions was so much a condition of her life, that she
had gradually evolved an outward air of compliance while
keeping her desires alive and intact inside her until such
time as she could satisfy them without anyone finding out.
Her aunt Lourdes, like her father and brother, was in the
right and must be deferred to. Estela had been given to
Lourdes, after all, by her mother when she was dying. But
this did not really alter anything. Estela wanted to go to
the movies more than anything in the world, and no amount
of arguments for or against could change that. Moreover,
she wanted to go with Mario. When Lourdes explained that
a girl could not go to the movies alone, and neither she nor

Rosario was free to go out at night and accompany her—
and of course there was never time to go out during the
day—Estela had been on the point of revealing that she
already had an escort. On thinking it over, however, she
had decided to keep this information to herself.

As she lay awake that night, listening to Misiá Elisa's
regular breathing next door, her secret glowed in her
thoughts as if irradiated by one of the flashes of blue light.
She lay quite still between the sheets, which warmed themselves around her body, and felt that she was keeping her
secret warm and safe next to her in the darkness. She
shouldn't go to the movies. Obviously. But if she really
wanted to, she would. She really would. She liked Mario
very much . . . very much indeed. She knew quite well what
it meant to feel like that about someone. And Mario was
going to take her to the movies. He would sit beside her in
the dark and explain it all to her. Mario knew everything
about this city which was still strange to her except for a
couple of streets.

5 ⚜   Saturday, Misiá Elisa Grey de Abalos's
birthday, the whole house was in an uproar. It might have
been a big reception they were getting ready for, instead
of four or five visitors whose main object in coming was to
express their amazement that the nonagenarian was still alive.

The visitors never lingered on the ground floor chatting,
but went straight up to the old woman's room, where they
remained, murmuring to each other, drinking little cups of
tea, and eating pastries and the tiny sandwiches which were

thought to be so much easier to digest. The gentlemen were offered a punch which was Lourdes's specialty, made to a secret recipe. It was not unknown, however, for the ornately plated punchbowl to be almost full by the end of the afternoon.

On this occasion, as on the señora's name day, Lourdes got up at dawn so as to have the whole morning to put everything in order, beginning by eagerly whisking off the dust sheets from the furniture in the library, the drawing room, and the hall. As the furniture emerged from its long concealment, it seemed as though a faint flush of life was stealing back into this cadaver of a house. Though somewhat moth-eaten, the ottoman in the hall, astonishingly, still retained all the vivid color of its garnet plush cover, and Lourdes would bustle about, wiping the dust off the leaves of the aspidistras standing behind it. The scaled-down reproductions of famous statues on imitation marble plinths, the innumerable bibelots scattered about the little Turkish salon next to the library, the books and bound collections of periodicals, the pianola cylinders, the plants, cabinets, and pictures, all these came to life under Lourdes's loving, careful hands as she cleaned away with a feather duster in one hand and a handkerchief tied around her head. It was a mystery how she managed to dust the gilded cherubs over the console mirrors, right up near the ceiling, but manage she did, and they shone forth in all their immaculate nakedness on the señora's birthday and on her name day. The curtains, released from their tiebacks, billowed out softly, letting in light, which for more than six months had not sunk into the thick carpets or gleamed on the tasseled fringe of the armchairs.

And all to no purpose. For years now, the visitors had gone straight up to the sick woman's room without so much as a passing glance at the reception rooms. But Lourdes held the view, which no one would have dared question, that everything must be just so for the señora's birthday; this was the way things had always been, and the way they must remain. In the old days the ground floor of the house had been her special responsibility, and she had cleaned and tidied it every day. This was not necessary now, but Lourdes revived the custom enthusiastically on these two days a year when the house resounded with her authority.

Andrés arrived some time around eleven in the morning. He went straight to the kitchen to ask Rosario what treats she had for his lunch, but she hustled him out, insisting that this was to be a surprise.

He ran up the stairs two at a time. He felt unusually happy this autumn Saturday. The sun shone soft and golden, and the people he saw walking in the park seemed to have nothing more serious on their minds than buying hot roasted peanuts and getting their shoes shined. And then there were the law students pacing up and down with their noses stuck in their books, heedlessly crunching the yellow leaves underfoot. This sight pleased him, too, because he had been a law student himself once and had known the pleasurable anguish of examinations and orals. Above all, the serenity that Estela's presence seemed to confer on his grandmother, which he had noticed on his last visit, helped to make him more optimistic just now than he would usually have been.

Andrés was panting by the time he reached the first landing. He had to remind himself of his age and proceed at a more restrained pace. He had brought his grandmother a bunch of late dahlias and a pink shawl that had been lovingly wrapped and beribboned by the salesgirl in the shop where he bought it.

"Happy birthday!" he cried as he went in and crossed over to the sick woman's bed to kiss her.

Estela was moving about the room, straightening the embroidered sheets, which were kept for occasions when the señora expected visitors.

"Good morning, Estela."

"Good morning, sir."

She had at last stopped calling him *patrón*. Andrés had asked Lourdes to tell her not to. And the girl's appearance, too, was noticeably improved. The rather skinny pigtails that dangled on her shoulders when she first arrived had now been gathered into a glistening black knot at the nape of her neck. Her shining cheeks, her starched collar, everything about her seemed to have acquired new dignity. Only her eyes, still downcast, were just as they had been, two slanting, glistening hollows. But she sometimes opened them wide now to look at something directly, and a vivid blue flame would flash out from their intensely black depths. Then the thick lashes would drop again, screening them. A peasant clumsiness still impeded her movements, however, and weighed down her large feet.

"How has my grandmother been?" Andrés asked Estela.

The girl hung her head.

"Why ask *her*?" said the old woman. "Do you think I'm so soft in the head I can't speak for myself?"

Andrés knew only too well the note in the cracked old voice, blurred as if the dentures had not been fixed into position behind the slack lips. This apparent feebleness, however, concealed a flicker of violence, alight and ready.

"How old are you, Grandma?"

"Don't change the subject. Nineteen. What difference does it make what age I am?"

"Are you sure you aren't twenty?"

"No. Nineteen. Just two years older than Estela here. You always liked them young, didn't you, you old goat? Now perhaps you'll fall for me."

Andrés's hope of a long period of peace and calm was
rudely shattered. It was going to start again, as it had with
the other nurses—quarrels, humiliations, filth that seemed
to adhere to everyone. In a moment or two—Andrés knew
from experience—that flicker of violence would flare up and
get out of control, searing, destroying, consuming everything in its path. He tried to console himself with the re-
flection that time and familiarity had so accustomed him
to the old woman's ravings that they only aroused his pity.
Not that he was given to emotional extremes in any case.

Estela smiled uncomfortably. Misiá Elisa gave a laugh
that sounded more like a muffled cough, or a cackle. In a
last attempt to turn the old woman's thoughts to a more
agreeable topic, Andrés smiled and said:

"Ah, well, if you're nineteen you'll look charming in
pink! Here. Open your present. Estela, would you put these
flowers in that vase over there."

"*You* open it! I can't manage these fussy modern bows
and things."

As Andrés shook out the handsome shawl to show it off
to her, the madness that had been accumulating in Misiá
Elisa's eyes gave way to a look of covetousness. She clapped
her hands together twice, gleefully, a gesture that sounded
more like dry bones clacking against each other than flesh
meeting flesh.

"How pretty!" she exclaimed. "Let me feel it . . . ah, yes,
yes, it's very soft." Then she added, with the travesty of a
smile on her cracked lips: "A black one would have been
more suitable for someone my age, though, a nice, cosy
little shroud."

And she laughed that ambiguous coughing or cackling
laugh again.

"This pretty shawl would suit Estela much better," she
went on. "It would look quite charming on her. Here, child,

look what your admirer has brought you—a pretty pink shawl, so you'll look all rosy when you wake up beside him in the morning. Here, try it on."

"Grandma, please," Andrés exclaimed faintly.

It was hopeless. Estela had retreated to the farthest corner of the bedroom. Andrés wished there was something he could do to, well . . . protect the poor girl. She was such an innocent. But he had no idea what to say or do.

"Estela-a-a-a!" The old woman's shriek foundered in the froth of bubbles streaming from her flaccid lips.

"For heaven's sake, Grandma, don't start all that again . . ."

"Don't start all that again—what mustn't I start again? Telling the truth, do you mean? That's what you're all frightened of, isn't it? Well, I *know* what the truth is. I haven't lived all this time for nothing. You think I'm silly, don't you? Well, I may be mad, but I'm not a fool. You don't fool me, *no* one fools me . . ."

"But why should anyone want to fool you, Grandma? Do be sensible. Remember it's your birthday today and you owe it to your guests to be at your best . . ."

"Don't you talk to me as if I were a little girl, Mr. Impertinence! I'm almost a hundred years old, I'll have you know, and by rights I should be feeding the worms by now."

"What's the matter? What's upset you? Look, let's talk about something else. What do you think of these dahlias I've brought you?"

"You're talking nonsense. Here, come here, you dirty half-breed slut!"

Estela did not move. She just raised her hands a little as if asking for help, and looked at Andrés. He had to avert his eyes hurriedly from those palms, as upset by the sight of that fresh pink flesh as by his grandmother's crazy accusations which had coupled them together so embarrassingly.

Where should he look, who could he turn to in search of order?

"Did you hear me?" Misiá Elisa screeched again.

The girl went up to the old woman's bed. It seemed as if nothing would ever again persuade her to look up or brighten those downcast eyes.

"Come on, girl. Let's see you try on this pretty pink shawl he's brought you. He wouldn't have chosen a shawl like that for me—it isn't the sort of thing you give to a lady with the virtue of a saint and royal blood in her veins. It's a whore's shawl, a whore's shawl, do you hear? Go on, you slut, try it on!"

The girl stood motionless, with tearful, frightened eyes, as if waiting for Andrés to do something. But what was it she was asking of him, mutely, with her eyes and hands? She seemed to be offering herself to him, and he was unable to accept the responsibility. Andrés's mind no longer obeyed him, his grandmother was blocking his thoughts, preventing the passage of any emotion save this, this quite novel one, which threatened at any moment to become stark terror. He could not check the macabre farce.

"So you thought you could fool me?"

"No . . . no . . ."

"No, no," the old woman mimicked. "You don't even know what I'm talking about. Do you think I haven't noticed? Do you think I didn't see those little glances you were giving each other when you first came in? So she's a good, sensible girl, is she? Sensible, pah!—she's sick! Do you think I don't know that this dirty half-breed slut is your mistress? They only made her my nurse so she could run off with everything I've got. Indian whore! You've been showing him your filthy tricks in bed, haven't you? *My* grandson, with my own pure, noble blood in his veins! A man who might have been a prince! Bitch, slut . . . !"

Estela pulled the shawl tightly around her. To Andrés she appeared pink all over, as if the nakedness of her palms had spread shamelessly over her whole body, as if Misiá Elisita's crazy accusations had stripped her naked in readiness for him. Andrés tried desperately to suppress this thought, but failed.

"You ought to be disgusted by the very idea of sleeping with this Indian girl! Lord knows what infections she'll pass on to you, depraved creature that she is! And don't try to tell me this she-devil comes from the country—a brothel would be more like it! What do you take me for—an imbecile? She says she's seventeen! Pah! She's thirty if she's a day, and as pox-ridden as a woman of fifty!"

Andrés stood up, trembling violently. His grandmother's madness had never threatened him so closely before. She had found a soft spot at last, a vulnerable chink in his armor of fastidious good breeding into which she could sink her poisoned fangs.

"Estela, go and get the señora's lunch."

The girl did not seem to hear. She went on standing there, fascinated.

"Why should she get my lunch? I didn't ask for it. I'm not hungry. This is my house and I give the orders here—not you! You're nothing but a pathetic, useless old bachelor. What have you ever done, eh? Why don't you tell me, since you've gotten so brave and bold all of a sudden? What have you done? Nothing! You just fritter your life away with your stupid walking sticks and books. You've never done anything, you're no good to anyone, you're just a poor old useless bachelor. And a wicked one too, because you're afraid of everything, most of all yourself! You're wicked, wicked! I'm the only good person here . . ."

Andrés, gazing at his grandmother with horror-stricken eyes, tried to take a step toward the bed, but the ground seemed to slide away under his feet. Everything around him had grown blurred. He wanted to speak, but the words stuck in his throat. As he struggled helplessly in a wave of doubt and uncertainty, old, familiar griefs and new, as yet undefined ones revolved like a viscous whirlpool about him, set in motion by his grandmother's words.

"Be quiet! You're mad. Be quiet, you mad, horrid woman! You don't know what you're saying. Can't you see Estela is listening?"

Misiá Elisa struggled up feebly, propping herself on one elbow, and fixed Andrés with her ravaged blue stare.

"How dare you insult me? How dare you call me a mad, horrid woman simply to protect Estela?"

Andrés could not look at her. Faltering, incoherent words poured from his lips. He hardly knew what he was saying, it was merely the outpourings of his stricken conscience as it sank under a sea of confusion and doubt. The old woman fell back on the bed, moaning faintly.

"You don't love me, you don't love me! No one loves me, not even Ramón. No one at all. And I've always tried to be so good, and sacrificed myself . . . and now I'm going to die!"

The old woman went on whimpering for a time. But her strength was soon exhausted, she was reduced to a white, insignificant bundle between the sheets, a body in which life barely flickered. Her hands, which held a rosary, were folded across her chest like a corpse's, but her lips still moved.

"Off you go," Andrés whispered to Estela.

Just as the girl was leaving, the old woman sat up in bed. "Whore!" she spat at her.

Then she flopped back again, a mere rag, a shapeless lump of living matter under the sheets. Her eyes were closed, and her hands, holding the rosary, were folded in

front of her. But she was neither asleep nor dead. Her lips
moved as she fingered the beads. Misiá Elisa Grey de
Abalos was saying her prayers.

6   Andrés stayed with his grandmother till
she fell asleep. When he went downstairs again, at lunch-
time, he was still bewildered, knotted up with doubt and
despair, incapable of the cool analysis that would have put
the morning's incidents into proper perspective. His arms
and legs had grown heavier, and he felt a dangerous
lethargy creeping over him as he devoured the chicken dish
Rosario had lovingly prepared for him, as she had all the
other dishes, each one a masterpiece of home cooking.

He climbed the stairs after lunch, leaning heavily on the
banister. He had never felt so old. He asked Lourdes to wake
him at five, so as to be ready when the guests arrived, and
then stretched out on the bed for a nap. Lying there with
the curtains drawn, on the bed he had had as a boy, he was
about to drift off into sleep when a thought flashed through
his mind, and he sat up again, guilty and worried. He had
forgotten to pay Rosario a visit after lunch to praise her
cooking and discuss the various dishes. How appalling! The
cook must be waiting for him now! And this little ritual of
courtesy had been his idea in the first place! Then he sank
back on the bed. No, this was not the day to wear himself
out over such trifles; he must rest . . . that, or force himself
to think seriously about vital, serious matters. But somehow,
as he lay there trying to sleep, his thoughts refused to take

shape in his mind. And as he slept his sleep was haunted
by the knowledge that he ought not to be sleeping. He ought
to think, and think, and think. Instead, trivial scraps of old
memories floated through his mind.

He was back at school.

It was a very big school, full of boys, most of them very
big too, and hundreds of priests in white habits and billow-
ing black capes that floated out behind them like wings as
they marched along the corridors, spying and watching. The
weather was wet and gray. The rectangle of gray sky
stretched like an awning over the playground clanged and
echoed with the bells that rang out the hours, the quarter
hours, and the half hours and summoned them all to
prayers. Those bells were slow and hoarse. But the bell that
rang to call them to class was shrill and urgent; its long
needle of sound stabbed down the corridors where boys
scratched their chilblains or stamped and scuffled about
because it was too cold and wet to play quoits outside.
Father Damián, who had a big cross like a red wound
across his chest, was always talking very loudly. It made
no difference where one went in the playground or how
much din the quoit players were making—the tragic cadence
of that harsh, sonorous Spanish voice penetrated everywhere. Sometimes Andrés would hide in the toilet to escape
from that voice with its burden of sorrow for all the sins the
boys had committed in the past and any they might con-
ceivably commit in the future. The toilet was a dirty place,
and Father Damián's voice could not go there because he
was a saint. Andrés would hide in one of the compartments
and bolt the door and then the priest's voice disappeared.
But the cold remained, a cold which froze his bare buttocks
during the long recreation period.

"I want you to make your First Communion next year on
the Feast of the Immaculate Conception. You are nine years

old now, and it's high time you started to learn the meaning of sin," his grandmother told him. "I want Father
Damián to instruct you. Would you like that?"

Andrés said that he would.

"It will be the happiest day of your whole life, and you
can offer up your holy communion for the repose of your
mother's soul."

His mother had died when he was born. His grandmother
had put a photograph of her in his inside jacket pocket so
he would never forget her.

"And for your poor father's too . . ."

His poor father had died a year later—of a broken heart,
some said . . .

"And you must always be good, and not say or think
nasty things, or you will go to hell."

And she would point to a colored print on the wall which
showed some wretched sinners writhing among flames that
looked a little like carrots but were frightening nevertheless.

Andrés knew that there was some connection between
hell and the school toilets. He rather liked the idea of hell
because Father Damián's voice would not be heard there,
but it frightened him too. But then, the school chapel was
another hell because Father Damián preached from the
pulpit there with his arms outstretched in the form of a
cross. *Hell* was the word he used most, and when he said
it his face and eyes went red and his mouth looked like a
black hole. They would all burn in hell, he assured them,
because they were all sinners. Andrés always shivered in
chapel. Either from cold or from fear. It was forbidden to
wear an overcoat or a scarf in chapel, for it was good to
make sacrifices. He gradually learned not to take in what
Father Damián was saying but simply to listen to the rising
and falling of his voice and to the word *hell* delivered with
threatening emphasis from time to time. Later he learned

not to see him. Or the host as it was lifted high above the altar. Or to hear as hundreds of boys prayed in unison, or to smell the odor of flowers and incense and tired boys crowded together. Father Damián was a saint because he made great sacrifices.

When they came out of evening benediction, it was time to go home. It was cold and windy and the muddy street grew dark early. Because he was a little boy, he had to sit on a bench in the icy-cold hall till someone came to get him. Being little was not very nice, being big must be nicer because not so many of the things one did then were sins. Andrés often waited alone in the hall till it was pitch dark outside before anyone came for him. The walls of the hall were hung with portraits of all the rectors the school had ever had. One of them, a fat gentleman with a fringe, looked very much like Lourdes. Andrés stared at him and he smiled back benevolently. He would much rather have had this kindly gentleman prepare him for his First Communion instead of Father Damián. The gentleman in the next portrait, though, stared at him with accusing, bloodshot eyes. This scared him, and he clutched his exercise books to his chest, where they pressed against the wallet in which his grandmother had put his mother's photograph, his poor mother, who had sacrificed herself to bring him into the world. He must respect and fear her, as one must respect and fear all good people who made sacrifices. People like his mother and grandmother and Lourdes and Father Damián. He was not sure if his grandfather Ramón was such a good person, but he was too small to find out. He seemed to hear Father Damián's voice booming around the big, dark, chilly hall as he sat there waiting for someone to come and get him. The only place in the school where that voice did not penetrate was the toilet, because that was a dirty place, that was hell.

". . . my brother's been to the whorehouse . . ." came the whisper of one of the big boys, talking in the lavatory. Andrés had bolted himself into one of the toilets. He was just going to pull his trousers up because class would be starting in a minute. ". . . and he is going to take me with him when I am fifteen . . ."

". . . our maid at home is a whore. She sleeps with my brother . . ." said another voice.

Andrés opened the toilet door. The boys who had been whispering got angry when they saw him and wouldn't let him go.

"You were spying in there," said the red-faced one who was so fat he seemed to be splitting out of his suit.

"I wasn't," Andrés said.

"Are you going to tell on us?" asked the other boy, who had long, yellow teeth.

"What about?" Andrés asked.

"You know what about, so don't try and pretend you don't," said the red-faced one, grabbing him by the lapels. "Go on, tell!" he shouted.

That was how Andrés imagined confession. Father Damián would grab him by the lapels, thrust his angry face into his, and shout: "Tell!" while shaking him savagely. And his blackened teeth would smell of tobacco and the tendons in his neck would stand out all tight the way they did on the anatomical figure they used to teach the different parts of the body. All the parts, that is, except one.

"Leave him alone, Velarde," said Yellow-teeth. "He doesn't know what you are talking about."

"You just watch out," Velarde exclaimed, scarlet and furious. And he gave Andrés one last shake. "You just watch out."

And that was how absolution would be.

One night, before Andrés was asleep, Lourdes came in.

She leaned against the foot of the bed and started going through his satchel to see if he had left any of the schoolbooks behind. Andrés asked her if she was a whore. Lourdes flew into a rage. All that decently brought up boys ever learned in those schools, she declared, was to behave like pigs. And she went off to tell Misiá Elisita.

There was a little room that opened off her bedroom which Misiá Elisa used to sew in or pray in when she was alone. Lourdes escorted him there one evening. The room was full of knick-knacks: plaster saints wreathed with flowers, prayer books, a work table made of lignum vitae, a small pink upholstered chair that looked like a naked body. Lourdes, who was beginning to put on weight, must look something like that chubby chair. Misiá Elisa was sitting on "Lourdes," as Andrés called the chair to himself. It was not very late yet, but the room was already quite dark. His grandmother did not say anything but motioned to him to come closer. Her beautiful sharp-featured face was shadowed by a look of great sorrow.

She asked him a lot of questions and explained a lot of things to him, but the only thing Andrés clearly understood was that he must never, under any circumstances, try to understand what he had overheard in the school lavatory. He must never even allow himself to remember what it was. It was something very, very bad, so bad that only very big people, his grandfather Ramón, for instance, were permitted to know what it meant. In doing so, though, they generally lost their innocence, and this was very sad. There were things she herself did not understand at all, and sincerely hoped she never would. He must stay pure too because he was her grandson. Velarde, Velarde, Velarde. Whose boy would that be? Ah, yes, he must be Luchita's youngest. Poor Luchita, such a dear good person!

"These men . . . starting to behave like pigs when they're

still little boys!" Misiá Elisa murmured as Andrés left the room. Lourdes shook her head sorrowfully.

Two days later, Velarde and the boy with yellow teeth summoned Andrés to the lavatory just as the others were going into class, and they hit him very hard several times. Then they told him lots of nasty things, and showed him dirty postcards and explained what they were about. Then they hit him again, harder still, for being a hypocrite and a sneak.

From then on, Andrés would shut himself up in his bedroom as soon as he got back from school. He dared not look at his grandmother or the maids. At night he dreamed that the pink chair in his grandmother's room had got into bed with him and was doing things to him, and they both sweated and sweated and sweated. The next day they would have to punish Andrés to make him go to school. He always went in the end, usually in tears. And wherever he went he heard Father Damián's voice going on and on at him, full of anger, horror, and contempt. He would try to hide during recess to escape from that voice, and from Velarde and his friends too. They were always lying in wait for him, and they said things about his dead parents and took him to the lavatory to show him more and more horrible things, and to beat him.

"The boy's become a problem . . ." Grandfather Ramón remarked listlessly as he leafed through the paper by the light of the drawing-room lamp. He was not going to the club that night because of a touch of kidney trouble, so he was wearing his velvet slippers. "What's the matter with him? He never used to be like this . . ."

His wife sat nearby, knitting. There were some things one simply did not talk about, so she remained silent. In fact, she had no idea what these unmentionable things were.

When Andrés came into the room to say good night, his grandfather looked at him.

"What is it?" he asked.

"Nothing," Andrés mumbled, glancing at his grandmother.

He was pretty sure she would not tell on him because his grandfather was a pig, like all men, and behaved like a visitor in his own home, always on his best behavior. His grandfather was afraid of his wife because she was so pure and it was this that made him spend every evening at the club and made his wife shut herself up in her room sometimes, to cry. Andrés could hear her crying from his own room, which was directly above hers. He would have liked to go to the club too, like Don Ramón, and escape from such a pure house. But his grandmother had hinted that it would be as well to talk to his grandfather as little as possible. Not that they had anything to say to each other.

When Andrés went to confession before making his First Communion, he kept quiet about Velarde and his friend and everything to do with them: about the postcards, the dreams, the chair called Lourdes, and all the rest. He received the Host in a state of mortal sin. It was not, as they had assured him it would be, "the happiest day of his life." He was damned and his flesh would burn in hell-fire throughout eternity. Only his grandmother, and Lourdes, would go to heaven.

"How many timeth, my thon?" Father Damián would have lisped if he had told.

"How many timeth, my thon?"

Andrés awoke and sat up in bed. It was three-thirty. Very early. He groped about for a glass of water on the bedside table but did not find one. Then he went back to sleep.

A friend of his grandmother's was asking him why he wanted to study law.

"I just do," he replied stubbornly.

This friend was a very learned lady, secretary of a club

where other ladies met to discuss burning topics of the day, and attend lectures. She was as desiccated as an old sea biscuit, and her nose was so hooked that Andrés was always afraid she might chew the tip off as she talked. He was feeling annoyed just then because the lady had patted his cheek as she assured him that he was the living image of his father. This was too much, having his cheek patted at his age, just when he was about to graduate! It was his grandmother's fault—she liked showing him off because he was first in his class and had read a lot of books. Andrés knew perfectly well that his grandmother's only reason for inviting this lady had been to show him off, like one shows off an animal at a fair, in spite of the fact that she disapproved of all the members of the club as suffragettes and freethinkers.

"My father was a lawyer, and since my grandfather Ramón is one too, I'll be able to get a good job with his firm."

"Have you considered going into politics like him?"

Andrés shook his head scornfully. His grandmother glanced at him, frowning, clearly disappointed by her grandson's pedestrian answers. The visitor, however, learned though she was, did not seem to have noticed the arrogant way he answered her questions, and the green feather in her hat bobbed about excitedly as she assured him that great things were expected of a boy with a grandfather like his.

Andrés did not clearly remember when or why he decided to take up law. Somehow his family had always assumed that he would, and the thought of studying anything else had simply never entered his mind.

". . . but don't let me influence you," his grandfather always said during their frequent discussions of the subject. "Study whatever you like. Engineering, for instance. Chile is first and foremost a mining country, and I foresee great opportunities in that direction. They still haven't tapped half this country's potential wealth—there is a lot to be done. That's where Chile's future lies . . ."

During the peroration that invariably followed, Don Ramón would pace up and down the room. Andrés was certain that if he were ever to take up any subject but law his grandfather would never recover from the shock.

"But law is such a nice, gentlemanly profession," Misiá Elisa suggested.

"It is undoubtedly a great profession, possibly the greatest," Don Ramón agreed, lisping slightly, for he had his moustache cover on. "Or you might take up medicine, like Carlos Gros."

Andrés knew that these speeches of his grandfather were largely meant to convince himself that he was a modern man, of an open-minded and liberal spirit. Thus it was that he took up law.

He never felt any great enthusiasm for the legal profession, however, and as the first, second, and third years of his studies slipped by, he came to speak with less and less conviction about his future career. University life amused him, but only from a distance; he never took part in any student activities. The lecture courses appealed to him chiefly as a form of self-discipline. He actually became quite interested in some of the curriculum subjects, but it was a mild sort of interest. It was the same with everything else. He was twenty-one and had full control of the fortune his parents had left him, and he really had not the slightest desire to practice his profession, despite Misiá Elisa's entreaties and Don Ramón's bitter disappointment. He proposed to devote himself quite simply to cultivating his tastes. He would take walks and he would read. He would *live*.

"There's one brilliant person in the Abalos family already —my grandfather. What's the point of having another? I have no ambition to be what they keep telling me my father might have been if he had not died. I really haven't. And people who refer to him as 'poor thing' make me sick," Andrés confided to his old friend Carlos Gros, now studying medicine with a passionate dedication which struck the law student as puerile.

"Yes, but what about you?"

"Me? Life is much too short to be spent sitting behind a desk, signing papers and defending cases I don't give a damn about. No . . . I want to live *my* life . . ."

But what *was* living one's life? How did one go about it?

Andrés's rather phlegmatic temperament was not the kind to lead him into adventures or excesses of any sort, and shyness made his dealings with other people awkward. As a compensation for direct personal contact, he read and thought a great deal. Calling upon rational arguments that were really only a mask for his childhood fears, he speedily demolished the religious faith through which his grandmother had caused him so much suffering. Once he had thrown all the ballast overboard, he felt he could really get down to living, and shaping his own way of life, a way neither imposed upon him from without nor inherited. He read a great deal. But somehow or other the conclusions put forward by the various philosophical and scientific systems never seemed quite final: they were projects, or plans, not constructions that could give life resonance or provide a definitive solution to the mysteries of life and death. Now he knew why the different philosophies had done nothing but contradict each other through the ages— in the last analysis, everything was a big question mark. And the more he read the more shifting and treacherous became the ground beneath his feet.

He used to dream that he was rushing across a long, long bridge slung out over a void. But the bridge abruptly came to an end before reaching the opposite bank, leaving a space in which there was nothing at all, only emptiness. In his haste and anxiety to reach the other side, Andrés always fell off the end, screaming with terror as he found himself hurtling through the void. He would wake up sweating and terrified. There was nothing in either philosophy or science —a point of view that provoked endless discussions with Carlos Gros—which gave him the means of arriving, whole and conscious, on the other side. Everything ended in a zero, in another question, the question mark of death itself.

He began to read poets and novelists—with the same result, except that these seemed to approach the same insoluble problems in different, disguised ways. Still, while reading the poems and novels, he did make one curious discovery: he actually enjoyed reading them. By concentrating on style and plot, he managed to slide over the troublesome questions, the dangerous, fascinating emptinesses that the great dissatisfied opened up behind them, and so they gave him a sort of forgetfulness: they were enjoyable. But presently this form of escape began to pall, and all the poems and novels he read began to seem identical. He no longer enjoyed them. And at night he once more fell screaming into the chasm at the end of the bridge.

He felt disoriented and anxious, and longed desperately for some kind of order and equilibrium. Then he began reading history, and this time genuinely succeeded in entertaining himself, most of all with French history: letters, memoirs, and biographical sketches. The odd, the picturesque details—how Henri IV spent the day, Walpole's amours with Mme du Deffand, the intrigues of Port Royal, of the Guise and Orléans families, of the ducs d'Enghien

and Cavour, in short, the minutiae of *la petite histoire*—
constituted a fantastic fictitious world, full of equally fictitious conflicts, all of which existed only in relation to each
other, preserved forever under the bell glass of time. Anyone who tried to relate this beautifully colored chess game
to some vital issue or conflict in the contemporary world
was nothing but a pretentious pedant. Yes, he enjoyed his
history! But he still dreamed that the bridge did not reach
to the other side, and hurtled screaming through the chasm
of his dream till the emptiness swallowed him up.

When he was twenty-four, at about the same time that he
finished his law studies, he suddenly stopped dreaming and
worrying. Andrés saw a lot of Carlos Gros at this period
and they often went walking together. Though Carlos was
naturally gregarious and talkative, he enjoyed his friendship with Andrés. Competing with Andrés was easy and
appealing: the worlds that medicine was even then opening
up to his marveling eyes seemed so much more immediate,
so much more alive than the law student's bookish existence.
Andrés himself, because of his shyness and also because of
his curiosity about some aspects of life to which Carlos
Gros's vitality gleefully drew him, never felt the need of
another close friend. His fellow students were acquaintances
only, never friends. During his frequent walks with Carlos
they would discuss all manner of subjects, both general and
personal, frankly and enthusiastically. Andrés was tall and
lean. His hair had already begun to recede, giving his forehead a pensive air. But his face was as soft as a child's,
and wore a faint perpetual smile, as if by adopting this
expression he hoped to exorcise all his fears and ills. His
eyes were already hidden behind glasses. Carlos, in contrast, was short and stocky, with good, strong features. His
smile, when it came, was a conflagration that illuminated
his whole face, but it would vanish again as suddenly as it

had come. They had been friends since childhood because their families were friends.

Andrés often preferred to go out without Carlos and walk about the streets for hours by himself. That is how it was on this particular warm day, one of those days when dusk falls early, leaving a ghostly light lingering in the sky for almost an hour after dark. Andrés was walking through streets whose general effect was one of monotonous sameness, although the rows of squat houses with identical windows and doors opening straight on the pavement were occasionally interspersed with an unexpected two-story building. The people here were neither rich nor poor, ugly nor beautiful, happy nor sad. They were just people. The street lights had not been lit yet. There was so little traffic that a gang of children was playing ball in the street. In a doorway an old woman sat on a cane stool, blowing at a charcoal brazier that had not been properly lit and gave off an unpleasant stench. A man passed him on his way home from work, jingling the keys with which he would open the front door of his house. Women were buying candles and bread and wine in the corner shop. It was very peaceful, the terror of nothingness concealed in its bosom.

"Four-eyes," a little girl called after him before returning to her game of hopscotch.

A second afterward, the little girl had forgotten him completely, never to remember him again throughout her entire life. That moment in which she had singled him out from the crowd would not make the slightest impression on this child, who would grow up to be a mother and then a grandmother. She was back at her hopscotch now. To her, Andrés was just a passerby, nothing more, alone among these people but no different from them. He looked up the street. The lights were going on. A man stood propped in a doorway, smoking, and a woman was watering the begonias in her window box. The squat houses had no architectural features that linked them with any particular country or time, and the lives they sheltered were like those in any street at any period in history.

At that moment the terror of time and space brushed past Andrés and left him reeling. His legs buckled under him, and his forehead was damp with the fear that assails those who need to know but fail to understand the wherefore of things. Standing there, on that tranquil dusky street corner, painfully wide awake, he felt himself about to plunge into the chasm at the end of the bridge, the ultimate horror which comes of realizing that all equals nothing. But a second before he gave in to despair and took the leap that would save or destroy him, a flicker of the instinct for survival saved him from the folly of demanding a final answer from himself there and then. This flicker took the form of an ironic remark.

"Everything is the same as it would be in . . . in . . ." he tried to think of the most remote, exotic place on earth, "in Omsk, say, and all these people were Omskians."

The atrabilious word made him laugh.

But of course, this street and these people were exactly the same as they would be in Omsk! His laughter brought with it a feeling of enormous contentment and well being, as if every one of his cells and muscles, every part of his organism had been renewed and was functioning perfectly. He saw people and things stretching out their hands to each other across centuries and kilometers; there were no longer any differences to make them objects of terror: all Omskians, himself included, were living a common destiny. They were all blind . . . but equally and universally blind amidst the chaos, a chaos that might be changed to order if one simply accepted the impossibility of arriving at the truth and stopped tormenting oneself with responsibilities and ques-

tions to which there were no answers. Compromises did not
exist. There was only matter, caught up in the phenomenon
of life, awaiting extinction. That was all. Was there anything to be gained, meanwhile, from seeking to understand,
driving oneself to question and demand, create and pro-
create, turning to philosophers, sages, poets, and novelists
in search of explanations? How could Carlos Gros be so
childish as to believe that science was the solution to everything, capable of carrying one across the bridge and over
the chasm into which all mankind must fall? He failed to
see that science, like philosophy and religion, has its origins
in a belief, in the mystery of that dark street, these lives,
Omsk itself. The only thing which was not a mystery was
the knowledge of one's own existence. Afterwards came
death, and then nothing mattered any more because everything there took place beyond life itself. He, Andrés Abalos,
was alive and had been born in a certain time and place,
among certain people. That was Omsk. Just as the woman
watering her window box had been born at a certain time
and place, among certain people. To rebel, try and give
meaning to existence, do something, cling to any belief
with which to try and cross the confines of the present, all
this was stupid, pretentious, and puerile. And responsibilities and compromises were still more so. The only reason-
able attitude was one of silent, passive acceptance. He liked
reading French history, didn't he? Well, then, he would
read French history. He liked walking through the quiet
streets in the evening, didn't he? Well, then, he would do
that.

For the first time Andrés felt as though his poor feet had
touched solid ground and he had succeeded in leaping from
the end of the bridge to the other side. For others, what he
had just felt might perhaps seem like a black pit of despair.
To him, however, it seemed like the justification for doing

nothing, risking nothing. It freed him from the necessity of making any compromises with life. The little girl was playing hopscotch. Houses with two windows and one door. A man smoking on a street corner while a woman laughed. He, Andrés Abalos, was merely one among them, a solitary wanderer at any point, any moment in the universe.

Andrés lit a cigarette. He walked on a few blocks through a world become wonderfully simple and clear. Then he took a streetcar home.

He described his experience to Carlos. The young doctor lost his temper, declaring that this Omsk business was nothing but an excuse for cowardliness and fear of responsibility. The important thing, he said, was to take up some position toward life, do something, leave behind some proof of having taken a chance and loved some activity or person above all else. Andrés was not much perturbed by this. He decided that what Carlos said was perfectly sound where Carlos was concerned, but quite unimportant, for Carlos's beliefs were Omsk too. They were the commonplace street as night fell, the solitary passerby trying to light a cigarette on a corner that seems to be a meeting place for all the winds on earth.

Andrés never dreamed again, and he forgot about the chasm at the end of the bridge.

And, after a while, his life adjusted itself to the Omsk concept and he was able to forget about that too. However, the word *Omsk*, but without its deeper significance, cropped up frequently in his conversations with Carlos, as a sort of code word denoting aspects of the city that seemed to them imbued with a special pathos and beauty. An organ-grinder, one Sunday, with a ring of bored, unimpressed children standing around listening, was Omsk. So was a man making love to a servant girl under the trees, out in the cold, shelterless street. So was . . . well, so were hundreds of things.

Some time later, on a sunny Sunday in early winter, Andrés and Carlos were strolling by the river across from the Parque Forestal. Above them, the dry net of interwoven branches fished in the light of a sky so clear it did not seem to be there at all. An ancient beggar was sitting by a tree, in the bed of a dried-up creek, mending an incredibly worn, patched shirt. His gray hair was dirty, and his bare torso was as hard and dark as leather. Various pots and packets disposed on the ground around him held his food, and in all probability all his worldly possessions as well.

"Look," Carlos exclaimed as they went past. "Omsk!"

"Mmm-mmm-m," said Andrés.

But he was not sure what his friend meant.

7 The old woman's insults did not make much impression on Estela. She was so used to hearing words like those—they were constantly on her father's and brother's lips—that they had lost all meaning for her. As for the accusations about her and Andrés, well, they were so absurd that they merely had the effect of bringing Misiá Elisa's madness home to her for the first time. Poor lady . . . she did not seem to realize that Andrés was an old man . . .

What did make her cry, though, was the violence with which the old woman charged her with stealing. At home in the country her brother had once stolen an old pitchfork from the *patrón*'s house, and her father had almost killed him when he found out. He whipped him and whipped him and then left him groaning right through the freezing-cold night, flattened like a dog in the stubble field alongside their house. She had stayed awake, appalled, listening to those groans. And she had felt something of the same horror when Misiá Elisa called her a thief. For the truth was that ever since Mario had asked her to the movies she had thought of nothing else but how to get hold of the key to the lock which secured the gate to the street, a massive rusty iron key that her aunt Lourdes always kept in the pocket of her apron. Being called a thief not only emboldened her to plan this small theft; it also made her recklessly indifferent to the consequences if she were found out. She *had* to go to the movies, even if it was only this once! So far there had been little difference between her life in Santiago and her life in the country, here as there what it all boiled down to was obedience and hard work. That was right, that was as it should be. But her desire to go to the movies—that inexplicable darkness, Mario, the blonde actresses—had made a breach in her submissiveness. Yes, she had to go, even if it was only this once.

As she fetched and carried trays of sugary cakes, empty glasses, and little embroidered napkins about among the few people who had turned up for Misiá Elisa's birthday party, Estela never once stopped thinking about the key. She offered refreshments to two ladies who were whispering together in a corner. They were cousins, nieces of one of Don Ramón's sisters.

"Won't you have something, María?" one of them asked the other. "No, not for me, thank you . . ."

María went on talking.

". . . three, *three* huge cases of quinces to make sweetmeats with, and I can't tell you how splendid, Inés, quite superb . . ."

"What did they want for them?" Inés asked, yawning.

While María told her how much they had cost, Inés

reflected that her unfortunate cousin, despite her recent
European tour, was still a simple country woman to whom
dulce de membrillo and the making of it ranked high among
the world's vital problems. How could she, with all those
millions to throw around, have chosen that particular hat
and that boring little dress in Paris? Still, if she were that
shape when she was forty-eight she probably wouldn't feel
much interest in clothes either, as long as she were decently
covered. It really wasn't surprising that Ramón, well . . .
she glanced over to where her cousin's husband, a youthful-
looking, conspicuously elegant man, was talking to Carlos
Gros's wife near the old woman's bed.

"Ah, but that's quite a bit more than Adriana paid for
hers," Inés said, for the sake of saying something, her gold
bracelets jangling as she moved her arm in a nervous
gesture.

"I saw Adriana's, but mine are much better—they're
superb, really superb." All the passion that her aging, un-
painted face could muster was concentrated in an effort to
convince Inés of the absolute superiority of her quinces.
"But you know what Adriana is like, Inés, she would do
anything to save money. Although Carlos Gros is made of
money, apparently. She has just bought a huge estate in the
south, near Parral somewhere, I'm not sure where exactly."

"*Another* one?" On Inés's gaunt face, whose brick-
colored mask of cosmetics could not disguise the traces of
years of spinsterhood, the glossy brows rose in a gesture of
envious admiration. Being poor herself, she had had to
satisfy her taste for luxury by opening a tiny, but immensely chic, little shop with another spinster friend.

"No, not another one, my dear, of course not! Carlos
isn't *that* rich! No, she bought it for Panchito, their second
son, to manage. You know they've never been able to get
him to settle down to anything. Mind you, though, they do

say that Carlos is tremendously well off! He gets a fortune for every operation he performs, you know."

"And there's what he hopes to get out of that great booby, Andrés . . ." Inés murmured.

Her parents had once thought of marrying her to Andrés, who was her second cousin, rich, impeccably well bred, and a bachelor. He had succeeded in extricating himself from the situation in the nick of time, leaving barely perceptible bruises.

"From Andrés?" María asked.

"Of course. After all, he must have been looking after Misiá Elisa for almost thirty years now . . ."

"Oh, I don't know. I don't suppose Carlos would sink so low as to send Andrés bills. We all know he likes money, but that would really be the end, Inés! But he has looked after my aunt magnificently. She's in tremendous form, don't you think, Inés?"

"Tremendous, nicer and livelier every day! I can't think why they all go around saying she's mad, I don't believe a word of it. Personally, I find her much more intelligent than she ever used to be. Do you remember what the poor creature was like when my uncle Ramón was alive? Ravishing to look at, of course, and as kind as could be, and tremendously well dressed. But didn't you think she was a tiny bit, well, silly? As though she were scared of something. And then staying at home all the time, sewing and praying with the servants. It can't often happen that people get nicer and cleverer as they grow older. It must be fun for Andrés having such an amusing grandmother. A grandmother who's going to leave him a nice pile when she goes, too!"

"Well, I'd just like to know what good all that money is going to be to Andrés! I think he's thoroughly selfish, myself. Why doesn't he come and live here with my aunt, in this splendid house, instead of letting those two monstrous maids get away with murder? Do you remember that dinner service my aunt has, the everyday one?"

"The Sèvres with the blue rim?"

"No, no, that wasn't the everyday china. As a matter of fact, I'm thinking of buying the Sèvres service if they sell up here when my aunt dies. No, the one I mean is the Limoges with the yellow rim and the tiny birds on it. It's a little old-fashioned now, of course, but you know what that sort of thing costs nowadays! Well, last year, on my aunt's name day, for some reason I suddenly took it into my head to peep into the kitchen on my way out. And do you know what? Rosario was pouring out milk for something like four cats, and every single one of them had its own Limoges saucer! Imagine! I'm positive none of these things would happen if Andrés came to live here. Now tell me if you don't think he's selfish."

"But of course he is!" Inés cried. "And I've told him so dozens of times! I don't mince words with Andrés, as you know. What does he get out of living alone, I'd like to know? It's not as if he led a particularly gay life. Leading the sort of life he does, he'd be perfectly happy under this roof. In fact, he'd really be much better off. He's so bored, poor thing, you can't conceive how bored he is! All he ever does is go from his apartment to the club, and then back from the club to the apartment again. Plus the occasional meal with Carlos Gros and Adriana . . ."

"I should imagine he would be going a bit off his head . . ."

"Oh, no, he's perfectly sound, poor fellow. Though sometimes . . . I don't know. But suppose he had some . . . how shall I put it . . . some secret vice, something a bit . . . odd? No, no, not *that*, my dear! Ha, ha, ha! He's never been accused of *that*! Who with, anyway? Just imagine how

ghastly it would be with poor Carlos, now that he's got so
revoltingly fat! Ha, ha, ha! No, not that. But something
much stranger, much worse. No, I don't know what exactly.
But don't you find when you meet someone so fantastically
quiet and virtuous and everything, the perfect gentleman
in fact, don't you find something the tiniest bit sinister about
him, like those Englishmen sipping tea in the movies? I
can't help suspecting him of being a hypocrite. Well . . . I
don't know why I'm going on like this . . ."

In the end, as Lourdes and Rosario had predicted, hardly
anyone turned up for Misiá Elisa Grey de Abalos's ninety-
fourth birthday party. Only Dr. Gros and his wife, Inés,
María and her elegant husband, and Don Emiliano Saenz,
who arrived very late. He gave the old lady a pinch and
assured her that he had never seen her looking so flourishing. Then he asked Lourdes in a voice half-choked with
asthma to bring him a man-sized drink, and sat down next
to Andrés and Carlos. They were both sitting in the small
room that opened off the bedroom, the one that had once
been a sewing room and was now used by Estela, who slept
on a cot, which had been folded away in a corner. Don
Emiliano, limping, coughing, wizened, and gay, thanked
Lourdes for the drink.

"How are you feeling, Lourdes?" Dr. Gros asked her.

"Not too good, Don Carlitos. I've been rushing around so
much I feel all worn out."

"You should go to bed early tonight, you don't look too
well."

He felt her pulse. A fascinated gleam appeared in the
maid's eyes.

"Who's going to clear up all this then, I'd like to know?
Rosario is already in bed—you know how selfish she is,
she'd be in bed on the dot even if the world was coming to
an end. Anyway, who's going to lock up the street door?"

"But that's what your niece is here for, woman." Andrés interrupted. "To save you work. Off you go then, you heard what the doctor said."

"Just try some of these little cakes, Don Carlitos, just taste one. You're still young, they can't do you any harm."

"But I'm too fat as it is. Adriana has put me on a saccharine diet. Well, all right then, I give up . . ."

He gobbled down several cakes. Don Emiliano drained his glass before putting it back on the tray which Lourdes removed. Then he seemed to fall asleep in his chair.

Andrés saw Lourdes handing the key to Estela. He still had a terrible headache. He felt as if his grandmother's remarks had buried themselves in his brain and blocked it up so that he couldn't think or feel anything but this pain which crushed his skull. He had just been giving Carlos an abridged account of that morning's scene in the hope that talking about it might somehow dissolve this mental block and relieve the pain.

"And you should have heard the other things she said . . ."

"Remember how squeamish she used to be? Do you remember that time we all went to spend the summer on María's father's estate when we were children, and your grandmother presented us all, boys and girls, with identical white pinafores so there wouldn't be any awkward questions asked?"

Andrés managed a laugh.

"And now she calls the girl a whore . . ."

"Poor woman."

"Yes, poor woman. And poor girl too. She was terribly upset by the whole thing. What worries me is that my grandmother may open the girl's eyes with all this talk. What shall I do if Estela does become a whore and a thief because she's constantly heard my grandmother accuse her of being those things?"

"Don't be ridiculous. I take it you'll send her back to the country when Misiá Elisa dies?"

"Will that be soon, do you think? Do you think she'll die soon?"

Silently, the question invaded Andrés's mind, dismaying him with its new, vehement desire. The question, formerly cloaked in a vague piety, now stood revealed for what it really was, the expression of a cruel hope. Oh, if only his grandmother would die! If only she would die now! That morning the old woman's mad intuition had plunged into Andrés's subconscious, uncovering fears and desires he had never dared to look at squarely, and showing them to him in the distorting mirror of her crazy words. Andrés could feel those fears fluttering within him now, naked, unformulated, still nameless. If his grandmother died, he might never need to identify them, he would be safe, free to take up his life again with everything tamed and under control. Like the criminal who envisages a second murder, that of the person who witnesses his first crime, Andrés found himself once more wishing, passionately, wildly: "Oh, if only my grandmother would leave me in peace!"

Carlos was speaking to him.

"What about you? How did you react? You've inherited all your grandmother's prudishness, quite apart from being an out-and-out hypocrite."

"Me? Don't be silly. Why should I mind? I'm too old, and I've lived too long."

Carlos interrupted him with a shout of laughter.

"*Lived*? You? Forgive my laughter, but you're the one who is being silly. You haven't lived, old man, you never dared to begin! You dropped out of the race years ago."

"What do you mean?"

"Don't pretend you don't know! You've never dared take the plunge into anything in your whole life, falling in love, least of all! Remember those insipid little love affairs of yours, nice handy little affairs which never threatened to involve you? *Have* you lived? In what sense of the word, I'd like to know? You are a reasonably intelligent man, with first-rate sensibilities. But you've simply wasted yourself, old man!"

Andrés stopped pacing about the room and came to an angry halt in front of Carlos.

"What right have you to . . ."

"What right have I?" Carlos, who had had quite a bit to drink, interrupted him. "The right that being your only friend gives me, that we have never kept anything from each other. I can't think what's got into you today, you're so . . ."

He broke off as Andrés collapsed into a chair, his forehead puckered with distress. After a short silence the doctor, rather apologetically and with a redder face than usual, once more addressed his friend.

"As a matter of fact, I'm in the most hopeless mess myself. I can't help envying your equilibrium, Andrés, and your freedom from the common appetites. I'm in love as I've never been in love before . . ."

Now it was Andrés's turn to laugh.

"I've heard you say that once too often, Carlos, my friend. You can't expect me to take it seriously . . ."

"You don't understand," Carlos said. "You don't understand a thing. I grant you your superiority and, as I said, I envy you your equilibrium and ironical detachment. But, do you know something? I pity you. When I think of your love life I feel very, very sorry for you."

Carlos, speaking with more than his usual intensity, suddenly asked: "Do you remember that woman you had a few years ago? That big handsome Jewess with the dyed hair?"

"Rebecca?"

"That's right. Rebecca. She was a nice convenient woman for you. You visited her a couple of times a week, at a certain hour, and I believe you were quite generous to her. But the moment you began to suspect that you were seriously falling in love with her, that you were becoming dependent on her, you walked out on her because that would have meant Rebecca wasn't a convenience any more. You might even have become involved. Carreños's handbook, which appears to have been the dominant influence in your life, for you are nothing if not a gentleman, must have something to say on the first page about gentlemen not marrying their mistresses, particularly when they happen to be Jewish. What would your family have said?—those four impoverished wretches who are all the family you have left and whom you never cared a damn about anyway? No, Andrés, you haven't lived, you've simply sidestepped life."

"You're talking like a complete idiot. Since when has love been the most valuable experience in life? Frankly, you sound like a schoolgirl who has read too much George Isaacs . . ."

"More of your irony! You don't understand what I mean, so you reject it. I am talking, if you will pardon the expression, in symbolic terms. The deficiency in you which prevents you from really falling in love with some woman is the same thing which keeps you from a passionate interest in some activity, or even some vice. What you lack is the ability to let yourself go, you lack faith, wholehearted enthusiasm, the capacity for emotional admiration which concedes to another person the importance of being unique, necessary . . ."

"You *are* being lyrical! Congratulations . . ." Andrés stammered.

"Let me finish, I'm drunk. But don't try and fool yourself, neither you nor I have made a success of our lives in any great or meaningful sense . . . consequently, love is the only great adventure left to us. No, no, don't look at me like that, I've always admitted to you that though my career has been brilliant I know I have failed myself in it, entirely through my own fault. But *you* think you're so marvelous you've never even descended to the level of needing anything, or anyone, and therefore, obviously, you have never been in love, poor fellow . . ."

Andrés laughed the convulsive, noiseless laugh characteristic of him.

"You've got a nerve, talking about love! You may have slept with a lot of women, but frankly you don't strike me as the person best qualified to preach about love. After all, you and your wife . . ."

"There is no need to bring Adriana into this. I respect her, I loved her very much once, she has given me three splendid healthy children and I have a marvelous home, a real haven. I would do anything in the world rather than hurt her, she is the one person I unconditionally respect. It's true that I am no longer in love with her, but I was once, deeply in love. I suppose you think it's funny that my extramarital affairs don't last? But what does that matter? I'm talking about attitudes. The fact remains that when I'm in love I live the experience with my whole being—it possesses me completely, in all my activities, my work, everything. It's as though I were falling in love for the first time, every time. . . . And I'm fifty-four, the same age as you. You, on the other hand, have always been a perfectly constructed human being from top to toe, without the slightest tendency to err. You are self-sufficient; you don't need either to give or to receive. But you have made the gravest mistake of all —you are quite alone. You are old now, and since your family goes to pieces early, you will soon be senile. Misiá Elisa will almost certainly die this year, and when that happens there will be nothing real, nothing except a few poor memories, to fill the gap. Your life won't have a center. I may be your only friend, but I must tell you, my dear Andrés, that in spite of my great affection for you, I would not be prepared to have you around more than once or twice a week—anything more would be a nuisance to Adriana and me. I can't lend you my life so that you can use it to create a factitious existence of your own . . ."

Andrés suddenly thought about his grandmother dying, and snatched, horrified, at the notion that she must never die, never, but go on living forever, because if she died he would cease to live too, assuming he ever had lived. How he envied Carlos what he had always regarded as his defects! There was a lot to be said against him. But it no longer seemed to matter that his schoolgirl gushing about love made him appear ridiculous; though certainly, with his short, plump figure, stubby fingers, and face like softened red Plasticine, it was both ludicrous and unaesthetic to imagine him making love. Moreover, he was ambitious and had let his youthful scientific passion be corrupted into a desire to make money and achieve a reputation. He was base, promiscuous, even lachrymose in his love affairs. He, Andrés, had frequently said things which had cut him to the quick. But he could not deny that Carlos always threw himself wholeheartedly into everything, whether for good or evil. He had given his instincts free rein, he had respected them, he had believed. When he was on his deathbed, he would have the consolation of knowing he had tasted a good portion of human experience with all the intensity he was capable of. And he, Andrés? He saw himself, suddenly, on his deathbed, and he was seized by a wild desire to run away, screaming with terror, go back fifty years and live through it all again, quite differently.

"Pretty little thing, that maid, nice legs . . ." Don Emiliano mused, watching Estela go by with a tray of empty glasses. Then he slumped forward again in his chair, like a mummy, and went back to sleep.

Andrés got up abruptly. Everyone seemed to have joined forces against him—his grandmother, Don Emiliano, Carlos, Estela. Every word cut like a lash into the tenderest parts of his being. He leaned out of the window, staring at the garden and the darkness which had just fallen. He wanted to think, think! But what good could it do him now? It was too late! How could he possibly blot out his whole personality and life with one stroke of the pen and try to build it all again, now, at the age of fifty-four? There was only one life, he saw that clearly now. His grandmother was going to die, and it would be as though he himself were dying. Then he too would die, and thousands, millions, thousands of millions of years would elapse and there would be nothing left of him, and the planet would go wheeling on through black, interstellar space toward its absurd, nonexistent destiny. By then he, who had never exposed himself to anything more demanding that his own convenience, would be reduced to a mere chemical substance in the process of transformation, a mineral, and he would never have availed himself of matter's infinitely short-lived privilege to be something more—life, consciousness, will—for one second in the millions of years in which everything that happened was accidental and arbitrary.

"Let's go, dear," Adriana said to Carlos. "Misiá Elisita looks tired. I must say, Andrés, she seems tremendously well, much livelier than last year."

They said that every year.

They all left. The large bedroom emptied out, and only Estela remained, silently picking up cutlery and dishes. The old woman dozed, gratified by all the fuss and attention. Thinking that she was asleep, Andrés leaned over her to kiss her on the forehead. The sick woman's eyes opened. She smiled sweetly at her grandson.

"What's the matter, child?"

Andrés stared.

"Nothing, Grandma, nothing at all . . ."

"There's something wrong . . ."

"Good night, Grandma."

"Good night, child, take care of yourself—you don't look too well."

Andrés went downstairs. The only sound in the great, deserted house was that of his soft footfalls on the red carpet. All the lights were burning and all the doors were thrown open in expectation of the visitors, who, as usual, had failed to materialize. Estela helped him with his coat. The pink bare palms, whose connection with himself had been pointed out by his grandmother that morning, were dangerously close. For a second he felt the girl's warm breath on the back of his neck. But he was terribly weary.

"Good night, Estela, thanks. It all went very well. Oh, you mustn't worry about what the señora says. You know she isn't well . . ."

"Yes, sir . . ."

He noticed that the girl seemed tired. She must be hoping he would leave quickly so she could get to bed.

"Will you be shutting the street door, Estela?"

"Yes, sir. My aunt gave me the key before she went to bed."

They crossed the dark garden. The girl softly opened, then shut the door. Andrés had a last glimpse of her haloed by the light of a street lamp which came filtering down through the branches of a tree.

"Good night, Estela."

"Good night, señor."

She stood watching as he disappeared from sight. Then she looked at the key, put it in her pocket, and squeezed it there, against her warm body. It was a quarter past nine. She would have to hurry.

PART TWO

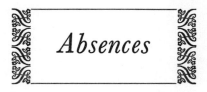

Absences

8 ⁂⁊ Everyone concerned took a little time to recover from Misiá Elisita's birthday party. The maids were tired, Estela was languid from her noctural escapade, and the lady of the house seemed incapable of distinguishing between the latest birthday party and all the previous ones. She kept asking why So-and-so—someone who had not visited her for more than a decade—had forgotten to bring her a gift to mark the occasion.

The old woman made Estela put all the presents in the bottom drawer of the bureau. Then she hid the key to the bureau under her pillow, where from time to time she patted it, as if to make certain it was still there. She had Estela show her all the presents every day for a week, and she inspected each one thoroughly.

"Mm-mm, they're all there. Those she-devils haven't stolen them from me yet. I have to go through them all, one by one, because you know what that Lourdes is like. I'm not saying she isn't a good, sober creature in many ways, but the poor woman just has this tendency to steal. Like Rosario. What's one to do about it? Everyone has his little faults, child, we are none of us perfect. You, for instance.

I know you are a good girl, but you're a little flighty, yes, yes, my child, a little flighty, so don't try to deny it! And hearing all these bad things everywhere, things you don't understand, you are in danger of becoming a loose woman and spending all your time in theaters and dance halls."

Estela sat nearby, doing some embroidery. She knew that it had been a very wicked thing to do, going to the movies. The movies were wicked, both Lourdes and Rosario said so, and Misiá Elisa too, and though she might be sick, she knew what was right and what was wrong. It had been such good luck, Lourdes giving her the key like that, though. It meant she did not have to steal it. But she had been dreaming lately that Misiá Elisa had turned into the sea monster who devoured the blonde actress in the turquoise-colored world of the movie she had seen, and was devouring her because she had caught her stealing the key. Misiá Elisa was devouring her because of her wickedness, for having been aware of Mario breathing beside her in the darkness, breathing, breathing. She awoke to complete silence. She couldn't even hear the old woman's faint snores in the next room.

". . . you'll see. First he invites you to the movies, acting all innocent. Then he makes you drunk and carries you off with him. And then, well, I just don't know, child . . . but nine months later there you are with an illegitimate baby to support—and don't fool yourself, you won't see *him* again! That's why a good, well-behaved girl like you needs to be very careful. Don't believe them when they start swearing eternal love and taking your hand, because that's how it always starts—men are all the same, all pigs! So be careful. I'm only telling you this because I know, and I'm fond of you . . ."

Estela dropped her embroidery. From where she was sitting on the ottoman, she could see through the thick glass panes to where the trees were waving and tangling in the afternoon breeze. Was it going to rain?

Misiá Elisa just didn't know what Mario was like! In the huge darkness of the theater, when she least expected it, he had quietly taken her hand. He just felt for it and laid his own hand over hers, quite naturally, as though it were the most obvious thing in the world. His hand was warm and rough-skinned, and a little shy too, and it was this shyness that told Estela that he really liked her. She had been waiting for him to look at her and smile, but he had been too engrossed in the submarine adventure. Then, abruptly, he began explaining the film to her, still not looking at her but with his hand covering her own small hand. All of a sudden he gave a shout of laughter and made a remark aloud which made everyone laugh; Estela was watching him out of the corner of her eye to see whether he expected her to join in the laughter. No telling. He was a little shy, and this was what pleased Estela most. She also liked feeling the weight of his hand over hers, both of them quite still, and hearing him laugh, and feeling him so near in the darkness.

She liked Mario. And Mario liked her too, she could tell. After all, it wasn't the first time in her life. . . . In the country, on her fourteenth birthday, Aurelio, Leticia González's idiot son who was always following her around telling her she was pretty, had given her a song-thrush called Pascual. Estela was nice to Aurelio because she could tell he liked her. The thrush, which was her only possession, for everything else belonged either to her parents or to the *patrón*, would call out "Tee-la, tee-la" from his little wicker cage in the hallway and poke his beak through the bars when he saw her coming. Estela would scratch his head softly and say:

"Here, birdie . . . here, birdie."

When the girl went away, Pascual started chirping again. "Tee-la, tee-la."

Fishface liked her in a different way from Aurelio. He wore glasses as thick as saltshakers and stammered and was sickly. Sometimes Estela managed to elude her sister-in-law Margarita's watchful eye and headed for the watermelon patch behind the tenants' orchard on the estate, where Fishface was waiting with a bag of candy for them to eat together. They would bathe in the creek at the end of the watermelon grove, in the concealing shade of a stand of old willows. Then they would stretch out almost naked in the sun, which tingled on their bare shoulders and dried them almost at once, and share one, two, three, sometimes four ripe watermelons, splitting them open on a stone. They only ate the cold red hearts.

"Like the witch in *Snow White*," said Fishface.

Estela didn't know who the witch in *Snow White* was. The boy told her the story, lying with the sun on his back, while Estela, listening attentively, cleaned his glasses or wiped the sticky watermelon blood from between his fingers with the damp hem of her petticoat. He was a year younger than she was, and his skin was white and smooth because he came of a very good family. She would sometimes kiss his face.

One day Aurelio saw them drying themselves in the sun. He went to Estela's house, took Pascual from his cage, and flung him against the tiles in the hall, leaving a little puddle of black feathers and blood and spilled entrails.

"It was Leticia González's son," said Margarita, sweeping up Pascual's remains.

It was bad and dangerous, then, to be loved the way Aurelio loved her. She felt frightened. Margarita put the broom away in a corner and then took hold of Estela and pulled her ears till they burned.

"Fool girl! Do you want the *patron*'s son to give you a

bastard? Don't you know what those rich people are like?"

Estela knew all about their legendary behavior. She knew that all gentlemen took advantage of silly girls and then pretended not to know anything about it after they had fathered a bastard child. Margarita questioned Estela closely on this score, and some of the questions made Estela laugh, but she must have been satisfied with what she heard because she gave Estela a slice of bread spread with fresh butter.

"All right, I won't say anything, but you must promise me this will never happen again."

Estela promised. She promised despite the fact that Fishface would never have done anything to hurt her, nothing she didn't want him to do. She often felt like doing things with him, but he was little still and didn't want to, and Estela preferred to wait till he did. The boy would stroke her bare skin, though, and tell her how pretty she was . . . then suddenly, catching sight of a thrush in the distance, he would get up and try to bring it down with his slingshot.

"When we are bigger," Fishface whispered.

Estela understood, and knew she must wait till he was ready.

She was not afraid of Fishface. But she was terribly frightened of her older brother, Margarita's husband. Several times when he had come back drunk and met her in the dark hall, he had tried to paw her and kiss her, his breath stinking of wine. He was dangerous, like Aurelio. Fishface would never behave like that, and neither would Mario, for his hand rested shyly on hers just like the patrón's son's.

Aurelio once talked to Estela's father about marrying her. This frightened Estela, because Aurelio had murdered Pascual.

"I'll kill you, I'll kill you, do you hear, if I ever catch you with that idiot of Leticia's!" her father shouted, brandishing his shining whip. At each shout his broad-brimmed hat flopped up and down on his forehead, which was light-skinned above the eyebrows and deeply tanned below. Estela trembled and cast down her eyes. She knew that her father, who was the *patrón's* grocer and the most respected tenant on the estate, loved her very much, more than anyone else, and his fury over the Aurelio business was only because he wanted someone better for her, someone like Mario, for instance. Her father taught her to obey and work hard so she would know how to make herself useful, and make the man she eventually married happy. Because of course she would have to marry. There was nothing dangerous or frightening about marriage. Loving Fishface was almost like being married to him because he was so nice. They had decided to wait till they were grown up so as not to hurt or frighten each other. They were grown up now, but it was a long, long time since Fishface had last been to the country. And now there was Mario, who was nice too.

Mario scarcely spoke on the way back to the house after the movie. But Estela understood how he felt, for every time they accidentally touched in the darkness Mario drew back hurriedly, almost imperceptibly, as if shy. When she smiled and said goodbye at the door, Estela thought he was going to come closer, but just as he was about to, he seemed to change his mind. He said something funny which made them both laugh, and then he left.

9   "No, I can't go," Mario said.

He was drinking beer with some friends, sitting at a table near the door of the Condor de Chile Sports Club, which was constantly swinging open or shut. There were few people in the bar because most of the members and their families had set off early to get a good place in the uptown empty lot where the Condor football team was playing against the Manuel Rodríguez team that morning. Things had looked pretty bad the night before, the sky was clouded over and rain seemed to be on the way. The club members gazed despairingly at the sky: they knew that neither Salvador Norambuena nor Muñoz, the team's two stars, played well on a wet field. But the morning brought a surprise, a clear blue sky perfect for flag-waving and good times generally. Even the team's most reluctant supporters allowed themselves to be persuaded to make a picnic lunch and climb into the crowded buses to go to the game.

Mario refused to go. His friends had been trying to persuade him for hours now, unsuccessfully. He was going to see Estela that morning. But there was no question of admitting this: if he did, his friends would jump to conclusions—the wrong ones—and ply him with questions and jokes. Ordinarily he wouldn't have minded telling them all about it—they told one another all about their conquests right down to the most insignificant detail. But Mario wanted to keep Estela's existence a secret. He didn't know why exactly, he just didn't want to have to talk about it, which explained his stubborn, ungracious: "No, I can't go, man."

They were all dressed up for the occasion. Black, slicked-down locks crowned their heads, and in the back their smooth helmets of hair ended in a freshly clipped line across the nape of the neck. Equally black and shiny were their shoes, allowed to go dirty all week but gleaming with polish now in the light that filtered down under the table through a palisade of trouser legs, all sharply pressed for the occasion. The Condor was only four doors down from the house where Mario lived, in a narrow street of mean dwellings where a gutter full of refuse separated the street from the sidewalk. The gang would gather there to drink beer, play pool, and hear the latest about love affairs and sports events.

"I've already told you I can't."

"O.K., O.K., you back out. I don't know what's got into you lately, you've been acting so peculiar . . . we hardly ever see you in the Condor these days," said Troncoso, the Little Hummingbird, with the authority conferred on him by the prestige of working in a garage that sponsored one of the most popular radio programs.

They kept at Mario to go with them. Cádiz, a colorless, insignificant specimen of humanity who echoed every opinion of Troncoso's, reproached him for having lost all interest in the Condor's activities. He accused him once more of avoiding them all since his promotion to the Emporium sales staff. This cut Mario to the quick. Realizing that he would have to use more substantial arguments to defend himself, he muttered:

"There's a chick I'm working on right now . . ."

This unleashed a storm of derision. Missing a Condor game for this reason meant you were pretty soft. In fact, it could only mean you were in love.

"Christ, what a nut!" exclaimed the Little Hummingbird. According to him, a customer who had the latest-model Oldsmobile was in love with him and sometimes they would drive out to a dark, deserted street somewhere in the suburbs . . . and afterwards she let him drive the Oldsmobile. "What's the point of working on her so hard? There are chicks going cheap right now, didn't you hear?"

"Is she any good?" Cádiz asked.

"Hell, of course. You don't think I'd waste my time . . . ?"

"I suppose it wouldn't be that chick who was walking around with you near your place the other day? She's only a kid! You'd better watch out, they're the serious ones . . ."

Mario bit his lip and said nothing. One of these days it would be his turn to laugh at Troncoso, who thought he was so tough and virile with his little black moustache and his girl friend with the Olds. He was about to take a swallow of beer when Troncoso nudged him with his elbow.

"I bet you haven't even kissed her . . ."

"Can't you see I'm drinking, you big dope? What do you have to go and make me spill my beer for?"

Hatred of the Little Hummingbird flashed in Mario's eyes. Why should he make excuses to him?

"Look what a baby he's turning into!" the Little Hummingbird exclaimed. "Can't even touch the guy since they promoted him at the Emporium. We're lucky we're allowed to look at him!"

Let them think that if they wanted to! But he wasn't going to let them get away with thinking he was a sucker. Because it wasn't true . . .

"Hell, of course I've kissed her!"

That was true. The night before, when Estela came out to meet him after the rest of the household were in bed, he had kissed her. It was cold in the street and Estela pressed so close against him under the tree on the corner that he hadn't really had any alternative but to kiss her. Mario's customary sangfroid at moments like these had deserted him. He was nineteen, but in spite of escapades and tall stories, he had never gone very far in his physical relationships with women. Out in the cold street, with Estela's warm lips beneath his own, he realized that this time it was going to go further than kisses and caresses, and the reason was that Estela was so little and innocent. Perhaps it was because of this that he felt an awkwardness with her that he never felt with more experienced women, although he wasn't frightened of her, as he often was of them. He stood there for a long time, just holding her. She was silent, a warm bundle pressed against him. The night was damp and icy cold, and he had left early.

"Do you really think I'd waste my time running after a girl who won't do it?" Mario added.

They all laughed, for the Big Hummingbird was a notorious Don Juan. The balance had been restored.

They were all pals, and they accorded themselves the right to meddle in each other's love lives as the most natural thing in the world—until one of these affairs turned serious, and then . . . well, then there was one member of the group who was always touchy and silent. A sure sign of romance in the offing. He would start taking his job very seriously, even attend engineering classes at night school, and finally he would take the disastrous step of getting married. Then there would be one less to come to the Condor, one less to discuss real and imaginary women with, one less to drink and play pool with, one less to feel young, gay, and manly with. One less, that is, till marriage, with its worries about buying shoes and medicines for the kids, had overshadowed love. Then he would come back to the club to grumble, and discuss women again, and football, and the last drunken spree he had not gone on.

But all of it in a very different tone of voice.

"Hey, take a look over there," Cádiz said to Mario.

René had come in to buy some cigarettes. He addressed the bartender, who was busy putting up a colored paper garland on the ceiling because the Condor's victory was a foregone conclusion.

"I won't be a minute, hold on," the man pleaded.

"Do you think you're paid to lie around sleeping all day? Get moving, will you—I haven't got all day!" René said.

Mario turned, recognizing the voice. René was leaning against the bar contemplating the thick white metal ring on his pudgy, hairy hands with their dirty, half-moon nails. His tight blue suit was shiny and threadbare along the seams, though if one looked at him through half-closed eyes, one might not notice this, or the film of poverty and shabbiness that enveloped the stocky figure he carried with such an air. But Mario's eyes were far from being half-closed. They were wide with alarm, as if on the lookout for the policeman's hand which might fall at any minute on his innocent shoulders. René's presence disconcerted him; it was a concrete reminder of his connection with the dark, ominous legends that had grown up around his brother. The anger in his brother's eyes, one black and the other grayish, focused on him.

"Come here!" he called.

"What do you want?" Mario asked, not moving.

"Come here . . ."

"Can't you see I'm having a drink with the gang?"

"Come here, I said, you little shitface . . ."

Mario went over to him. No one would have guessed that they were brothers. The elder had none of the younger's clear-cut features, well-proportioned limbs, or generous movements. The depressing atmosphere of the pawnshop, with its accumulation of long-neglected objects gathering dust, seemed to have settled over his short-legged body and thick neck, giving the lie to any pretensions to dash and elegance. His mouth was flat and thick-lipped in the jaundiced face, its shape accentuated by the fine hairline moustache which carefully reproduced its curves.

"Take this cash and look after it for me," he said, handing Mario some bills.

"Why do you want me to look after it for you?" Mario asked.

The roll of bills felt conspicuously bulky as he fingered it in his pocket. The thought of his brother's reputation struck him suddenly, and he glanced nervously toward the door, and then at the table to see if anyone had noticed anything.

"Just keep it for me till tonight, and shut up about it. Didn't you see how Dora tried to grab it off me this morning, and then bawled me out for not taking her out more. Now that I have some money, she says, I ought to take her to the game at least. The fucking cow went on shouting till she was blue in the face, all about how badly I treat her and what a fool she was to make all the sacrifices and never have any good times. She says everything that's happened is my fault. I don't know what got into her! Fucking cow! You know what she's like."

"Why didn't you offer to take her out this once to keep her quiet?"

"She *made* me offer to take her out, the cow, she *made* me! Do you think I like people laughing at me? Haven't you noticed what a shabby old hag she looks like these days? The idea of being seen around here with that vision of loveliness doesn't appeal to me. You know how well known I am. I'd get a bad name. All I'm going to do is take her for a little trolley ride uptown, that's all, but the silly cow's gone and taken it into her head that I'm going to take her to the game. That's why I want you to keep the money, otherwise she might even get the idea she wants to go to the movies. I'm not going to parade around with the silly bitch, and spend my money on her too!"

"Are you going home to get her?"

"No, she's followed me here. She's waiting outside now, keeping an eye on me to make sure I don't try and run out on her through the back door . . ."

As she waited for René in front of the club, Dora reassured herself that the cotton dress and jacket she was wearing, though threadbare after years of wear, would be

warm enough after all because the sun was shining, softly
gilding the almost deserted street. Before going out, she
had run a comb through her lank hair and anchored it
behind her ears with two clips. Then she had pinned a
brooch with a couple of stones missing to her neckline. She
was singing happily.

"Shut up, shitface!" René had shouted from next door.

It didn't matter, a remark like that didn't matter a bit
today, Dora thought to herself, flattered that it had not
been as difficult as she had expected to persuade René to
take her out. He must love her really, in spite of everything.
And she went on with her preparations, singing a little more
softly.

René was taking longer than he should to come out of
the club. Dora began walking nervously up and down. She
knew he was capable of any cowardice or meanness. A small
boy, probably from some other neighborhood—Dora didn't
recognize him—threw a glass marble against a loose paving
stone, chasing after it delightedly when it bounced off at an
unexpected angle. Then he sat down by the door of the club
as though waiting for someone.

When René emerged, the boy told him his father wanted
to see him immediately. A shadow fell across René's face,
and he went off with the boy after telling Dora to wait in
the square nearby. He would be back in ten minutes. She
tried to follow him at first, afraid he would give her the slip
and then she would miss her outing. René turned on her,
fury kindling his odd-colored eyes, and shouted:

"Go to hell then, if you won't wait!"

Then he went off.

Dora waited for him, tearful and furious, and without
much hope of seeing him again. It was such a long, long
time since she had last been able to go out that she found it
hard to resign herself. She waited for an hour and a half

sitting on a bench in the little square. She was impatient
and hungry. What would the neighbor who had agreed to
look after the children say if she caught her creeping back
this early, with her tail between her legs? Besides, she
didn't want to miss this Condor game. Everyone in the
neighborhood would be talking about it for months.

When she saw René coming back, Dora fell on him in
a fury. He needn't think he had got out of taking her to the
game by coming back so late, she cried. She wanted, she
insisted that their friends should see them together at least
this once.

The odd thing was that René's mood seemed to have
softened. He was all smiles. Wasn't there anywhere else
she would rather go, he asked, have lunch downtown perhaps, or go to the movies? Goaded to fury by what she took
to be his reluctance to show her to his friends, Dora went
on insisting at the top of her voice that she wanted to go to
the football game, even though the game would certainly
be ending by now.

They waited on the corner for the trolley. After a lot of
shouting and weeping, Dora was gradually calming down.
René, a smile playing on the thick lips beneath his moustache, stood screwing his eyes against the glare. It was a
private world they gazed into, those odd-colored eyes of his
. . . a different, better world. He had never dreamed that
good fortune would come his way as simply as it had a
little while ago. If the deal the boy's father had proposed
to him came off, his life would straighten itself out, at least
for a time. He would leave for Valparaíso that evening, stay
there two or three weeks, and come back with bulging
pockets. Not rich perhaps, but with enough money to treat
himself to some months of decent living. Best of all, it was a
deal the police could hardly have an inkling of.

What if it was such a good business that he got enough

money to go away, go up north, or somewhere, get away
from all this and open a little bar, for instance?

The smell of Dora's much washed clothes next to him on
the bus instantly killed the thrill of excitement produced
by this wildly desirable prospect. No, no, it was impossible.
He could never bring himself to abandon Dora and the kids.
He had never been able to, all these years, though the
thought entered into every one of his schemes. Dora revolted him, he couldn't stand her, and the children were
nothing but a nuisance, but René knew he was too much of
a coward to accept the guilt feelings that would pursue him
if he abandoned them. If only he could hate Dora! But she
only inspired revulsion in him, and this emotion was not
powerful enough to drive him to hurt her, and leave her
without a word of explanation or farewell. He would never
be able to go anywhere unless this business turned out so
exceptionally well that it left him enough money to be able
to send something to Dora each month. And that sort of
plum didn't just drop into one's hands, not into his hands.
Unless, that is, he were prepared to undertake something
which had often tempted him when he was feeling desperate
about his cowardly inability to drop his family and run,
without a backward glance or a pang of remorse. Other
fears, however, had always made him steer clear of *that*.

Not that René ever put his hand to anything criminal
exactly. He dealt in small frauds and lies, but nothing more;
he was not an honest man, but neither was he a criminal.
In his desperate eagerness to better his wretched condition,
though, he frequently hobnobbed with thieves, pickpockets,
promoters, small-time smugglers, all the types who supplied
the pawnshops with which René did business. That was
why in the neighborhood he had the reputation of being a
thief—though he maintained a precarious balance on the
outer perimeter of the underworld, he inevitably drew on

himself some of the dread and suspicion that attaches to
malefactors generally. His small frauds brought him a few
pesos, which went on supporting his family and on standing
some crony a drink with the idea of gaining his respect and
friendship. And, occasionally, on some cheap tart. Still,
living in a world in which theft was commonplace, he could
not fail to realize that the only reason he had not stolen
anything yet was that the takings had never seemed rich
enough to encourage him to break the law. He would never
master his fear either, unless something came along that
could set him free from wife, family, and guilty conscience
all at once. Meanwhile, as he waited for this chance, he
trembled inwardly at the thought of having to face it when
it did.

Well. Fantasies like these were too beautiful to be prac-
ticable. Still, he ought to have enough money when he got
back from Valparaíso to get Dora fixed up with some teeth,
and earn himself a little peace and quiet.

"What about all that money I spent getting your teeth
put in?" he would be able to say when she drove him mad
with her nagging and complaining. "I hope you realize that
we never went through a civil marriage ceremony, so
legally I don't have to give you a cent."

Then Dora would be forced to shut up and treat him like
a king when he visited her; naturally, he would only come
home from time to time.

"I'll get myself a girl," René thought to himself. "A
really nice girl, young and lively so it'll be fun being seen
around with her. A nice midtown girl, not one of those
downtown sluts."

If he told Dora this deal would involve leaving town that
evening for several weeks, she would want some money
from him, and except for the five thousand pesos in hundred-
peso notes that he had given Mario to look after, René had

no money. If he left without saying anything, though, the silly bitch was quite capable of going to the police and asking them to look for him.

He had a better plan. This was to spend the day with Dora and bamboozle her thoroughly—something she was always accusing him of doing. All right then. Let people see them together! Let them think they were a loving couple! It would be worth swallowing his pride this once because it would mean that Dora would cherish such fond memories of him that it would never occur to her to go to the police in retaliation for his desertion. On the contrary, she would be prepared to endure the bitterest hardship, feeding her hopes with recollections of the afternoon they had spent together and the small kindness he had shown her then. That very evening he would leave for Valparaíso, without saying a word to her.

To strengthen Dora's loyalty, he decided to tell her that he was on to a good deal. Listening to him as they sat together in the trolley, Dora slipped her arm through his. She drew closer still when he ended by assuring her:

"And then I'll get your teeth fixed."

The remainder of the drive was happy. Commenting on a woman who struck her as well dressed, Dora observed that when she had her teeth fixed and could dress like that and had gained a few pounds, she would look even better. She admired several large mansions surrounded by gardens. René answered in monosyllables. In the bright light his pale-colored eye looked tawny yellow; the black eye reflected the light like a jet bead. Those eyes of his contemplated a better, richer world than Dora's.

Uptown, the buildings began to thin out. The trolley turned into a very broad, paved avenue with street lights and young trees, and off it side streets named after flowers and obscure politicians. There were not many finished

buildings or buildings under construction; only a few
dividing walls. On one rough plot of ground some rickety
geraniums leaned toward the sun from a battered chamber
pot standing on the roof of a hut where there were also some
winter squashes drying.

—— They got off at the trolley terminal. René bought two
apples at a kiosk and took off his blue suit jacket, which he
gave to Dora to carry. He wore his green sweater tucked
into his trousers under his suspenders. Dora draped René's
jacket over her shoulders. He did not look at her—if he
had, the temptation to run away and leave her there and
then might have been too strong for him. He loosened his
greasy tie and frayed collar.

There were very few people left on the site chosen by the
two teams for their game. Judging by the expressions of the
people who passed them on their way home, René and Dora
felt sure the Condor team had won. The ground was littered
with picnic remains, paper, fruit peels, and empty cigarette
packs. Two boys were getting out of their scarlet shirts and
into their Sunday suits. René went up to them and asked
who had won.

"Condor . . . ," one of them replied, dejectedly, ". . . six
to one."

They went on dressing in silence. Then they walked
slowly away, the bags in which they carried their football
clothes slung over their shoulders.

Soon the sun would start climbing down through the clear
sky. The heat diminished minute by minute, but the light
remained bright and golden. Westward, beyond the dark
puddle of the city, the hills gradually lost their bulk and
detail till their blue profiles looked like cardboard cut-outs
against the sky. No one moved in the labyrinth of streets
along which not even the phantoms of future houses had
settled. All around the football field dry grasses, fennel, and

hemlock made a sort of rough garden where an evil-looking pony was grazing, tethered to a stake. Eastward, the transparent air swept down beyond a distant suburb of the city, then up over the hillside toward the sharply jagged bulk of the cordillera.

The words of a song from a distant radio carried with astonishing distinctness in the clear air. Dora joined enthusiastically in the chorus.

"Ay-y-y-y . . . my heart calls to you
So desperately-y-y-y!"

René slipped off his suspenders and sat on the grass to peel an apple. When he had eaten it, he belched, lay back on the ground on his jacket, and half dozed, smiling, with his hairy hands crossed over the bulge of his paunch.

Meanwhile Dora, as if keeping guard over him, was gathering wild herbs nearby: balm to flavor the maté with, mint because it gave such a delicious smell in the warm hollow of her hand. As she bent over, stiff-legged, to break off a stalk, her tight skirt climbed above her knees, past her rolled stocking tops. René, half asleep, caught sight of this patch of bare skin. To escape from this intrusion into the beautiful imaginary world his drowsiness had conjured up, he rolled over on his face and fell asleep.

He did not remain asleep for long. Presently Dora came and stretched out beside him and woke him, pressing up against him. René lay motionless beside her, face down, eyes closed, not moving a muscle, like an animal shamming death at the approach of danger. His wife's characteristic odor began to mingle with the scents of the field: the smell of old clothes that could never be got quite clean, in spite of endless washings; the smell of paraffin smoke in her hair. She was so close that René could feel her sharp hipbone.

"René, baby . . ." Dora murmured in his ear.

He jerked about a little, mumbling disconnected words, like someone dreaming. Dora stroked the hard skull of his dried gourd of a head. Her eyes were deep and tender in her faded face, to which the kindly sun lent a passing freshness. When she noticed her man moving, she pulled a frayed thread off his unbuttoned collar. Then, unable to stop herself, she slipped a hand under his collar and caressed his hairy shoulder.

"Can't you see I'm asleep? What are you fucking me around like that for?"

Dora's eyes clouded over, but she went on stroking René's shoulder.

No. Important as it was to leave a good impression behind him, he just couldn't do it, René reflected. He just couldn't. Although they slept in the same bed, he had not touched his wife for over a year. Why bother when there were real women to be had? He generally managed to arrange it so he went to bed in a bad temper. Other times he would return home late, knowing that Dora was unlikely to wake up after a hard day's work. On the last occasion he had been so revolted by his wife, by her aging, evil-smelling body, and even more by her passion, her yearning, frustrated sensuality, that he had stayed away from home for several days. On his return he had told Dora that if she ever forced herself on him again he would leave her for good.

He felt some blades of grass tickling him, under his double chin, his ears and ankles, under his trouser cuffs. The heat, an insect crawling around his waist under his shirt, the smells, all these conspired to dissolve his powers of discrimination and his resistance. He put his arm around Dora's recumbent body and let his hand lie over her flat breasts. The feel of his hand encouraged her. With a great effort she rolled his inert body toward her, using both hands. She strained up against his warm body, cleaving to him, murmuring over and over:

"My baby, my pretty baby . . ."

Dora's eyes were closed. Her hair was wreathed with dry herbs and grasses, and desire had lent color to her face, making it softer and prettier. A look of fierce triumph appeared there as she noticed René's body responding to her touch. René would not look or think; he let his body carry him along, no more. Dora took little bites at his neck and ears, but he refused her his mouth, which she sought hungrily. And there they were, making love in the wasteland, while a startled bird circled for a long while high over the recumbent pair, keeping watch in the perfectly blue lookout post of the air.

10 ᨏᨏ   The bird soon tired of circling over them. Toward the west, twilight would soon be darkening the fresh blue of the air, and René and Dora were certainly not the only couple taking advantage of the unusual autumn weather to make love out of doors.

The bird flew off toward the hills, wheeling above them for a while as the aerial map of the city turned golden in the tiny beads of its eyes. Down below, the countless couples who had come to the hillside from their various neighborhoods after wandering through the streets and parks were waiting a little wearily for the afternoon air to turn chilly and show that it was time to go home. The bird glided over the lovers lying in the grass as if it wanted to inspect them before making a choice, and finally circled above one particular couple locked together in the bushes on a slope that faced the setting sun. Gently, softly, as if they were afraid of hurting each other, they drew apart and lay quietly side

by side in the slanting light which painstakingly traced the
outline of each blade of grass as it fell.

"Look . . ." Estela whispered to Mario, pointing out the
bird which circled overhead.

In silence they stared westward, where rows of squat
houses clustered around patios, some small, some spacious.
Out of them occasional palm trees sprouted, like ancient
waterspouts bubbling up from past ages when the city had
been different, and yet the same.

Estela closed her eyes slowly. But this time they did not
close because of the old shyness that had so often kept them
fixed on her feet, but because they knew there was nothing
more to see that could possibly add to her joy. A great
kindly wind seemed to have cleared the shadows from her
young face. Her lips, still darkened by love, curved in at
the corners with the suggestion of a smile. This deepened
when Mario, settling himself into a more comfortable position beside her, brought their bodies closer together. The
girl's eyes, screened by lashes still damp with tears, dreamily
reviewed the events of the day as if caressing them.

Lourdes had gone all solemn when her niece had asked
permission to visit the zoo on the hill. She was slightly
annoyed, too, that Estela could not curb her curiosity long
enough for her varicose veins to get better so she could go
with her.

". . . and I'm not letting you go alone," she announced,
with finality.

"But weren't you going with Mario?" Rosario asked.

"Oh, well . . . in that case," Lourdes, vacillating, left her
sentence unfinished.

At this point Rosario plunged in and convinced Lourdes
quickly that it was eminently suitable for Estela to go out
with Mario. Not only had he just been promoted to salesman
in the Fornino Emporium, but he was, above all, a boy with

sound, old-fashioned ideas, altogether trustworthy and responsible.

"And aren't you going to have lunch?" Rosario asked Estela.

"I don't know . . ." the girl said.

"Look. Go get Mario, child, and bring him to lunch here with us. What's the point of throwing your money away when there's more than enough food here for us all now that Don Andrés hardly ever comes?"

During lunch, Lourdes appeared to be warming up to the idea. She always had difficulty reaching a decision—but now Rosario seemed to have decided for her by treating Mario not just as Estela's friend but as a friend of the house. This meant that Rosario would be responsible if anything happened, an accident or something like that. This thought dispelled her last trace of uneasiness, and she chatted and joked with Mario as if they had been old friends. Silently savoring a feeling of power, Rosario noticed that Lourdes was chatting a great deal more freely than usual to the Fornino clerk. Her lips puckered sardonically, as if she were reminding herself what a fool Lourdes had once been.

Mario and Estela both breathed a deep sigh of relief once they were out of the house. The feel of Mario's hard, strong arm under her own, a feeling at once familiar and long-awaited, banished all suspicion and caution from Estela's mind. As they strolled through the sunny streets this Sunday afternoon, his arm through hers, Estela felt proud of being seen with Mario.

It proved difficult to drag Estela away from the cages of monkeys, lions, and parrots; she appeared to be oblivious of her companion except as someone to whom she could put her excited questions. It wasn't till he held out the bag of peanuts for her to put one, nervously at first, in the elephant's trunk or the monkey's paw, and their fingers touched through the paper, that their eyes met briefly. As the afternoon wore on and the cones of peanuts were used up one after the other, Estela's eyes lingered more and more on Mario's and her torrent of excited remarks and questions gradually dried up. Later on, when they were both tired, he took her hand and she let him guide her, jumping over shrubs and little streams, toward a secluded slope.

When he pulled her down beside him in the grass, in the shelter of a copse of young pines, fear of what was to come blotted all the tigers and parrots from Estela's mind and checked the questions on her lips. She trembled a little too: although what was about to happen didn't happen with Fishface only because they had both been so young, she somehow didn't feel nearly as safe and confident now as she had then.

But as she noticed how clumsy Mario's advances were and realized that he was in some respects even more frightened than she was, her doubts disappeared. Although he was much bigger than Fishface, he was a lot more like a child! With this Estela offered her love to him, quite simply, holding him closer and closer so that in the meeting of their warm bodies he might share some of the confidence born of the certainty that this was as much the first time for him as it was for her. And when in his inexperience he whispered desperately: "Help me . . . I don't know . . ." Estela forgot everything—the stones digging into her shoulder, the boy's belt buckle which was cutting into her. With her eyes wide open and fixed on the glowing sunset beyond the trees, which soon grew dark as the ecstatic pain tore through her, Estela gave herself joyfully and confidently.

Stretched out beside Mario, she remembered it all.

As she lay with her eyes closed, Estela was aware of Mario studying her profile, still warm with kisses, her fluttering breast, and the damp armpits that she exposed to the last glow of daylight when she crossed her arms behind her head. That first time in the movies, Mario's gaze had deserted her; from now on, though, she would follow his eyes so they could both look together.

She opened her eyes and smiled at her lover, who blushed and buried his hot face in the girl's shoulder. Now he had his eyes shut and hers were open, looking at him. She saw the way his powerful neck rose up between the straightest of shoulders under the unbuttoned white shirt, and how these were transformed magically into the arms which held her so tenderly. She looked at his hair. Her fingers trembled remembering the warmth they had found beneath that tousled thatch, close to the skull.

Estela took a stalk and tickled him under his nose. Mario tried not to laugh, but first a snort, then a great guffaw burst out of him. The last glimmer of light mellowed as it lit up his love-struck eyes. They embraced again.

"Here, look, you've torn your shirt," she murmured.

"Damn. It was the only good one I had left."

"I've got a needle and cotton in my pocket. Take it off."

"Br-r-r-r-r, I'll freeze! What do you think my skin's made of—leather?"

"Take it off," Estela repeated, threading her needle.

He sat slightly hunched, with his arms crossed over his chest, trying to ward off the chill that was seeping into the evening air. She went on with her sewing, sitting very erect on the ground. Her fingers, absorbed in repairing Mario's shirt, stitched away with the same proud dexterity with which her sister-in-law Margarita used to patch her man's shirts when they were torn at work or in a brawl. All she thought about was making the darning as perfect as possible: she knew, in some dark corner of her mind, that her real life was beginning here, at this moment.

Mario did not feel at ease. He said he did, but he didn't.

For a few minutes the triumph of his first conquest had filled him with boastful confidence. The sexual conqueror had carried off the first foray with honor and preened himself accordingly. He exultantly pictured to himself the countless women he would possess in the future and the endless discussions in the Condor about their good and bad points, discussions that would reduce the Little Hummingbird to insignificance. How jealous Cádiz would be when he heard proof that Mario wasn't one of the fools who got stuck with a girl who refused to come across. It took an experienced eye like his to assess which ones were worth fooling with! How calmly he would be able to affirm, between beers, that women were all the same!

She was little and unsophisticated, and she had given herself to him. In other women he had sensed a threatening desire to enfold him, seduce him, conquer him, but never to give themselves to him. Estela had given herself. That was why it had been so perfect.

"Help me . . . I don't know . . ."

Suddenly those words, spoken in a moment of passion and bewilderment, came back to him and crushed his pride. He looked at this woman, sewing there so contentedly, as if to destroy her for having found him out, for having exposed him as weak and helpless. Those few wretched words had trapped him, he wouldn't be able to talk about it to the boys at all. Well, he wouldn't utter a single word even if they laughed at him when he avoided answering their questions. The best thing, really, would be not to go back to the Condor. Estela had reduced him to the level of a man in love! He was shocked by the sudden wave of hatred for her which swept through him. *He* wasn't going to fall into that trap! In love? That was all right for the saps who didn't know what women were like. But he knew all about them now. After all, hadn't he tried the old seduction routine on Estela, move for move, and hadn't she fallen for it just like all the rest? Yes, they were all the same. Only a fool would deny it . . .

"Ouch! I pricked myself!" Estela exclaimed, sucking her finger.

Mario felt as if a needle had been jabbed into his own flesh. He looked at Estela in astonishment. How pretty she was! His discovery of Estela's beauty as she sat there on the ground, sewing, swept his doubts away like a tidal wave. She was pretty! Other women knew their way around, were sophisticated, but Estela was different—she was pretty. He remembered the warmth of that dark smooth cheek, the size and weight of her waist, and his cheek and arms were warmed by the memory. In a last effort to suppress these tender feelings, he tried to think of other waists, still softer cheeks . . . but failed. Estela was unique, and now that his imagination was focused wholly on her, he found there was no room in it for anyone else.

They would have to part in a few minutes. He would be going home to more of Dora's eternal complaints, and Estela to that big cold house. She would go to bed alone miles away from him, near the bedside of an old madwoman. What would Estela be like asleep?

"Hey, do you snore?"

"No," she said, not looking up.

Mario pictured her asleep. And himself sleeping beside her, in the double bed they had bought. He imagined a cupboard filled with blue glasses, china, plates. All by themselves, they would be, miles from René and Dora and Lourdes and the old madwoman. When he went out to work in the morning, Estela would stay home, sewing and preparing their dinner. And when he got back home, if he wasn't too tired, they would go to the movies and sit in the orchestra, not the balcony, because he was now a member of the Emporium sales staff. And all of it, Estela and everything in that room, would belong to him and it would all be as clean and shining as the gold watch that gleamed on his wrist.

"Here you are. Look, it hardly shows."

They got up. Estela held out the shirt while Mario put his arms into the sleeves. But as he was doing it, a sudden wild uncontrollable wave of despair seized Estela. She threw her arms around his waist and buried her face in his shoulder. He turned toward her, his face serious and his white shirttails flapping in the breeze. They embraced, and almost without realizing it, slid down happily onto the grass once more.

11 ❧ It was a good five weeks since Andrés Abalos had last visited his grandmother. He had sensed so much danger in her and in everything that had happened in her house on the day of the wretched birthday party that he had found he could not go back to visiting her once a week as he had done before.

As time went by, his distress only seemed to increase. He could not think why the whole thing should have left such a deep impression on him, or why his grandmother's mad chatter—after all, the old woman's delusions were not new to him—should have shaken him so badly on this particular occasion. He was only inwardly shaken, though; outwardly he managed to behave as usual. But the terror produced in him by the conviction that his accustomed way of life was threatened, and his days as a punctilious, orderly, intelligent caballero were numbered, made the passing hours unendurable.

He searched within himself for some explanation of this violent distress. Why was it that ever since that birthday party the knowledge that his grandmother's death would leave him free, free as air but without any use for his new-found freedom, why should that knowledge torment him so profoundly? He had vaguely known this for a long time, though up to now the idea had merely inspired in him a mood of melancholy dignity, a mood eminently becoming to a man of his age and position. And now, all of a sudden, nothing in his past and nothing that his future seemed likely to bring seemed to have even a particle of nobility or value. He might as well throw all his past experience, attachments, interests overboard, they were so pathetically meager! How dreadful to die without ever having taken a bite out of life! But, worse still, to find oneself propelled along by this new, corrosive dissatisfaction into doing just that—taking a bite out of life!

Brooding in the gloom of his study, Andrés asked himself why it should be that the more insidious danger to himself lay in his grandmother's senseless remarks rather than in Carlos Gros's cruelly accurate diagnosis? Why should he constantly recollect the stab of shame which his grandmother's monstrous accusations about him and Estela had inflicted? Was that the answer? Could that be the cause of his present distress? No, it would be too adolescent . . . he couldn't see himself in such a ridiculous role. But was he attracted to Estela? To prove that he was not, he adduced the fact that he had no recollection whatsoever of the girl, and that thoughts of her rarely, if ever, crossed his mind. What did she look like? Tall or short? Dark or fair? He didn't even remember! Emboldened by these reflections, he went further . . . what if he *were* attracted to her? He had been attracted to many women in his life. He was quite capable of satisfying his desire without becoming involved or losing his head. A sort of mist softened and blurred the outline of these thoughts . . .

Whenever Lourdes phoned him, however, he would be thrown into confusion at finding himself in direct communication with his grandmother's house, as though that were the source of all danger. He avoided replying to the maid's veiled reproaches:

"Oh, the señora has been in excellent health, Don Andresito, you mustn't worry . . ."

"No, of course not . . . I haven't been to see her because, well, one has to take care of oneself at my age . . . as you know . . ."

"Of course, take good care of yourself, that's the main thing. Do you need anything? Would you like Rosario to make you a little chicken to see if it makes you feel any better?"

A little chicken!

Andrés forced himself to go on as usual. But his life refused to obey him. It remained intractable, stubbornly centered on this sense of dissatisfaction, which devalued every minute of his day, as though lying in wait behind every one of his domestic pleasures was some shattering revelation about himself.

He went as usual to the Union Club, where he would install himself in the most peaceful corner of the library to leaf through the latest French magazines. *Histoire* had an article on Mme de Castiglione. It might prove interesting. But then the cheap paper on which the magazine was printed, the profusion of vulgar advertisements forced him to abandon in disgust what would once have amused and interested him. He moved to the card room. His usual fellow-players were all there, passionately absorbed in what suddenly seemed to him the most puerile of fictitious adventures. Only those who had never known, or had rejected, what is moving and stimulating in real life could bring such enthusiasm to a card game. How pusillanimous they must be to be content with this! He walked out of the room without greeting them, leaving them astonished at his strange behavior.

In a salon on the second floor two of his friends were having tea. Their heads, both perfectly bald, bobbed in satisfied agreement with what they were saying. They called Andrés over to join them.

"Here, Andrés, you're something of an artist, isn't it true that nothing in the arts today can compare with opera as we used to know it?"

Andrés was gratified at hearing himself described as an artist, though he was quick to detect a slightly deprecating edge to the compliment. It was as if his mildly artistic leanings were enough to keep him from being totally accepted in his friends' absolutely stable world, a world in which he had hitherto felt so secure. They now thought of him as an outsider, his sensibility made him suspect, an eccentric.

How else could Vicente Castillo see him? A man whose secure position as a wealthy landowner who had married off all his children to his satisfaction now entitled him to sit in judgment on everything and everyone with supreme arrogance?

"Of course, you are quite a bit younger than we are," Vicente went on. "But you remember how in the old days one would meet artists everywhere. Walking along Huérfanos Street in the morning; at someone's house in the evening where they had been invited to sing. Not like now . . . in those days everyone accepted artists socially. Of course they did. And why not? They used to be civilized, decent people like ourselves, not what they are now . . ."

The nodding which underlined these dogmatic views was

echoed in the nodding of his friend, who now gave a reminiscent chuckle.

"Remember when your father lost his head over that soprano . . . what was her name? Oh, yes, Terrazzi, a tall redhead, handsome too . . . though a little on the plump side now that I come to think of it, here and here especially. But then they all were in those days, unlike now. And remember how your mother got so angry she refused to go to the opera all season, and the family box was empty the whole time, so that people would notice, as an insult . . . ?"

Do you remember? Do you remember?

"Do you remember the time Tita Ruffo hit a wrong note?"

"Do you remember the time Miguel sang at a benefit for the Araucanian Indians?"

"Do you remember how the family box was lent to the poor relations toward the end of the season, when we had seen *Aida* ten times and *Lucia di Lammermoor* fifteen times?"

"Do you remember?"

"Of course. Of course I do. Not like now . . ."

Andrés stopped listening to this fossilized conversation, which once would have passed the time so amusingly. Now it made him feel dizzy, as if it confronted him with a yawning abyss from which there was no escape . . .

A group of young men, with an air of owning the whole world, had installed themselves nearby. One of them greeted the agriculturist briefly, and another saluted Andrés. They were talking about politics, the stock market, business; they were serious and responsible, and never once doubted that the government of the country would eventually fall into their hands. Andrés listened. Pesos, pesos, shares, bonds, the board of directors. They discussed a certain Matías who had risked all his money in a fraudulent business scheme and had fallen foul of the law, dishonoring his name and drag-

ging his family to the gutter. Poor Matías! They would
have to help him because he was a friend and a relative.
But gambling away all of it! Ah well, Matías had never
been very bright, even in school. But he was one of them,
with their gray suits and white shirts, each identical to the
next, with not the faintest suspicion of idiosyncrasy to flaw
the crystallized surfaces of their personalities. Ambition
simmered behind everything they said, the ambition to become wealthier, more powerful, better in every respect than
the others but without departing even momentarily from the
socially accepted pattern of behavior.

Andrés, though he knew them to be horribly mistaken
in their values, listened enviously nonetheless. This Matías
who was capable of staking his all on something as trivial
as money must be something of a hero. Why had he, Andrés
Abalos, never felt this love of money which drove men to
take risks, to live? It would have been so easy! And such a
mistake! Andrés found a certain beauty in this mistaken
notion of theirs, however, when he compared it with his
own mistakes. They were capable of the most dangerous
and ruthless enterprises, of sullying their consciences forever, of going under completely, but perhaps one of them
would once make a noble gesture or take up a courageous,
authoritative position. Yes, the risk involved in their enterprises lent them a certain beauty. And, besides, they had
time on their side. He, on the other hand, had almost no
time left; he had wasted it in learning to distinguish between
right and wrong. What use was this knowledge if, in spite
of it, he had never stepped over the threshold of action? And
he had almost no time left . . .

He stood up, curtly excusing himself. Then he asked for
his coat and went out into the street. All he wanted to do
was run away, run anywhere at all.

The week before, he had had lunch with Carlos Gros and

his family at the doctor's home. Observing that Andrés
seemed out of sorts, Adriana had asked him:

"Tell me, Andrés, why don't you take a nice long trip to
Europe? You are always talking about France and how
much you'd like to go there. I can't see why you don't . . .
you can't be short of money . . . unless you're turning into
a miser . . ."

Even avarice struck him as an admirable passion. But it
wasn't that in his case . . .

The idea of a trip had been germinating in his mind for
a week. A trip would solve all his problems. At night he
would wake to find himself sailing, softly sailing along,
through the air or over the water, and it seemed that he
sailed and sailed and sailed and the port receded farther
and farther and the airport vanished from sight. His vessel,
whatever it was, never touched ground.

He remembered the trip he had made after finishing his
law course. He conjured up the smell of certain London
shops, and of the Uccello in the Bodleian Library. He
remembered the blue of the Ionian Sea near Brindisi, ruffled
by the very breeze which had driven the boat where Virgil
lay dying. He pictured himself once more in certain Parisian
salons to which he had had introductions, salons of faded
gray *boiseries*, where conversation with fashionable women,
all a little disillusioned and a little intelligent, tended to take
on the same diluted coloring as the corners of their rooms.
Every ornament in these rooms, every rare and finely bound
volume looked as though it must have decorated that little
table or this particular bookshelf from time immemorial
and would doubtless continue to do so for the rest of time.
In those surroundings, where the solutions of the past
modify the present with serene continuity, it might be
possible to find a refuge from the questions life constantly
harassed him with now.

He returned home in a more tranquil frame of mind and went to bed early, taking with him a magnificent illustrated book about the history of the Château de Blois. He was soon so pleasantly absorbed in his reading that he lost track of the passing hours, unlike the past few days, in which the passing of each minute and each second had been a torment. The ringing of the telephone broke the spell. It was one A.M. He recognized Felipe Guzmán's stammer.

"Look," Andrés said, rather crossly," it's one A.M."

"I just had to tell you—you're the only one sensitive enough to appreciate my discovery."

"What discovery?"

"No one, absolutely no one has ever brought up this extraordinarily interesting point about her life . . ."

"*Whose* life?"

"Marie Antoinette's life, dear boy."

"Ah," Andrés murmured.

"It seems incredible, but do you know, Marie Antoinette, Queen of France, never once saw the sea in her whole life? How about that? I have just finished re-reading more than thirty biographies of her life and I've proved it beyond all possible doubt. I didn't call you before because I've only just now gotten all the facts together. Don't you think I should write a piece for one of the French magazines, to make this astonishing fact known? Andrés, Andrés . . ."

But Andrés had put down the receiver. He had just discovered that Felipe Guzmán, whose life was devoted to reading monographs, texts, memoirs, and works about the Bourbons and the Habsburgs, was dead . . . quite dead. And by the same token so was he: his liking for what was beautiful and historical was merely another way of dodging life and marking time pleasantly—above all, pleasantly—till the hour of his death. It was then, on that night which had begun so auspiciously, enveloped by a darkness that had

suddenly grown menacing in that civilized apartment of
his, with the incessant drumming of the rain outside, that
Andrés realized that there was no point in taking any trips.
The only reality he would ever know, the one vital experience he could aspire to, was death.

One of Andrés's greatest pleasures was taking an evening
stroll through the streets, directing his steps toward various
second-hand bookstores or one of those little shops—usually
found in working-class districts—which deal in antiques and
every kind of second-hand article. He had picked up the
habit in his youth. On his twenty-first birthday he had come
into the fortune left to him by his parents and thus had suddenly found himself with considerable spending power but
without the least idea how to dispose of his money, though
he had every intention of doing something with it. There
was something about the brightly lit shops in midtown, and
about the goods sold there—a sense of urgency that reminded him unpleasantly of the passing of time, an im-
personality that had nothing evocative about it—all of which
killed his enjoyment in the adventure of buying. In the
second-hand shops, however—dusty, untidy places presided
over by seedy gentlemen of doubtful origin, as in all those
objects and volumes which knew more of history than he
did—he found an indefinable something which brought him
a mysterious feeling of confidence and peace, as though
those rooms full of old furniture and books were deliciously
domesticated; they did not have the sterility of shops selling
new things. This pleasure was related to his liking for
wandering through the streets in the poorer districts of
town, some swarming with life and noise, others silent, a
solitary anonymous figure, till at length he reached some
shop where a cat would be warming itself at a charcoal fire,
along with one or two people who scarcely spoke, like himself. Andrés never acquired anything of great value, nothing

rare or catalogued; this would have made him a connoisseur, a professional collector, and so would have curtailed his freedom. But from time to time he allowed himself to be tempted by some insignificant trifle, a small table of pale wood which had been polished by time and use, or a piece of porcelain whose simple lines gave impeccable form to a fine white glaze.

What he liked most was buying walking sticks. Once, when he was about twenty, he had broken his ankle and to help drag his leg along in its plaster cast he bought himself a stick in an antique shop. Then, when he no longer needed them, he bought more. But he never allowed himself to have more than ten at a time in his collection. If he wanted to acquire a particularly irresistible stick, he would first sell one of the ones he already had; in this way he never trespassed beyond the set limit but constantly improved the quality of his collection. He eventually came to possess ten outstanding specimens: chinese-ivory sticks carved with trees and figures; an ancient Toledo blade in a sheath of polished cherrywood; a perfectly plain mahogany stick with a chased-gold handle. It gave him intense satisfaction to hold and caress those handles which in far-off times and places other hands had warmed.

Shopkeepers and private dealers soon knew that Don Andrés Abalos would pay a good price for anything exceptional in walking sticks, and he was received with great deference when he appeared in an antique shop.

The evening after his visit to the club, Andrés sat down, as he often did, in a leather chair beside one of the windows in his apartment, through which the light was gliding rapidly toward dusk. He examined his sticks one by one, polishing and cleaning them with unusual care, and rubbing the handles made of precious metals. This generally left him feeling satisfied and contented.

But this evening it was different: the beloved ritual failed to restore his peace of mind. He needed to do something, not simply sit and contemplate what he already had.

Suppose he bought another stick? One which would take him over his self-imposed limit? His enjoyment of life might return if he spent a lot of money on something to gratify his taste, something unlooked for which would induce him to break his rule of ten at a time. Donaldo Ramírez had phoned him only the week before to tell him that in a few days he would be in possession of a really outstanding stick. Oh, if only this could dispel the sense of death and stagnation which was poisoning his life!

Donaldo Ramírez, then, was the man to see!

Andrés put on his coat and walked to Ramírez's large house, behind the Plaza Brazil. The dealer reserved only a couple of rooms in it for his own use; the rest were rented as furnished rooms to students from the provinces.

"They are all my children!" Tenchita would exclaim. She was Donaldo's wife and they were childless.

Andrés never observed the slightest trace of maternal feeling in her toward her tenants. She kept it all for Donaldo, whom she treated like a delicate, spoiled only son. And Donaldo treated his wife like a mother, a mother who must be fussed over and obeyed. It was an incestuous relationship and it made them both very happy. Andrés admired their happiness. But he admired still more Donaldo's eye for exceptional pieces, sometimes of great value, which he could spot under the most untoward exteriors. His professional knowledge and competence were astonishing. His talks with Andrés might well have proved of great interest to the collector and of great usefulness to the dealer if they had not been invariably interrupted by Tenchita with a flow of small talk that managed to turn any conversation, business conference, or consultation between experts into a

stream of animated chatter. Donaldo always seemed
charmed by the interruption.

Tenchita was huge and ripe, like an enormous fruit. She
rolled her mascara-rimmed eyes as she smoked on her long
holder, and between puffs her smiling lips never stopped
moving. There was a provoking rasp of silk as she crossed
and uncrossed her plump calves, which she did as frequently
as her excessively tight skirts would permit, thereby dis-
playing tiny feet in shoes with the highest of heels. They
were the last word in shoe fashion, and Tenchita liked to be
up to the minute.

Andrés was constantly surprised that there should be no
conflict of taste between husband and wife, but their house
gave proof of the most harmonious adaptation. It was
crammed with things. On the walls, engravings in the
eighteenth-century style popular at the turn of the century,
and machine-made tapestries representing the different
stages of a Venetian idyll, alternated with innumerable en-
largements of family groups in heavy, ornate frames. It was
incomprehensible how the massive Tenchita managed to
move about in the labyrinth of tables, consoles, footstools,
chairs, all of them recently rejuvenated with a coat of
golden varnish, the work of the loquacious mistress of the
house.

"The Louis XV belonged to Donaldo's family," Tenchita
confided, "and we wouldn't part with it for all the gold in
the world. I don't like antiques myself, but something which
has always been in the family is different. When you aren't
a millionaire, you need something to show you come from
an old family, Andrés."

Andrés suspected that no one had ever made them an
offer for the grotesque, cumbersome pieces which formed
the stable population of these rooms. But in addition there
was another, changing population that never failed to sur-

prise Andrés on each of his visits. On the one hand, the astonishing objects Donaldo acquired to sell privately to the representatives of large firms, and on the other, Tenchita's own ubiquitous personal touch. A curtain in absolutely the latest style would almost immediately be replaced by another whose ruffles would be arranged in a still more modish manner; an embroidered runner on which stood a large vase of moulting pampas grass gave way to a woven mat like the one in the latest picture magazine.

Donaldo was precise and spare. He had once, a long time ago, been in the army, and he still retained the immaculate appearance, ramrod back, and squared shoulders which his wife so admired. These were not what Tenchita most admired in her husband, though. She had once confided to Andrés that her husband was a Ramírez but—and it was this "but" which Andrés found so touching—connected with the Alvarez de la Serena family through his mother.

Donaldo himself came to the front door to let Andrés in. His face lit up with a welcoming, genuinely affectionate smile and a flash of false teeth around which his face seemed to have dried up without actually aging.

"And how has Misiá Elisita been?" he inquired.

He liked talking with this restrained familiarity about the widow of a well-known public figure such as Don Ramón Abalos.

"Well, very well, Donaldo. And Tenchita?"

"Not too well, Andrés. The poor thing seems to have a touch of mononucleosis in the early stages. It's a new illness, you know, and you've seen what Tenchita's like with anything new. It appears she's passing it on to everyone else . . ."

"Who was that, my love?" came the invalid's lilting voice from next door. "Don't tell me it's that ungrateful Andrés Abalos . . ."

"Yes, it's me . . ."

"Oh, Andrés, how marvelous of you to come! I've been dying to see you. But I'm in bed and I look terrible . . ."

While Andrés sat down, Tenchita rattled on: "I've so wanted to see you I think I'll get up. But you must promise not to look at me."

Andrés was wary of the effect Tenchita's loquacity might have on his poor bruised spirit. He didn't want to see her! All he wanted was to buy a magnificent walking stick in defiance of the ridiculous limit of ten he had set himself. Oh, if only that would dispel the miasma of disquiet and death which clung to him! Still, he entered into the rallying, flirtatious vein Tenchita had adopted.

"How could I possibly not look at you, Tenchita? It would ruin my day . . ."

Donaldo meanwhile was poking around in the cluttered corners of the room, looking for the stick with which he proposed to tempt his client and friend. He was smiling happily, delighted by this fresh proof of his wife's skill in transforming business relations into intimate, sophisticated gatherings. Andrés, on the other hand, was asking himself how a man with such an excellent eye for unearthing beautiful, authentic objects could be blind to his wife's appalling meretriciousness.

Tenchita presently appeared, wearing a silk dressing gown. She looked like a large pink cake decorated with rings and pins and touches of whimsy. She poured her curves into a chair facing Andrés, her silk garment clinging to her body.

Andrés refrained from looking at her: her presence merely intensified the anguish of these last few weeks. He felt as if he were being painfully severed from the old Andrés Abalos of before his grandmother's birthday, that quiet man who had succeeded in burying all his problems. The split had begun with his grandmother's incision that morning. Any minute now, Tenchita's vulgarity might deepen the wound, perhaps irrevocably. She was describing an engraving she had liked very much but which Donaldo had refused to buy. Getting to her feet, she explained that the picture showed a woman leaning against a tree.

"Like this . . . and she's practically naked!" she added, affectedly switching her large posterior from side to side.

How absurd she was! And how was he to shield his genuine, lonely sufferings from this blighting triviality? Perhaps everything he was experiencing, this nameless thing which was causing him so much pain, was really only ridiculous? But what right had this monstrous woman to be the one who fatally destroyed what was left of his composure?

Pleased with her little bit of mime, performed under her husband's fond eye, Tenchita sat down again and launched into an exhaustive account of her mononucleosis. The fever made her shiver, she complained, drawing her pink woollen shawl closer around her shoulders. Donaldo stood flourishing a walking stick, obviously waiting for a pause in his wife's torrent of words to show it to Andrés. But Andrés was no longer interested in it. He was only interested in the fine pink shawl.

"Go on, Andrés, don't be mean—tell me you like my shawl."

This request was Andrés's undoing. He could not think or see. What right had this awful woman to drag up these images from his unconscious, images still—but only just— faceless. Why should she be the one, why had she been chosen to give his poor agony a face?

"Donaldo gave it to me last night, as a present, you see how he spoils me! He said he wanted to see me all rosy beside him when he woke up in the morning . . ."

As she gestured toward her husband, Andrés caught a glimpse of the palm of her hand, pink, moist, raw. Andrés stood up. He saw not Tenchita but Estela, wrapped in the shawl he had given his grandmother . . . Estela waking up beside him in bed. He felt the girl's young warmth and the slight dampness of a body warmed by sleep. He felt Estela's breath sharp against his neck as she helped him with his coat, and the naked danger of those palms flashed before his eyes.

Had his grandmother, in spite of her madness, perceived something that he had never dared to see? Perhaps madness was the only way to see deep into the truth of things.

Andrés retreated toward the door.

"Don't go yet, look at the stick I've got here for you."

Sticks! Like Rosario's chicken!

"Why should Andrés want sticks, dear?" Tenchita exclaimed. "He's just a boy! Why, you might almost think he was in love! Tell us your naughty little secret, Andrés, you'll find we're very modern and broad-minded."

"Shut up!" Andrés shouted.

Tenchita's archly wagging finger froze in mid-air. She and her husband both stood, instinctively drawing together for protection.

12   Andrés slammed the door and ran down the stairs into the street.

He had no recollection later of having hailed a taxi, or why he gave the driver his grandmother's address. It was not until he noticed that the taxi was pulling into the street where she lived that he realized he must have told the driver to take him there.

He told the man to stop, and got out. He would walk the rest of the way.

He glanced at his watch. Nine o'clock. A light mist

blurred some of the detail of trees and houses, leaving them apparently floating in the depths of the gardens. Rings of misty light haloed each street light so that it seemed embedded in a drop of cold. A car tore up the silence of the damp pavement. As Andrés went past, he could see into the brightly lit rooms behind the windows where lives were going on as usual: people were talking, getting ready for bed, laughing.

Andrés walked on. But his life was not proceeding as usual. A shape loomed out of the fog and walked by without looking at him; Andrés briefly registered a high collar and an air of hurrying back to a familiar destination: everything was in order in that life, now vanishing into the mist once more. But he, Andrés Abalos, was no longer the person he had once been . . .

His eyes were moist with a sudden joy. He had at last succeeded in breaking the mold that imprisoned him. He stopped under a street light. His body, enveloped by the chilly mist, glowed with a new and wonderful warmth.

But why? Why?

His imagination had only to stretch up to pluck the answer—he wanted Estela. Just that. But it was not the fact of wanting her which was so important, he had often felt desire before. It was this vital tremor, this feeling of being recharged with power and energy throughout his body, which was so wonderfully new. Now he might howl with hunger, or dance with delight, or groan with pain; the old Andrés Abalos, still halted on the threshold of himself, was powerless to stop him. Was this the truth which Tenchita's ludicrous caricature had brought into his consciousness? Might it not be the gestation of this force within him which had so disturbed his peace of mind during the past month?

He wanted Estela. His clenched hands thrust into his coat pockets imagined the naked softness of her palms, and her black eyes sparkled before him. His neck tingled reminiscently as he recalled her warm breath on his neck as she had helped him into his coat more than a month ago. Yes. He wanted Estela. He wanted her more than he had ever believed he could want anyone.

Andrés walked on with his eyes half closed. The urgency of his desire was ample proof that, contrary to what he had believed and Carlos had suggested, he was not dead at all. He was not, after all, one of those people who have so pruned and curbed their sensibilities that they no longer know how to let go. On his first meeting with Estela he had felt a tremor at the sight of those moist, pink palms—it could only have been, he now realized, a sudden stirring of desire. But then, unnerved by his grandmother's obscene accusations, the desire had become submerged again. Yet it had gone on growing in the dark depths of his mind until Tenchita's grotesque caricature had excised it as skillfully as a surgeon's knife and forced it on his attention. It was all so simple! He, Andrés Abalos, now found himself right at the center of life!

Andrés shook with silent laughter. He laughed silently for the length of an entire block, walking slowly so as to postpone his arrival a little. So he wanted Estela? Well, it would be easy to procure her for himself. She was innocent, alone, and poor. He was rich and experienced. He would devote all his experience to seducing her, shower her with gifts, introduce her to a life she had never known, a life of new and enriching interests and enthusiasms. The girl might not fall passionately in love with him, but she would at least come to value and respect him. After all, fifty-four was not so old that one must renounce all hope of awakening desire. It might be argued that it was a contemptible action on his part to seduce an innocent young girl merely to appease his desire. But if she were to fall in love with him, and this was not impossible, what heights Estela's life might soar to! Anyway, he could not afford to overlook any opportunities for sampling life, he had too little time left. And besides, Estela would have ample time afterward to repair any damage which might have been done.

He crossed the muddy little square. A stone bench, wet with rain, glistened smooth as a mirror under a street light until a leaf, withered by the frost, ruffled its shining surface. Beyond the brightly lit windows, other lives pursued their old, contented habits in an atmosphere of warmth and light. When he reached his grandmother's house, two blocks farther, the lights there would be lit too, so he might reign in their brilliance.

Before he got there, he stopped suddenly at a corner.

A man and a woman were talking to each other near one of the street lights. The woman put out her hand to brush something off the man's sleeve, while he went on talking, apparently intent on explaining something. That was all. But Andrés could tell from the tender angle of the woman's head as she listened, and the touching trustfulness and self-abandonment he sensed in them both, that they were in love. This was nothing impure or fortuitous, there could be no doubt that what he saw before him was real love, young love at its fullest. They could not be friends, or brother and sister; only what they were—a man and a woman, in love, alone together in the cold, frosty night.

Andrés took a step forward, then another.

By now the girl was recognizable, but still Andrés could not bring himself to formulate her name. He was just about to take another step, his legs poised in mid-stride, when the name struck him. Estela. It was Estela!

Andrés stepped back. Something inside him seemed to have overturned, leaving him in a state of agonizing indecision. The doors which a moment before seemed to be opening in welcome were all closing. His heart hardened in his breast as he watched Estela in love talking to a man, a stranger but clearly in love too, under a street light. It was all so simple and natural. Another instance of the one truly rewarding human relationship repeating itself endlessly, trivially but perfectly, a relationship that now excluded him as he had once sought to exclude himself. But now he needed to be part of it!

He peered through the mist, trying to see the man's face—it was a boy! He took a few cautious steps forward, but the lovers saw nothing beyond the ring of intimacy that enclosed them. Estela drew nearer to the boy, looking at his lips not in search of words or explanations but for the warmth in them.

Andrés thought of his own lips. They were well shaped, and ironical, but bloodless. Estela would never look at them the way she was looking at her companion's now.

His whole edifice of hope was shattered.

Shattered, he now realized, because it was not simply desire he felt for Estela but love, yes love, and this knowledge sliced through him like a knife. Desire alone would not have been powerful enough to deliver him from the void and from death, from the flat monotonous days of his past and the yawning chasm of the future whose chill he felt about him already. Only young, harmonious love like the love these two felt for each other could have redeemed him: Estela would have to stand close to him and pluck a loose thread from his sleeve just as confidently as she had from her friend's a moment before. No more than that. No more, but it would have to be done with as much love, with the same surrender proudly etched in the inclination of her body, and the same spontaneous affection of her gesture. Yes. That was what he needed.

But it could never be. Andrés had left his youth behind him years ago, intact, almost unused. It could never be. Estela was young and he was not, she was beautiful and he was not. There wouldn't be a grain of poetry in a relationship between them because he had forfeited his right to poetry. It was grotesque to imagine himself making love to Estela! But it was beautiful and satisfying to think of those two young bodies making love. If he succeeded in seducing her, he would only be what his grandmother had called him—a vicious old man, the kind who stroke girls' knees furtively in the theater, or contrive to press themselves against a little girl in the anonymity of a crowded bus. Oh, he was well aware that fifty-four is not old! But in craving the love of a seventeen-year-old and envying her young gallant his youth he turned himself into a ridiculous old man. Had he felt this way about a mature woman, the whole thing would have been simple and straightforward, with nothing sordid about it. But now . . . the ugliness of his age punished him with the immense distance it placed between him and the faintest hope of beauty. Only the beauty of what those two standing there under the street light felt for each other could satisfy him.

The mist seemed to be thickening. A chink of light glimpsed through a curtained window showed that life was going on within. They would be eating, sleeping . . .

It was all his grandmother's fault! Yes, it was her mad insight which had introduced this idea into his mind and left it to putrefy there. And he had momentarily believed it to be feasible. Now he knew that someone who has chosen to exist like a corpse cannot come to life because he suddenly feels like it, because the thought suddenly appeals to him. But he had believed it could be done, and that was the worst of all . . . he could never resign himself now to the mummified existence he had led before. And yet, to drive away the horror which stared him in the face, he must instantly realize his longing for a young, full love! Impossible, impossible. No, the horror of death must serve as his reality, as it had for his grandmother.

Estela drew closer to the boy. She clung to him softly, leaning on him, their faces almost touching. Andrés stopped breathing. When they kissed, a corrosive fury seized him.

What about his grandmother?

Didn't he pay the girl a good salary to look after his grandmother day and night, as she needed to be looked after at her age? Estela had no right to desert the old woman to come and kiss and cuddle with some good-for-nothing out in the street! Well, this might not be the first time, but it would certainly be the last! She had only been working there three months, too—yes, his grandmother was quite right, Estela was definitely bad, practically a prostitute! His grandmother wasn't mad at all, it was these young people who were mad, rotten, corrupt!

Estela took the boy by the hand, opened the gate, and led him into Misiá Elisa's house.

Aha, so the girl not only neglected her duties, but brought men into the house too, did she? The old woman, in her folly, had often insisted that former nurses had invited men in to make filthy love together in the next room, believing her to be asleep. Was it possible that all the filth in the old woman's mind was not the result of delusions at all but plain fact? Certainly this wouldn't be the first time Estela had done this . . .

Andrés trembled as he turned the handle of the wrought-iron grille which Estela had opened a moment before to go inside with her man. The silhouette of the house with its crenellations and moldering carvings was lightly sketched in the misty garden. The keys jingled faintly in Andrés's hand as he entered the dark hall. The house was silent, but after a few seconds Andrés became aware that there was life behind one of the doors to his right, though no noise came from it and there was no light.

"Lourdes!" he shouted into the darkness.

He waited, motionless. His keys went on jingling in the silence left by his cry.

"Lourdes!" he bellowed.

A moment later Lourdes's dark bulk appeared framed in the lighted doorway which had opened suddenly into the servants' quarters.

"Why, bless me, if it isn't Don Andresito! Heavens, what a fright you gave me! Why don't you come into the kitchen, it's a little warmer in there. Come in a moment. The señora's asleep, you know."

Andrés followed her in.

The yellowish light made the kitchen look small and warm and full of life and familiar odors, in contrast to the bleak street outside, and the cold hall. Rosario greeted him with delighted surprise. Estela smiled. The boy, sitting before a bowl of steaming broth, put down the spoon he had been in the act of raising to his lips.

"What's he doing here?" Andrés asked.

The boy stood up.

"He's a friend of ours from the Fornino Emporium. It was cold and we thought a bowl of soup . . ."

"I want him out of the house at once."

The expressions froze on their faces.

"What's he doing here?" Andrés shouted wildly, clutching the key so tightly it hurt his hand. "What do you think this house is, Lourdes? A boardinghouse for your niece's admirers? Eh?"

"But we all know the boy, Don . . ."

"I won't have any boys, known or unknown, around the place. Who's looking after my grandmother? I thought you brought your niece here because you thought she could be trusted to behave herself—well, I've just seen these two cuddling outside in the street! What's to keep her from carrying on with everyone else too, and getting this house the reputation of being some sort of brothel? I'll throw all of you out, do you hear! The whole lot of you, for negligence and thoughtlessness! And I'll stay here alone and look after my grandmother by myself. All alone . . . and you're a shameless pair too! You ought to be ashamed of yourselves, covering up for the girl like that!"

The boy had started to move toward the back door.

"Come here," Andrés ordered. "You heard me—I won't have this sort of thing going on in my house. And I shall send Estela back to the country tomorrow, yes, tomorrow, you wait and see . . ."

He went out, followed by the boy. In the garden Andrés opened the gate and after closing it behind Mario he said: "If I catch you here again or I find out you've been talking to the girl, I'll tell Don Narciso to fire you, and I'll call the police."

Mario vanished into the mist. But he waited at the corner.

13 His limbs felt heavy as lead. He kept his agony of mind isolated in a mist of weariness so that none of the hostility accumulated in the world around him could impinge on his thoughts. He was too exhausted, too shattered to go back to his apartment that night. To take another step, to try to cope with a perfectly ordinary situation like walking along the street or hailing a taxi, would expose his nerves to the most dreadful ravages. This weariness was his only protection against having to look at himself clearly on the edge of the abyss. He yielded to exhaustion.

Lourdes got the room ready for him quickly and silently, helped by Estela. He climbed to the third floor listening to his footsteps on the stairs. Each tread marked a second, each step took him nearer in time to the point, the moment when things ceased to be. He met Estela on the threshold of his room. She was on her way out, carrying a bundle of sheets. The girl lowered her eyes and shrank against the door as if afraid to brush against Andrés or to come too close to him in the narrow doorway. Her fear brought home to him the ugliness of his desires and he too averted his eyes and shrank aside, hurt by her fear of him. He was tempted to spring on her and make the whole house re-echo with her screams. The girl sensed this, and it was that which made her avert her eyes and hurry down the stairs till her footsteps were swallowed up in the silence of the house. Andrés undressed quickly and was overtaken by a leaden sleep as soon as he lay down.

Down in the kitchen, the two maids were going around turning off the lights before going up to bed.

"I don't feel like listening to the serial tonight," Rosario murmured.

"Neither do I. I'm so tired . . ." Lourdes answered.

"So am I. I guess it will go away."

Rosario gave the faucets a last turn so they wouldn't drip at night.

"Poor Don Andresito," she said.

"Yes. He's getting just like the señora with his rages. He'll be going on about things being stolen next, and I don't know what else. Poor soul . . . and I expect we'll have to look after him too then. Poor soul . . ."

"I'm going to bed. Good night."

"Good night. Estela, child, would you go out and make sure the gate is closed. Good night, dear. I'm going to bed now, I'm worn out . . ."

Estela went out into the street. Mario was waiting on the corner.

"My aunt says he's going mad like the señora," she told him.

"Old goat . . ."

Mario was not interested in Don Andrés. After all, gentlemen were very different from people like him, and anyway they had a right to behave as they pleased at home. The rich could go crazy if they wanted to, and create whatever problems they dreamed up for themselves. Naturally, they were completely ignorant of the problems of raw reality, like the ones that had recently unleashed themselves on Mario. At home, Dora went on moaning and complaining day and night. She even seemed to do it when she was asleep. It was more than two months since René disappeared, and there was no money to buy food for the children. She could have put up with that, though. What was really appalling, unendurable, was that she was unmistakably pregnant again. She took all sorts of miracle pills and potions, visited old crones who prescribed nostrums, inhalations, massages, and every imaginable remedy, but they were all useless. She stayed pregnant, complaining endlessly about how uncomfortable she felt and how inconvenient it was, until one of her children appeared and then she seemed to find some relief from her own misery in scolding the child at the top of her voice or beating it for no reason at all.

"I hadn't noticed before that he was peculiar . . ." Estela murmured. She seemed preoccupied with Don Andrés.

"Come over here, there's less light . . ."

Mario did not touch Estela. They were leaning against the gate side by side, hidden in the shadow of the branches through which mist drifted slowly.

"Listen," Mario said suddenly. "I bet the old guy has his eye on you . . ."

"Yes, he has."

"How do you know?"

"Huh!"

"You watch out then, they can get very fresh with girls . . . these old fellows . . ."

"Come on, he's so silly!"

"Remember all that money he's got!"

Estela's forehead took on the same worried frown as Mario's.

"Have you got anything left?"

"Not a cent."

"Here."

She gave him fifty pesos, which Mario took without looking at it.

"And René?" Estela asked.

Mario shook his head.

"Not a peep. He could be dead, for all I know."

Estela shook her head sympathetically. Mario bit his nails, then went on speaking in the harsh, violent way he had adopted lately.

"They make me want to go and sleep under a bridge somewhere! That bastard René! He's really fixed me! I haven't even got anything for a smoke. Look at the crap they gave me at the Emporium."

He lit the cigarette he had shown her, and as he did so, the flaring light showed that his watch was missing from his wrist.

"Where's your watch?" Estela asked.

Mario hid his hand as if ashamed of it.

"I pawned it," he muttered despondently.

Estela's eyes filled with tears. The watch was the last straw. She knew that that little gold mechanism which it had taken Mario so long to pay for was what he loved most in the world. As he talked he would move his wrist in the sunlight so the imitation gold reflected back into his smiling eyes.

"Why didn't you ask for an advance at the Emporium instead?"

"I already have, that's why," he snapped. Then, more gently, he added: "They won't let me have any more."

"What about where you live?"

"Do you honestly think they'd lend me anything, knowing René's reputation like they do? For all I know, he may be in the can somewhere for what he's been doing. And maybe they'll throw all of us in too because of him."

They parted a few minutes later.

While Estela was locking up, she thought of what Misiá Elisa had said only that morning. She had forgotten about it during the day, but now, in her distress over the pawned watch, the words seemed to float up to the surface of her memory under their own weight.

"See? One, two, three, four, five thousand peso notes. I'm putting them right here under my pillow so you can steal them from me. I know you will steal them from me, because you're a wicked girl . . ."

Estela had handed her a little box which was kept in a drawer in the dressing table. She took the notes out and folded them away under her pillow. Estela put the box back in its drawer, hardly aware of what the old woman was saying.

"It's to tempt you, you see, to make you steal . . ."

Estela knew just what she had to do. If Misiá Elisa accused her of stealing now, no one would believe her; she accused everyone of stealing from her all the time. No one knew how much money she had in the little box because she had been hoarding it away for ages and refused to let anyone see how much the box contained. Then Estela would give Mario the money so he could get back his gold watch. She wouldn't have to tell him where she got the money, he needed it so badly he'd believe anything. And it wouldn't be like René's stealing because René was bad and she wasn't. She had to take those notes from under the pillow because if she didn't they would only molder away in the little box and no one would ever benefit from them.

She opened the door stealthily, feeling her way up the

stairs with one hand on the banister till she reached the old woman's room. The money was under the pillow . . . and her father was a long way away, in the country . . . and Mario missed the watch so much. She opened the door . . . a little oil lamp glowed on the bedside table, red like the sacred flame in church. A step, then another. There was really no need to move so quietly; Misiá Elisa slept very heavily. Estela stopped by the señora's bedside and bent over her. The old woman's toothless mouth was half open. Her breathing came and went so imperceptibly she seemed scarcely alive. But deep down in those bronchial tubes which old age had silted up, the air was trapped, making a tiny subterranean noise.

Estela could not bring herself to do it. She went into the room next door and lay down, and she tossed and turned interminably before finally falling asleep. The old woman's breathing sounded very near, almost in her ear, and Don Andrés seemed to be snoring in the room above. Finally, without knowing she had been asleep, Estela found herself wide awake. The cold dawn was washing the ragged remnants of night. And the fog, hovering out there, was the same fog of the night before, when she and Mario kissed in the street.

She went into Misiá Elisa's room and slipped her hand unfalteringly under the pillow, feeling around till her fingers closed on the notes. Then she went back to her room and hid the money where no one would ever find it. And she went back to sleep.

Andrés stayed in his grandmother's house that night too. And since the next day was rainy and colorless, he spent most of it tossing in bed, half awake, only dimly aware of the shaft of light that entered between the curtains, vaguely registering the passing hours. The consoling warmth which had accumulated around his body between the sheets made a protective cocoon that kept him from having to think, and so he lay there and passed still another night in his grandmother's house. The following day, a little more wakeful but still insulated from full consciousness by a cloud of weariness, he asked that some of his things be brought over from his apartment—a change of clothes, toilet articles— with the idea of spending just one more night in the house. He would leave, without fail, the next day. He must not stay here. His grandmother was alive in the room below. With each frail breath the old woman seemed to knit him closer and closer to the agony of the previous days, which he had succeeded in evading briefly in the blessed torpor that hung over him.

He must leave because he needed absolute tranquillity. Above all, he needed to forget that Estela was moving about the rooms on the floor below. And he needed the feeling of independence that the couple who looked after him in the apartment gave him with their impersonal manner. Lourdes's attentions were part of the malicious plot to tie him to this house for the rest of his life. The maid was forever coming upstairs to lay another rug across the foot of his bed, or offer him some tempting little snack. She stirred his tisanes and smoothed the covers so diligently that Andrés was finally provoked to order her, in his most cutting voice, to leave him alone. But he shivered when he saw in Lourdes's good-natured eyes the certainty that he would never leave the house again.

"Which he should never have left in the first place," Rosario remarked in the kitchen.

"Did you see the state the poor man's clothes were in? It made you feel sorry for him. There was even a button missing from his drawers, imagine! This new couple he has working for him must be a lazy good-for-nothing pair. And did you see her? All dressed up like a real lady!"

"And they must be millionaires, with the money he pays them."

They shook their heads in disapproval. A second later, Lourdes murmured: "He asked me to take him some cognac after his meal . . ."

"How strange . . ."

"Mmm. That's what I thought. I told him to be careful, it might upset his stomach—you know how sick he's been these last few days—and you know what he did? He shouted that I wasn't to interfere in what didn't concern me!"

"He shouted? He never used to."

"Mmm. That's what I said."

Andrés did not go back to his apartment the next day, or the day after that. There was a core of inertia in him from which decisions and feelings rebounded limply and ineffectually, keeping him anchored to his grandmother's house.

He wandered ceaselessly from room to room in his dressing gown and slippers, carefully avoiding the old woman's room and any chance encounters with Estela. His anguish hung as if suspended between these two poles—his grandmother and Estela. He fled from both, a perpetual flight that kept him adrift in a twilight existence, between life and death, as he wandered from one room to the next. He never went out into the garden. He seemed beyond hearing, thinking, seeing. At the most he might slump for a moment in an armchair or peer at the dripping trees through the gaps in the plush curtains. He picked up a book, only to drop it again as Lourdes appeared with a bottle stained with the traces of time and damp, to ask him if this was the cognac he wanted. Once he asked the maid for the keys to a cupboard near the dining room, where Misiá Elisa's huge collection of silver was stored. The cupboard had not been opened more than a couple of times in the past ten years. But he never got around to opening it. Instead he picked up a magazine, months old, but discarded it almost immediately to leaf through an album of ancient photographs he had found in a chest of drawers he opened in passing, and where, except for the album, there had been nothing but a few mothballs.

——Catching sight of Estela disappearing down a carpeted corridor, his eyes would glide over her as if they didn't see her, or as though his mind refused to register the girl's image. But a few minutes later, sitting on the edge of his bed, cutting his nails, he would catch himself meditating as to why Estela's beauty should have this lacerating effect on him. And leave this terrible feeling of injustice. Why should a shade more pigmentation in the skin, a few millimeters less nose, a certain suppleness about the movements, a liquidness about the eyes have this terrifying power to torment him merely because these ineffable proportions added up to his conception of beauty? Why did he feel the urge to possess this and not some other type of beauty? Why? Why?

The days passed, and Andrés did not leave his grandmother's house. The days lengthened into a week, a week and a half, two weeks. He telephoned his apartment to tell them to send whatever he might need. He did not ask for anything specific, however, nothing which might anchor him too decisively, just a few changes of clothing, handkerchiefs, a suit he thought he might wear if he decided to dress the following day. But he did not dress. He wandered about the house, oblivious of time, and collapsed into bed in the evening, when Lourdes would come up to keep him company for a while. Sitting at his feet, the old woman would launch into an interminable monologue, a meandering stream of details and observations which long ago had lost their pungency but which effectively undermined Andrés's last shreds of will power.

—— One night Andrés heard an unusual commotion in the

room below his. Something was going on there. His attention was caught by his grandmother's voice, which began by complaining softly and then rose to a feeble moan of pain. Apprehensively, he sat on the edge of his bed, his feet thrust into his slippers, and waited. What if his grandmother died? Suppose she died that night? His nerves, suddenly alert and sensitized, tingled up and down his body, sending a wave of blood pounding in his ears and filling up his dormant self, waking it up. This could be the solution to everything! A wild tremor of joy ran through him at the thought that right now, this instant, the poor travesty of life was being snuffed out in that body down below and that henceforth his suffering too would stop. The house, Lourdes, Estela . . . above all, Estela . . . all would be dispersed to the four corners of the earth the moment the old woman drew her last breath. And then it would be as though none of it had ever happened; they would become no more than ghostly figures in a dream. He strained his ears in the darkness of this charnel house to catch that last exhalation of breath which would set him free. But then the terror of the void poised over him as he reflected that this freedom would mean that he himself no longer existed except as the walking corpse he used to be, with his walking sticks—but only ten at a time—leading a colorless existence in that apartment of his which was simply an antechamber to . . . to nothing, another and still more horrible nothingness than this one because there would be no Estela to pass through it and remind him, even at a hopeless distance, that something existed. His grandmother must not die! If she died, Estela would go off with her boy, leaving him to polish and twirl those ten beautiful canes, the better to admire them, without so much as a qualm about the health of his ninety-four-year-old grandmother to disturb his peace.

His grandmother must not die!

He wished this so feverishly that he stood up, determined
to go to his grandmother's room and keep her from dying.
With his hand on the doorknob, he paused—what about
Estela? She would see him with his face all blurred by
sleep, his hair disheveled, absurd, ugly, useless in every
way. She would be standing beside him, in the same room,
and the thought of the girl's flaunting youth made him
hesitate. He went back and lay down again on the bed.

Misiá Elisa's lamentations suddenly stopped. The tone
of the old woman's voice as it filtered through the floor was
not one of despair but of exhaustion. Then he heard Estela's
voice. Was she singing? Crooning softly so her mistress
would fall asleep? Yes, that was it. Her voice was soothing!
As she sat by the sick woman's bed, naked under her coarse
cotton nightgown, she would be bathed in the rosy light of
the little lamp on the bedside table. Andrés found this soft
singing of hers anything but soothing. The song became
the rhythm of the blood pounding in his ears, and the weak
or wrong notes were his nerves scraping inside his body.

He did not stay in bed. Instead he walked up and down
the room all night, till dawn stained the borders of his
drawn curtains and he heard the first steps and voices echo-
ing through the icy house. Later, after a shower, he put on
the suit he had sent for a few days before.

"How pale you look, Don Andresito!" Lourdes exclaimed
when she brought up his breakfast. "Didn't you sleep well?"

Lourdes explained that the commotion of the previous
night had been due to a simple attack of indigestion. This
astonished Andrés: his grandmother scarcely ate; she pecked
away like a bird and then only at the most digestible foods.
Had Rosario not prepared her food properly then? No, it
wasn't that, Lourdes said. It was just that the señora's
stomach, being so old and tired, was subject to these attacks of indigestion for no reason at all. They caused her
great discomfort, but it was all right, they only lasted a

few minutes. The señora had awakened feeling so well that she had actually asked Estela to paint her nails for her.

He must put an end to this situation. Imprisoned within himself, and within the walls of this house, Andrés was reduced to the plaything of Estela's presence and his grandmother's indigestion. He must find some loophole and escape, but where?

Carlos Gros!

— He set off for his friend's house. He had not seen Carlos Gros for a month. Under the pressure of recent events, the doctor's face had vanished from his mind and he had to make an effort to dredge it up from the debris of his memories. His excuse for coming so early in the day was his grandmother's indigestion. If Carlos proved a sympathetic listener, he might gradually make some reference to his present plight to see if his friend's compassion was aroused, and if he recognized his error in believing Andrés incapable of intense feelings. Then, and only then, he would tell him everything.

He got there just as Carlos Gros was emerging from his bath. He wore a pale green towel knotted around his sagging belly and was wreathed in steam from the shower which was starting to condense and trickle in great tears down the tiled walls, which matched his towel. Carlos, both feet squarely planted on the plushy floor covering, wiped the mirror and began to shave. Surrounded by everything that could possibly minister to bodily comfort—thick towels, pleasant warmth, bottles of English cologne—he resembled a very plump, elderly priest officiating in the temple of pleasure. Andrés found it impossible to contain himself and his secret burst out of him, raw, without embellishment or preamble. Ashamed and embarrassed, he cast about for a subterfuge or subtlety with which to shield his modesty, but for all his efforts the words burst out naked.

Carlos Gros finished shaving with his usual care, although his intelligent simian face was clearly concentrating on what his friend was telling him. Andrés talked on without stopping as they moved into the bedroom where Carlos slowly dressed and Andrés sat down beside a table to continue his confession. His eyes never left the doctor's face, but he did not seem to see him. When his tumbling words reached what seemed to be a climax, Carlos, who had been selecting a tie, turned and asked him:

"But why does this make you suffer so much, Andrés? What's so wrong or dreadful or abnormal about what you've just told me?"

Andrés stared at his friend for a moment with the tears streaming down his gaunt cheeks. At this, Carlos's heart knotted with pity and shame.

"But what's wrong, man, what's wrong?"

He started toward Andrés, to comfort him, but stopped halfway across the room, revolted.

"What does it matter? What's wrong with it? I don't see . . ."

"I don't know, I don't know what's bad about it. All I know is that it's ridiculous, ugly, that everything I feel is absurd, undignified . . . ignoble. Can you seriously imagine me walking down the street in broad daylight . . . holding Estela's hand?"

"Is that what you want?" the doctor asked in astonishment.

Andrés nodded. Carlos kept knotting and unknotting his tie so as not to have to look at his friend, who nauseated him.

"But she's only a child," he murmured without conviction.

Andrés sat looking at him. He wiped the tears with the back of his hand and swallowed, like a little boy.

"Yes, I know. I know what you're going to say. Who should know better than I, with the empty mirror of my life to gaze at myself in?"

The unaccustomed rhetoric of this remark touched Carlos much more than the story of Andrés's love for a little maid servant and the maid servant's love for some boy, rather banal occurrences when looked at dispassionately. In this absurd, incongruous rhetoric, however, Carlos perceived a real disorder in his friend's psychological make-up which alarmed him. It seemed to manifest itself in a pathological compulsion to retreat, escape from something, everything—or was it nothing—return to an adolescence he had never had. This was dangerous. Dangerous, chiefly, because it was so absurd. His brief impulse toward pity was instantly suppressed as he reflected on the risk of encouraging such absurdity.

"Careful, Andrés!" he exclaimed. "You're beginning to talk like a madman."

"You don't understand . . ."

"You mean you don't want to listen to me. Well, if that's the case, please don't waste my time. I'm late at the clinic as it is. I can't give up a whole morning to hear still another version of the story of your cowardice."

"You'd better go then. I don't need you . . ."

"Yes, you do. You do need me."

"You're wrong, Carlos, I'm quite self-sufficient now. I'm more alone now than I have ever been, totally and permanently excluded. But there's this pain here in my chest, burning me!"

"Stop, stop, Andrés! Can't you see that all you're doing is inventing phrases to make something quite simple seem terrible and complicated? Don't be silly, man, don't you see you've got everything all wrong? What you are doing is taking revenge on yourself—a phony revenge, of course—

for having lived so little. To convince yourself of your
capacity to feel, you've dreamed up this imaginary tragedy.
I must say I never believed you were so simple, Andrés.
Don't you see that you're simply dressing up a perfectly
normal physical desire as love, just to prove yourself capable
of it? You must see that."

"Is that what you think of me?"

"No, no, no, it's precisely because I think so much of
you that I'm telling you this. You deserve richer experiences,
Andrés, and fuller ones. You mustn't let yourself be carried
away by a nightmare situation. Persuade yourself that it's
a simple case of animal desire."

"What a limited, unimaginative person you are! If it
were only that, do you suppose my grandmother would have
been able to grasp what I felt, out of nowhere, before I
even knew I felt it? Do you suppose she could have done
that if it hadn't been genuine?"

"You mustn't let Misiá Elisa's delusions affect your own
mental balance, please, Andrés. Don't you see that the situation might have been expressly designed for you to create
this imaginary drama for yourself? The girl is desirable,
as all, or almost all girls are desirable, and I agree that
there is something touching, painfully beautiful about
youth. She is in love with some boy, the way thousands of
other little servant girls are, and this naturally means she
is less likely to want to accept your advances. This whole
grand tragedy you are trying to get going boils down to
one hugely simple problem—you are jealous, nothing more.
And so you clutch on to this problem and you construct
yourself a tragedy of unrequited love; worse still, a tragedy
of ugly, suffering old age—which is not even accurate in
your case—confronted with the beauty of youth. Why don't
you seduce Estela? Why not try and teach her to love you,
since that seems to be what you need? You're rich and

intelligent, and everyone finds you charming. I tell you, in spite of those fifty-four years of yours, which seem to upset you so much, you're a great deal more attractive than a mere boy. But that won't do for you. The señor must have his tragedy. He wants to feel deeply, to suffer in order to prove to himself that he can live in the fullest sense of the word. But still without taking any risks, Andrés, or living in earnest. My advice to you, Andrés, is to take great care, that way lies madness. Try to make her fall in love with you, or seduce her, as any normal man would. Then I'll believe you. And if you fail, I'll sympathize with you and feel for you. But this . . ."

Andrés stood up angrily.

"You don't understand because you're a trivial person," he exclaimed. "Can't you see that it's poetry I want? What poetry is there in a man like me seducing one of the maids under his own roof, whatever his intentions? No, no, what those two have is natural, it just happened. That's what I can't have and what hurts so much. All you care about is the cold pleasure of sleeping with the girl a couple of times. I want more than that . . ."

This was too much for Carlos. The situation was so monumentally absurd that the doctor found himself sharing his friend's humiliation. He was flushing with the embarrassment that Andrés's tears and tone of passionate desperation had aroused in him. Anyway . . . the whole business wasn't really that important. Knowing how short-lived Andrés's enthusiasms were as a rule, Carlos thought it likely that he would soon recover his composure.

"If you go on deceiving yourself, you'll go mad."

"Go mad? I only wish I could. That would solve everything. The only orderly thing about life is its chaos and injustice—insanity might very well bring me closer to the truth. Then I would never have to look death and extinction

in the face, in broad daylight and in the full possession of
my senses. What a marvelous escape it must be from . . .
from that! What could be more perfect than the mysticism
of madness, with its gift for living the truth? My mad
grandmother is the only person I know who is capable of
perceiving the truth. You don't come anywhere near it with
your cold reasoning and compartmentalized passions."

Carlos reflected that his friend was only too transparently
taking revenge. It was a fact that since youth he had always
enjoyed presenting himself to Andrés as a model of passionate naturalness, not only in love, but in all his attitudes, in
life, politics, his profession, as well as in financial and business affairs. These attitudes gave him a certain advantage
over Andrés, who rejected all that as cheap and vulgar and
sought different spheres in which to shine. However, in
all this, Carlos had undoubtedly overlooked the problems
germinating darkly within Andrés. He had been guilty of
egotism, undoubtedly, but then he too had problems, many
of them serious, some insoluble, which Andrés had never
suspected.

Suddenly the disgust Andrés's revelations had aroused
in him turned to hatred: he had been made to feel guilty for
no reason at all.

"Good. Well, that's enough of your adolescent stupidities," he exclaimed angrily. "What do you expect from me?
Pity? Do you want me to embrace you and tell you that your
sufferings are mine? I'm sorry, Andrés. I can't do it. You
disgust me. Your troubles don't move me—they aren't real
. . ."

"Not real?"

Glaring haughtily at his friend, Andrés left the room
without a word. He would never speak to Carlos Gros again
in his life.

Now he was really alone, though the wound of his love

for Estela was still there, keeping him company, affirming that he existed. Carlos might say it was not real, but he felt it and to him it felt real.

Andrés spent a long time that morning wandering through the muddy streets.

On one corner two men were fixing canvases over the loads in their trucks. They were young, rough-looking, and ill-shaven, but the flame of life sparkled in their eyes. They began talking about their machines and the price of gasoline; they compared radiators, discussed cranks and tires, steering wheels, batteries, and condensers. The truck headlights were pale at this time of the morning. Andrés pictured them at night, their yellow beams piercing the rainy darkness of a bad road somewhere down south, as they traveled from unknown village to unknown village, the drivers' faces sleepy behind their streaming windshields, their eyes intent on the bright beams with which the headlights sliced the rain-swept darkness. He imagined those men swearing at someone who annoyed them, arriving at some village where you asked a stranger for a light and it didn't take long to become friendly over a few glasses of wine or a few bottles of beer. So many needs, appetites, hungers, and desires were written in their eyes! Money was one of their ways of settling a fundamental acccount with life. Perhaps they had wives to give it to, children or parents to provide for, wine awaiting their parched lips behind the counters of thousands of remote bars. And all this they loved, they knew intimately, like their trucks, which held no mysteries for them. They knew every piston, every spark plug in the engine. They would sit at the wheel of their beloved trucks and set off for remote villages, drawing nearer to or farther away from the people they loved and needed, from their hunger and thirst.

The men said goodbye to each other. They were just about to set off.

What if he asked one of them to take him along? Andrés
thought to himself. To Perquilauquén, to Curanilahue or
Tinguiririca? Andrés laughed at this absurd caprice. He
was fifty-four and a man of culture and refinement. The
truck drivers looked at him. Andrés could not resist going
up to them, saying something which would allow him to
partake, even momentarily, in that vitality of theirs from
which he was shut out.

"Could you give me a light, please."

They did, and Andrés walked away through the murky
morning.

14   As soon as the silence of night extended
over the wretched mud roofs, René would appear in Mario's
dreams. Perhaps it was not René but someone else, someone
even more hostile, but he looked like René with his burning
bloodshot eyes. He called out to Mario, dragging him toward
something terrifying, through whole battalions of policemen. The policemen weren't friendly like the ones whose
clean, smiling faces, no longer surmounted by their fierce-
looking caps, made them look like any boy next door as
they ate a sandwich in a restaurant. The policemen in
Mario's dreams did nothing but deal out bloody punishments
to René, and to him too. Because he was no better than
René and was judged equally reprehensible by this squad of
policemen who swarmed and multiplied like ants, covering
everything in sight in his dreams. Mario would wake up
groaning: he did not know what they had condemned him
for.

His dreams were preferable to reality. Dora's pregnancy
made her cry all day long, and the kids, their noses stream-

ing, never stopped their unspeakably noisy games except to whine for something to eat. Mario did not know where to turn, or what to do. Forcing down his repugnance, he had approached each of René's "business" friends to ask if they knew where he was, but all he got was dark looks and answers muttered through clenched teeth. At the Emporium, Don Segundo gazed at him with those little oozy eyes, as if to say: "You'll end up badly. Didn't I always say that boy would end up badly?"

And Mario began to be afraid that Don Segundo was right.

He thought about Estela continually, especially when René's evil influence seemed about to consume him. All he had to do was imagine the girl's face and the little room with a dresser full of blue cups and plates, and René's world and all its terrors would vanish. Most of the time when they were together, though, Mario was harsh with her. The five thousand pesos that he had used to redeem his watch, which once again adorned his wrist, made him feel like the girl's prisoner, obligated to her, suffocated, no longer free to move or breathe. And it was hard to believe Estela's account of how she came by the money. A dark suspicion, implicating him as much as it did her, made him lose all his gentleness and trust. He scarcely ever saw her because the señor spied on her all the time and kept her from going out.

"What else does that old goat do to you?"

"Nothing."

"What are you complaining about then? You're getting like Dora."

"Nothing . . . it's just that he looks at me, when he sees me, as if, well, as if he was going to jump on top of me. He frightens me sometimes."

"These old men can't do anything."

"Then why did you tell me to be careful?"

"I was just kidding. That old man's got nothing left in him."

"And when he shuts all the doors and windows at eight sharp . . . you'd think he was doing it just to keep me from coming to meet you. And the way he looks at me, honestly!"

One afternoon a letter arrived at the Emporium addressed to Mario. He read it with his hands shaking.

"Come," it said peremptorily, adding, besides an address and some curt instructions: "Bring money."

René had finally stretched out a hand to get him. And the frightening pain that had often made him fight people who called his brother a thief, the mysterious terror that made him glance behind him in dark streets, all the suspicions and anxieties that had haunted his life from afar were suddenly made real by this letter: he would have to go and find René and join him.

He crumpled up the sheet of paper and dropped it into the water which ran along the gutter and watched it bobbing along ahead of him on the trickle of dirty water toward Misiá Elisa's house, which was at the end of the block. He followed the piece of paper a little hesitantly, patting his pockets in the hope of finding a cigarette. But he was so poor that there wasn't even one. His nerves were all on edge, keyed to expect their dose of nicotine. To think he once would smoke a whole pack in an evening, and expensive ones, too! All of them, Dora, René, Estela, and that old nut, all they wanted was to lock him up and keep him from having a good time. He would have to go and join René, though: anything was better than this uncertainty, the eternal hope in the kids' faces and in Dora's, and the fear that left his nerves sharp and rasping like a saw, so that he was permanently tense, on edge, about to explode.

When he reached Misiá Elisa's house, he rang the bell. Estela came to the door at once.

"Why did you have to go and ring? What if the *patrón* had come to the door?"

Her voice was veiled; it had a new gravity about it. Mario looked at her, surprised, as they walked along without speaking or touching. Estela gave him a bundle with bread and cold meat and four ten-peso notes, looking at him insistently, the way people do when they are trying to drive the wedge of their own problems into someone else's.

"What's the matter?" Mario asked.

Estela took him by the wrist and pulled him toward a doorway as if she wanted to hide in its shadow. Mario watched the beams of a car's headlights traveling across her face. Then they passed and it was in darkness once more. Why was Estela hanging on to his watch, which he had redeemed with money from such dubious origins?

"Let go of my watch," he said.

. . . the watch which would be traveling the well-worn route to the pawnbroker next day. No. It would be better to sell it this time, get rid of it once and for all, so he would have some money to take to René . . . sell it and cut all the ties that bound him to his old life. Goodbye to the Emporium and the bicycles and Don Segundo, goodbye to the Condor and his friends, goodbye to his nickname of Big Hummingbird, goodbye to everything.

Goodbye. What now?

"Listen," Estela whispered.

"What?"

Estela did not answer. She stood silent beside Mario as he took off his watch and dropped it into his pocket along with the money, and then held it there for a moment as if taking his leave of it.

"Listen . . ." Estela began again.

She was crying silently. Mario turned to look at her and just then the lights of another passing car lit up her face, which was distorted with weeping.

"What the hell are you blubbing for, eh? Eh? Can't you tell me, instead of just standing there crying?"

Mario's frightened eyes searched for Estela's in the darkness. Estela had the words on the tip of her tongue, but she couldn't say them because she was crying too hard. Mario took her by the shoulders, in a sudden fury, and shook her.

"Goddamn it, what's wrong? Eh? What's the matter with you? Why are you crying? Do you think I don't know you stole that five thousand pesos? I know you're a thief, for Christ's sake!"

Estela covered her stomach with both hands as if to shield it. That was all. Mario's hands relaxed slightly on her shoulders. But almost at once a new wave of anger swept over him and he began shaking her again, much harder.

"Are you pregnant, you fucking bitch? Are you pregnant? Are you?"

His voice trembled as he repeated the question again and again and again, appalled, furious, rigid with anger. He shook Estela as if he wanted to tear her apart, limb by limb.

"Yes . . ." she whispered.

As though René's spirit had suddenly invaded his body, Mario struck her savagely across the face with the flat of his hand, and she whimpered like an animal in pain.

"You're trying to screw me too, you bitch!"

And he ran off, leaving Estela standing there, with her hand on her cheek.

Mario ran for a long time before slowing down to his normal walking pace. His body shook and shook and his heart pounded as if his organs and his blood were trying to burst out of him. He searched himself for cigarettes but found none. He never had anything on him these days, not even a cigarette. A frenzied craving for tobacco assailed his mouth and nostrils. He longed for the oval shape of a cigarette between his dry lips, the smoke making his eyes smart, and its slight warmth against his face and fingers.

He sniffed his fingers, but he smoked so little these days that the odor of tobacco had gone, like the ocher stains on his fingers. He walked on and on through half the streets in the city, streets that were filling up with gay evening faces lit up by the neon signs, by street lights, open doors, by the light flooding from shops, garages, drugstores, parked cars, cafés. He was neither cold nor hungry; the only thing he was conscious of was this craving for tobacco. He remembered the few notes Estela had given him and fumbled around in his pocket for a few loose coins he had there. Then he went into a cheap café to buy some cigarettes. There were crowds of people milling about outside the Coliseum Theater. A streetcar rattled by, up the Avenida Matto, clanking so loudly it sounded as if it was about to disintegrate at any moment. Mario tore open his pack of cigarettes with clumsy fingers, standing on a street corner in the wind and drizzle. He used up half a box of matches before he managed to light the cigarette. His lungs felt huge and soothed as they filled up with the smoke they had been craving for so long. Mario felt himself coming to life again. He was cold and hungry now, and the tobacco was clearing his brain little by little as though the gulps of smoke had absorbed the blood which filled his head a moment before and calmed the pulse beats there.

Mario knew that the ring of danger which always hovered menacingly about him was closing in on him at last, imprisoning him. He had no choice but to go off the next morning to join René, and destroy himself along with him. René said he would show him a different style of life, and perhaps, when the time was ripe, later on, they would go off somewhere together. Perhaps this was where his whole life had been leading. He suddenly realized that this was what it meant to become a man. What would he have to do? Kill someone perhaps? Well, then, he would kill with the powerful hand on which the blow he had given Estela still

smarted. Estela! Huh, he wasn't one of those greenhorns
who let themselves be hooked by the first woman they got
into trouble! It wouldn't be the first time it had happened;
it had happened to lots of his friends and they always
managed to hide out somewhere for a bit, or run away till
it blew over. Anything was better than getting hooked!
Especially by Estela, who was nothing but a thief anyway.
Yes, a thief! It was no use, her trying to pull the wool over
his eyes—she stole those five thousand pesos! And she
wasn't going to get around him by crying either. Did she
think he'd marry her then, just like that? Not on your life!
So that he had to work like a horse while she went around
nagging and complaining all day long and turned into a
hideous scarecrow like Dora after the second or third kid
came along? No. The boys at the club were right to laugh
at him for getting serious all of a sudden. Why get hitched
to her, what on earth was the point when the world, especially René's world, was full of women who would give you
a good time without that? He was going to steer clear of
that sort of thing now, he belonged to himself and himself
alone. Anything he might earn or come by in the future
would go on amusing himself, on women very different
from Estela, on buying much better watches than the one he
would sell in the morning.

He walked on, shivering with the cold. He felt an urge
to weep swelling inside him, but he resisted it. Weeping
now would be much more dangerous than joining René.

Dora kicked up such a fuss and commotion when Mario
told her he would be leaving to go to René the next day
that Mario began to be afraid she might go out of her mind
completely. He managed to get her into bed at last, and
after that she gradually calmed down.

Steeled in his new role, Mario glanced at himself in the
fragment of a mirror held up by a couple of nails driven
into the bare wall. He grimaced as he squeezed a pimple

that had appeared on his chin. Then he smoothed his chestnut hair, which used to come down over his forehead in a lock but was now all lank and greasy, and he flung himself down on his bed without undressing, and stared out beyond the grimy, whitewashed ceiling.

15 🙟 Around this time a drastic change took place in Misiá Elisa Grey de Abalos's house. It was silent no longer. Astir with meaningless bustle from cellar to attic, the house seemed at last to have emerged from the drowsiness that clung to the worm-eaten timbers, the sealed sashes, and the eaves where mice and swallows had found homes in the crevices and crannies.

What it amounted to was that Andrés himself had changed.

He no longer trailed his wan shadow through the dusty rooms, restless, unthinking, struggling feebly and spectrally to shake off the web in which Estela had entangled his thoughts and feelings. One fine day, for no good reason, he woke up determined that the routine of this household, which had continued unchanged for so long, must be altered. This house, whose windows he himself closed punctually at eight, where the maids spent day after day listening to serials on the radio in the kitchen, or chatting idly and knitting or embroidering in the vine arbor when it was good weather, suddenly revealed itself to Andrés in his new frame of mind as the center of world sloth. All that anyone ever did there was waste time shamelessly.

Henceforth, at his command and under his watchful eye, a ceaseless activity filled the great house. He ordered all the windows opened every morning so the house could be given a thorough airing. He had the sheets stripped off the furniture and put away. By the light streaming in through the drawn curtains every worn spot on the velvet chairs, every faded patch of wallpaper, every moth hole, every chip on the marble statuary leaped into dreadful prominence. At night Andrés turned on all the lights in the downstairs rooms. Walking about on the immense carpets, he seemed to acquire an artificial, useless kind of life.

He also demanded that delicacies be served to him at all meals. He would spend hours over his dinner, which he usually took at a little table Estela had placed in a corner of the library. Observing the girl's face, which anxiety had made heavy and stupid, he came to the conclusion that he must be responsible for her unhappiness, and he hated her for making him feel guilty ... But he could not allow Estela to go out right under his nose to meet a young man at night. The moment she left the room, though, Andrés's imagination gave her face back all its old brightness and transparency, and his pain and longing surged up again.

Lourdes and Rosario were delighted with these changes. They felt as though they had suddenly, unexpectedly, been granted a new lease on life. Rosario would leave for the market at the crack of dawn and never failed to return with something quite exceptional, a fresh-water fish, an unusually delicious fresh cheese, some tiny brussels sprouts. Lourdes shed twenty years overnight. Who but she was skillful enough to clean the hundreds of curios and ornaments in the display cases: Don Andrés's baby shoe cast in bronze; the menu of the lunch held in Don Ramón's honor by Don Pedro Montt and Misiá Sara in La Moneda; the china and crystal trinkets, the travel souvenirs and miniatures? Once, while her enthusiasm was still at its height, Lourdes clambered up a ladder to clean the immense oil painting of Don Ramón which had been done from photographs in Paris. She scrubbed it with two halves of an onion to remove the dust and flyspecks, and she wiped off the smelly scum with a damp cloth. Then she stood back to admire the magistrate in all his newfound splendor, with frock coat and handlebar moustache, standing against a background of broken Corinthian columns in a twilit park. She even ventured the hope that things might return to what they had been in Don Ramón's days.

Gradually, however, the two women realized that things were not going to be as delightful or as simple as they had first imagined. A few days had elapsed, but Andrés did not give them a single moment's respite, or any free time for their personal affairs, whatever they might be. He hounded them continually, a merciless slave driver, inventing point-less, unheard-of things for them to do.

"You don't seem to be doing anything, Rosario. I'd like you to paint the rosebush stakes, they're in a dreadful state."

"But why, Don Andresito, why . . . ?"

"Because they have to be painted."

"You'll have to get a man to do them then. I'm a cook and I don't know how to paint rosebush stakes."

"Don't be silly. You've got nothing else to do."

Wounded in her culinary pride, Rosario put on a battered straw hat and toiled away in the rose garden from morning to night, with frequent rests, squatting on her haunches with one big can of white paint and a smaller can of red, till the rosebush stakes were all done.

Uncharacteristically, she was full of complaints.

"Oh, how my ribs ache, Lourdes! I'm too old to spend the whole day crouching on the ground. What will Don Andresito think of next?"

Lourdes's eyes were half closed with exhaustion.

"Mmm," she answered. "I can't go on like this either. What's got into him, for heaven's sake!"

They both yawned and rubbed their haunches.

"Maybe he'll decide to give a party, now that he's decided to stay," Lourdes suggested, her eyes sparkling with excitement.

"The other night he stayed up till Lord knows when, poking around in all the drawers in the house."

"And the other evening he rearranged all the books. And you know how many there are!"

"If he's going to stay here, why doesn't he tell that couple of his to bring his things?"

"Perhaps he will. Listen, do you know what he's had me doing all day?"

"Yes, I saw."

"Imagine! That boy made me take all the silver out of the cupboard, mountains of it there are too—you know, Rosario—and now he's making me clean it all, piece by piece."

"Did you finish?"

"Are you out of your mind? How could I finish? You don't seem to remember how much stuff there is. Look, come and see," said Lourdes, heading for the dining room followed by Rosario.

She switched on the overhead light, which was reflected in the dark polished lake of the table and the mahogany sideboards. Scattered all over the room were pieces of silver dulled by tarnish, except for a few of the smaller pieces, which Lourdes had already restored to their former brilliance. These were grouped in military formation around a cloth covered with greenish-black stains. Everywhere there were tea services, trays, punch bowls, cruets, and figurines.

"What pretty things! I'd forgotten all about them," Rosario exclaimed.

"Well, they've been put away for so long. Doesn't it look like a wedding reception, though, with all the presents laid out? Look. Remember those pheasants we used to put in the center of the table when people came to dinner?"

"Of course. It's going to take you a long time to clean all this."

"Ages."

The next day Andrés woke up with a new idea. He sent for Lourdes after lunch and told her to leave the silver where it was for the moment, and go on cleaning it in her spare moments, with Estela's help. He wanted her to help him with something much more important now. They were going up to the attic.

"Up to the attic?" Lourdes cried, terrified. "But what do we have to go up there for, Don Andresito?"

Andrés did not answer.

"But listen, Don Andresito. How do you expect us to do it all ourselves? We need someone strong to help us lift the trunks and move things around. It must be a dreadful mess up there."

"I'm quite strong enough. I'll help you. Anyway, Estela can lend a hand if we need her."

Lourdes thought to herself that her niece was in no condition to lug heavy trunks around. City life just didn't seem to agree with her. She must miss her family and the country air—she looked pale and a bit sickly lately, and she was more silent than ever. Lourdes made a mental note to ask Rosario to make Estela a little balm tea to see if that livened her up.

Andrés and Lourdes went up to the attic, which was in the highest part of the house. Lourdes puffed and snorted—there was barely room for her to squeeze up the narrow, steep stairs. As they went in, they noticed little gold sequins of light glinting in the chinks of the immense room with its low ceiling and uneven floors, its musty, dusty silence broken only by a scurrying mouse or a bird alighting on the garret roof. Lourdes squeaked with fright as a spider's web stuck to her forehead when they moved forward in the semi-darkness.

Andrés pushed open the four little round windows one after the other and light flooded into the dust-covered room, sparkling on a rivulet of broken glass and the many spider's webs. The place was littered with cartons, trunks, suitcases, briefcases, gutted pieces of furniture, a headless mannikin of Misiá Elisa's figure perched on one leg like a heron with a human torso, hatboxes, piles of ancient magazines, a *chaise percée*, a large china tub decorated with swallows and blue ducks in a forest of reeds.

"What a lot of stuff!" Lourdes exclaimed. "And look how filthy it all is!"

Andrés looked around him calmly. He felt perfectly at ease amid this hoard of objects that life had bypassed. A quiet smile lit up his tired face.

"What's in this trunk?"

"How do you expect me to remember, Don Andresito?"

They opened a trunk made of chestnut-colored leather, with the initials R. A. stamped in black on one side.

"Look, Lourdes, some of my grandfather's clothes. This Spanish cape—do you remember? When I was little, he used to put it on sometimes when he walked in the garden in the evening."

Both he and Lourdes seemed oblivious of the world around them. They had gone back through time to a period they felt perfectly secure and happy in because there they knew the value of everything. They opened up bell-shaped leather hatboxes and took out shiny top hats which emerged immaculate from their red silk nests on which the name of the London manufacturer was inscribed below a crest that said: BY APPOINTMENT. They poked about in boxes full of gloves and shook out the moth-eaten fur collars on the overcoats. The thick layer of dust on the lids of the trunks seemed to have preserved everything so perfectly that the period in which these objects had seen active use was precipitated whole and intact into the present.

Andrés tried on a top hat.

"It suits you very well, Don Andresito."

"Clean this mirror," he told Lourdes.

While the maid rubbed a clean patch in a mirror that had been blinded by dust, Andrés wrapped himself in the Spanish cape.

"I'm going to take these things downstairs, just in case," he remarked mysteriously.

They found some women's clothes in a trunk and shook them out. Lourdes took out an embroidered silk gauze dress much dilapidated by time.

"Look at this! What a shame . . . it was so pretty once!"

Andrés fingered the gauze delicately, holding it up to a window to inspect the embroidery in the light. He stood there for a long time gazing thoughtfully at this fragile object on the verge of disintegration. It was feather-light across his arms, and the embroidery sparkled amid the dust.

"Do you know something, Lourdes—I can't remember a single occasion when my grandmother wore this dress. And yet, when I think of her as a young woman, she always seems to have this dress on and not any of the others which I connect with particular incidents. I always think of her wearing something vaporous like this, with big sleeves like shining cloud-wings floating around her body. Funny, isn't it? Even now, when I see her lying there all sick and querulous, I keep trying to imagine her in this dress—it helps me forget the horror of her madness."

"You mustn't call the señora mad, Don Andresito, or God will punish you . . ."

They were busy all afternoon, quite oblivious of the time as they chatted happily and poked about, having forgotten that they had originally gone up to the attic to clean it.

"We can go on cleaning up here tomorrow," Andrés said as they left. His eyebrows were white with dust, and his face was covered with smudges.

Among the various bits and pieces Lourdes had collected, with Andrés's permission, was Misiá Elisa's gauze dress and a long, moth-eaten feather boa. Andrés went downstairs wearing the top hat and wrapped in the cape.

After dinner, Lourdes sat down at the marble-topped kitchen table, under the green-shaded light. Rosario sat opposite, sifting through a large bundle of dried aromatic herbs in search of some balm to make Estela a tisane with, as Lourdes had asked her to do. Lourdes was straightening out little pieces of bent wire and lovingly cleaning a quantity of little flowers made of silver threads and tiny fragments of mother-of-pearl.

"Don Andresito gave them to me," she explained.

"What do you want them for?"

"Don't you remember those two candle screens in the señora's sewing room? She broke one of them after one of her first quarrels with Don Ramón. The two that were exactly alike, covered with these little flowers?"

"Oh, yes, of course. But what do you want them for?"

A gentle smile of malice and superiority curled Lourdes's lips.

"I have an idea . . ." she said.

"An idea?"

"I'm making a little present for Misiá Elisita."

"But the señora will recognize them, Lourdes, and think you stole them."

"I don't think she will. I'm making her a little crown, a little crown of silver flowers for her saint's day, which is coming soon. You know how she calls herself the Queen of Europe and says she should have a saint's crown for having been so good always? I'm going to give her this gauze dress too, but first I have to mend it very carefully because it's full of holes. And I'll give her all these presents on her saint's day."

"There won't be many people."

"Is it time for the serial yet?"

"It was over ages ago."

"What a shame! No, there won't be many people . . ."

"Don Emiliano died in his bath they say . . ."

"What of?"

"He just died suddenly."

"Ah well, that's the way to go . . ."

"Poor soul. He was such a devil."

"And much younger than the señora, too."

"No, not much. How strong the señora must be, though! She'll see us all into the grave, you mark my words."

"Well, she deserves to, poor good lady that she is. And here she is, getting perkier and cleverer every day! A good person like her ought to live a long time so she can be a good example for the world."

"That's right."

"And she's ninety-four."

"Mmm."

"Or is it ninety-six?"

"Mmm . . ."

"No, it's ninety . . . I've forgotten. Can you remember?"

Rosario had dozed off. She really was worn out.

"Ninety—what is it, Estela?"

"I don't know, Aunt," the girl said. She had come in silently and was sipping her balm tea out of a plate, blowing to cool it.

Mario's desertion had dealt her a wound which still hurt constantly, but she had long been conditioned to the idea of male brutality and unreliability and she found it hard to give up the hope that the boy would come back. This hope came to occupy a very hard, bright little space, like a nut, in the midst of the pain which filled her hours.

In the evening, when the dim light entering through the tall windows set Misiá Elisa's great vessel of a bed afloat on the shadows, and the furniture lost its sharp outlines, Estela would tiptoe across to the windows to close them. From one of them she could see Santa Lucía, its battlements rosy in the last glow of sunlight. Mario had promised to take her there one Sunday . . . and now he never would. It was then that her faith in his eventual return crystallized inside her, piercing, shrinking till it was so small it almost disappeared. Estela thought of her father's whip hanging from its rusty nail in the hallway at home in the country . . . and she thought, too, about the child. She tried to make herself jump out of the window, telling herself over and over that Mario's absence was just a momentary interruption, another insignificant absence in what had come to be the even monotony of her life. When the windows were all closed and the curtains drawn, Estela would switch on the light and suddenly the precise shape of the furniture clicked into place in what had just been patches of darkness.

One night Don Andrés passed so close to Estela in one of the halls that she shrank frightened against the wall to avoid touching him. She felt on her face the caballero's breath, reeking of liquor, and saw his hands outstretched to touch her. Somehow Estela managed to summon up enough presence of mind to murmur, very low and rapidly: "Just because my mother gave me away . . ."

Andrés's hands fell to his sides, trembling, and he went away without touching her but with a look on his face which frightened Estela. Was he mad? Drunk? Sick? The next day Andrés made Estela a present of a length of cloth, which she accepted only because she couldn't think of a way of refusing.

To hide the deterioration in her looks, Estela started painting her lips and cheeks, but the cosmetics only made her look sicklier than before. One evening while she was sitting, knitting, beside Misiá Elisa's bedside, the old woman suddenly roused herself.

"Go and wash your face, girl," she ordered. "You look

like a whore. Do you think I want people to say I keep a brothel here?"

Estela washed her face and returned to her place by the bed.

"I said you were a thief, didn't I?" the old woman went on. "You stole those five thousand pesos from me, didn't you? The ones I hid under my pillow here? I said you were a corrupt creature, and a thief."

Estela held her knitting close to her eyes to count the stitches, as if she hoped this childish maneuver would hide her guilty conscience. Misiá Elisa and Mario were right to call her a thief.

The sick woman's mind had never been so clear and perspicacious as it was at this time. She could explain correctly every single noise in the house, even the most distant ones.

"Don Andrés is getting too old to run up the stairs like that . . ." Or: "They're giving me an omelette for lunch. Rosario is beating the eggs."

At the same time her delusions grew more pronounced, or perhaps it was just that they had spread till they covered her mind completely. Endlessly, persistently, the wild words came pouring out. ". . . and Ramón laughed at me because he thought it was all lies, but I know he envied me secretly. Well, naturally, since I was related to all the kings and nobles of Europe. They looked down on me here in Santiago because my father wasn't a Chilean and they said Ramón had married a foreigner. Who wouldn't be a foreigner in this country of Indians? When my mother was a girl, she went to a ball in someone's palace, I can't remember whose, but it was somewhere in Europe and she danced all night with a prince. She wore a crown too, being of noble birth, as I am too, of course. She was such a good person, my mother, so good and pretty! And a real Christian too, like me. I tell you, child, I've been a saint all my life, and have

the right to a saint's crown as well as a noble's. I was so
good, so moral, do you know that never once in all my
married life did I let Ramón see me naked! Not once, though
we slept in the same bed. Now tell me if you don't think I
deserve a saint's crown? God will reward me in heaven for
my sacrifices . . ."

She went on talking for hours in her cracked voice, without a change of tone, the voice rambling on without inflec-
tion, spinning out her madness from between the white
sheets. Estela did not understand much of it. At first, when
she had just arrived from the country, she had found a
certain fascination in the phantoms conjured up by Misiá
Elisa. They gave her a glimpse into a style of life with which
her young mind had no acquaintance. When Mario came
into her life later, she stopped listening to the old woman;
she was always thinking of him.

One evening the old woman was watching Estela as she
went about the room cleaning it and putting it in order.
Suddenly she cried out:

"Estela!"

"Señora?"

She went up to the bed where the old woman was half
sitting up and tried to get her to lie down again.

"Don't touch me, you vile creature!"

Estela snatched back her hands as if she had burned
them.

"Kneel down!" Misiá Elisa ordered.

Estela looked at her in terror as though some dark truth
were finally going to be revealed to her.

"Repent!" the old woman commanded.

Estela hung her head, murmuring almost inaudibly:
"Why must I repent, señora?"

The old woman's frail voice seemed to infiltrate every
corner and cranny of the room, filling it with menace.

"What do you mean why? The impudence! As if you

didn't know, you vile creature! Don't try and play the un-
tarnished angel with me. Repent your sins."

"What sins?"

"Do you dare tell me you haven't sinned? Be careful, or
you will damn yourself to hell for all eternity. The sin of
the flesh is the worst of all, the filthiest and most terrible.
Look at that picture . . ."

She pointed to a colored print of Our Lady of Mount
Carmel gazing at a well of flames where sinners writhed in
agony.

"See. You will burn in hell like that because the only love
that interests you is the love of the flesh. Aren't you afraid
of hell and the Lord's angry face as he damns you for dis-
obeying his chief commandment? You are a whore, a corrupt, perverted woman, and wherever you go you will be
pointed out as one of the damned!"

Misiá Elisita was sitting up in bed now, staring with
blazing eyes at the trembling Estela.

". . . and the man who ruined you was only interested
in one thing too, his own selfish pleasure, a brutish animal
pleasure, like all the rest of them. That's all any man ever
wants from us—to make use of us, and their pleasure is
filthy and obscene. Life is a cesspool and you must take
refuge in religion to escape being dragged into the pit and
defiled. Repent! You must learn to hate this man, and yourself too, for being so weak and thinking you were in love
when your love and his were nothing but filth. And don't
tell me that he will return, because he has satisfied his lust
now, and left you defiled . . . sinner, sinner!"

Sinner!

Estela covered her face with her hands and sobbed. The
señora was right, she was right! What she had done must
be very wicked if so many punishments—her father's when
she went home with her child in her arms, and hellfire itself—awaited her. How could Mario be anything but a

scoundrel, if he had persuaded her to commit so many sins for him, including stealing? Yes, God must be punishing her for her sins, making Mario abandon her like this, with the new life growing inside her. Everything was false, evil, treacherous; only the señora was saintly and good. She knew the truth . . .

Estela knelt down, her face streaked with tears, and began to pray, accompanied by Misiá Elisa in her small, dry voice. She confessed her sins, swore never to see Mario again, and denied that he could ever have loved her.

In the days that followed, Estela did nothing but cry, all alone, in the hallways, in her own room, in every corner. Her eyes were permanently fixed on the ground, and all the light seemed to have gone out of those oblique pools under their thick lashes. She spent hours with her rosary, reciting one Hail Mary after another, not daring to leave Misiá Elisa's bedside because everywhere else held such terror for her.

"The child is like a ghost these days!" Lourdes remarked. "And they all said balm tea was so good . . ."

16   During the next few days the old woman fell into a state of such great agitation, haunted by ghosts, cursing, calling for repentance, that they were unable to make her eat even a mouthful of food. She grew so weak that Dr. Gros was sent for. He gave her the most perfunctory examination and seemed to have very little to say about her condition.

"Aren't you going to examine her a little more thoroughly than that?" Andrés asked, rather disappointed.

"No. Why?"

"I don't know. But, well, she is still alive . . . like you or me."

"What do you want me to say, Andrés? The only thing wrong with your grandmother is old age, and there's no cure for that. I can only say what I've said a hundred times before—we must wait and see. She is on the verge of a senile marasmus, the exhaustion of all her bodily functions. The matter she is composed of is tired of living and is beginning to prepare for its repose when it is reduced to mere substance again. The circle is closing, that's all. What more can you expect at ninety-odd?"

They went downstairs in silence, Andrés in front, looking a little petulant, like a child who is not being taken as seriously as it would like. Going down behind him, Carlos noticed that the hair was growing down the back of Andrés's neck. He had never known Andrés so old or so childish, as if reduced to his smallest factor—like Misiá Elisa herself. He recalled Andrés as he had been only six months earlier, admirably maintaining his *tenue*—a word often on his lips, a term of approval—master of discreet refinement, unobtrusive elegance, a lively and informed conversationalist when subjects that interested him were touched on. Was there such power in the beauty of a little seventeen-year-old that it could reduce a human personality to rubble, leaving only this ill-shaven old man who seemed to have lost all self-respect, who walked down the stairs gingerly as though they hurt his feet? Anger at Andrés for letting himself be demolished so easily dampened any pity Carlos might have felt. He wanted to push him downstairs, shake him, rouse him somehow from his self-absorption. Lourdes was waiting at the foot of the stairs, her hands folded over her stomach, a smiling, kindly figure at the heart of her own immutable domestic world.

"How are you, Lourdes?"

"Me? Very well, very well indeed, Don Carlitos, you

know what we old women are like—it takes more than a
cold to finish us off. It's the young ones who need looking
after. Like Don Andresito here. Reduced to skin and bone,
as you see. And he never leaves the house. I keep telling
him to go and enjoy himself . . . after all, we only pass this
way once . . ."

Andrés, who had been looking impatiently at the floor,
now looked up sharply at Lourdes.

"Once, Lourdes? What about the afterlife?"

"Ha, ha, ha, the things he comes out with! That's something else again, Don Andresito, it's not for having fun in!
Didn't I say this boy was acting strangely? The things he
says! The afterlife . . . ha, ha, ha . . . didn't I say he was
getting more like Misiá Elisita every day?"

"That's enough, Lourdes, that's enough. I've got a lot to
talk about with Don Carlos. Bring some drinks to the
balcony, will you."

"You see, Don Carlos? He's even short-tempered with me
these days. Listen, though, there is something else I wanted
to mention. Now that you're here, would you look at Estela?
She goes around all day with a sick face, you'd think she'd
seen a ghost. I've been making her drink balm tea because
they say it's good if you're not feeling well, but the child
doesn't seem to improve. And she says she's got a stitch
here, as if . . ."

As she led the way to the room where Estela was waiting,
Lourdes gave the doctor such an exhaustive account of her
niece's malady that he was soon in no doubt at all as to the
reason for her mysterious symptoms.

They found Estela stretched out on the bed in a servant's
room which had not been slept in for many years. The girl
at first refused to be examined, or to answer questions, till
Carlos finally sent Lourdes out of the room. She went
reluctantly, murmuring: "It's just that you've got such a
reputation, Don Carlos . . ."

This remark, aside from being offensive, acted as a sort of spark that let Carlos see something clearly—he had been disturbed, on entering the room, with its smell of unaired mattresses and empty cupboards, by the animal presence of Estela lying there on the bed. He stood some distance from her, questioning her curtly. But the questions were unnecessary. The girl's faintly distorted silhouette and the symptoms Lourdes had innocently rattled off told him all he needed to know. Estela was pregnant.

With her forearm the girl was shielding her eyes from the light of the naked bulb hanging from the middle of the ceiling, and the muscles in her arm raised her breast under her blouse. Carlos gazed at the moist pink of the palms that Andrés had described so agitatedly to him, and felt a strong desire to feel the girl, to touch her. It could easily be arranged. All he had to do was tell her he must examine her. He thought of the dreary afternoon that stretched out ahead of him, driving his car back through the rain-drenched streets, his friends all out, Adrianita at some charity tea, the children all pursuing their hobbies and interests. He was alone. And there was the girl, stretched out on the mattress.

No, no, it couldn't be! Carlos forced himself to move away from the bed. The answer he gave himself was both positive and negative. It would be ugly. Ugly, unnecessary, and unsuitable. It would reduce him to the level of Andrés . . . or lower still. Injecting a note of gentleness into his voice, the doctor said: "It's all right, I know what's wrong . . ."

"Please don't say anything—don't tell my aunt!"

"I won't. But you must come to the hospital tomorrow for a complete examination. Tell me, who is the father?"

"Mario."

Just Mario. Estela was crying, and her face was dirty, but everyone must know Mario because he was the center of her existence, the only Mario in the world.

Carlos went to join Andrés. A new silence fell between the
two friends, a silence peopled by the rocking chairs, palm
trees, ferns, and begonias on the balcony, though these had
always been there. In the fading light, Carlos heard the
tinkle of ice cubes in the glass Andrés was holding, and
he helped himself to a drink. Through the glass-enclosed
conservatory, beyond the trees, dark blots of clouds could
be seen racing dizzily by, occasionally disclosing strips of
sky crowded with stars.

"Have you got a match?" Carlos asked. "Oh, it's all
right, I've got my lighter."

Andrés leaned toward the doctor as if expecting him to
say something which would put a spark to his dry tinder.
Carlos stood up abruptly, stubbing out his newly lit cigarette in a pot of ferns.

"Estela is pregnant," he announced.

Andrés slumped back into his rocking chair, which
started to rock softly. He asked, very quietly: "Why tell
me?"

"In the last resort, you are responsible."

"Me?"

"Of course. You brought her here in the first place to
look after your grandmother."

The rocking chair went on rocking to and fro, but more
slowly.

"She said the father was called Mario," Carlos went on.

One foggy night under a street light Estela had touched
the arm of a boy called Mario. That was all. But from then
on everything had slowly deteriorated for Andrés, whereas
in Estela's belly two lives had coupled beautifully to make
another, thus completing a cycle of perfection while he found
himself standing naked beneath a hostile sky which revealed to him only his own insignificance and the pointless
brevity of his existence. Andrés, with his pain laid bare,

groped through time, through the millennia of years to come and the millennia of years past, and thought of all the beings who had learned how to prolong themselves by uniting with other beings. Swaying almost imperceptibly in the old rocking chair on the balcony, in the calm of the evening, Andrés allowed a piercing anguish to enfold him, moistening his tired eyes.

"We'll have to talk to this Mario," Carlos said.

"Of course."

A moment later Andrés added: "You examined her because she is young, but you scarcely looked at my grandmother. I bet you wouldn't look at me either . . ."

"Don't be silly, Andrés. What do you expect me to tell Misiá Elisa? That she's dying?"

Andrés, who had been staring at a remote star suddenly revealed in a bare patch of sky, stood up abruptly.

"Don't talk to me about that, don't talk to . . ."

"About what?"

"I won't have people talking about death! I won't! I won't!"

"But look here, old man . . ."

"Don't you see that what you've just said strips me of everything which might have helped me hide my terror of death? Now all that's left is the terror, staring me in the face!"

"But this is a terror we all share . . ."

"Ah, but you all have your past achievements and future conquests to defend yourselves with. I've got nothing . . . no life or faith, or rational beliefs . . . nothing . . . nothing but terror."

"You're talking nonsense . . ."

"What have I got to my credit? Nothing, my walking sticks . . . And now what is left to me? Death, that's all. I can't think of anything else. And I think of that with terror because I know only too well that all the philosophical theories, all the pleasures of living, all the religious beliefs are false, all lies to ward off the great panic of extinction . . ."

"But don't you see that all life, every act of creation in whatever field, every act of love is simply a revolt against extinction, and it doesn't matter whether it's false or not, or whether it has results or not?"

"Oh, if only I could find some way of lying to myself!"

"What you're saying is morbid and unpleasant. Why think about things like that?"

"Morbid! Why think about it? You'll be telling me next to whistle in the dark. What do you suggest, that I should acquire a religious faith the way you buy a pair of socks? I can't do it so easily. I would give anything to get back my faith. Think how handy it would be. But, unfortunately, religion only makes me laugh. Don't you see it's only the old instinct of survival in a different guise, a safeguard against the horror of non-existence, a pathetic attempt to enlarge this appallingly meager life of ours with the help of lies? 'No, my son, don't be afraid,' the Eternal Father tells us. 'Don't be afraid, don't believe in extinction. Death is only a game. You are to play at dying and then I'll give you a much longer, nicer life than this which you'll enjoy much more.' Whistling in the darkness of extinction. Of course it would be convenient! But I can't help despising people who can delude themselves, consciously or unconsciously, with this formula for eternal life. How easy it must be for them to face death! How restful!"

The ferocious intensity with which Andrés delivered this speech left Carlos stunned. It was like standing there, unable to defend yourself, while someone smashed your face to a pulp. Of course there were defenses by the thousand, true and valid ones. One thing was quite obvious to him, and that was that Andrés was converting what should be a passing mood into an attitude toward life. Carlos found it hard to think clearly, such was the force of his friend's words. Also, he seemed to have caught a chill—he could distinctly and separately feel each heartbeat, each pulsing of the blood in his cheeks, the end of his nose, his finger-tips. These throbbings caused by a chill seemed to define him in some way, reassure him that this was his shape in space, that he was at least alive here and now, and this shape was him, Carlos Gros, alive and fully conscious.

"Don't you realize that everything is a mess, an injustice, a mad trick played on us by the Cosmos? If there is a God who watches over man's destiny, he must be a mad God. What could be more absurd than giving men the faculties to perceive the chaos and terror around them, and not giving them anything to conquer them with? No, Carlos, don't lie to yourself—the only truth is madness because the mad are the only ones who see that everything is chaos, and that explaining, clarifying, reasoning are futile. Being helpless, they realize that the only way to reach the truth is to let themselves be swallowed up by the greater madness. To sane men, like ourselves, all that remains is the terror . . ."

In the silence this terror Andrés spoke of appeared to Carlos like a solid, permanent threat. He only had to move, or make a small mental concession, and the terror would have him. No. No. It was enough to have a cold, to feel one's fingers and nose throbbing and the blood pulsating in one's burning-hot right ear, to make the terror recede farther than that star sparkling in the farthermost corner of the sky. It was a genuine experience undoubtedly, but surely not one which need change one's life or undermine one's personality. Andrés was still talking.

". . . and when I'm dying, let me tell you, I'll struggle and scream and abase myself. I'll be violent, cowardly, ridiculous, contemptible, and wretched, and with my last breath I'll implore you to save me and I'll curse you for letting me be exterminated."

Carlos jumped up as though to strike Andrés.

"Shut up!" he shouted. "Shut up, you damned fool!"

They stood there face to face, staring at each other for a minute. Then, as if mutually agreeing not to come to blows, they sank back into their chairs.

"Do you want to destroy everything, you idiot?" Carlos asked. "Is this your way of protesting because a servant girl won't sleep with you? You think you're a philosopher, but you're just hysterical."

"That's a form of madness, and of truth."

"You don't seem to realize that life is only what you make it. All of us, even the most ignorant, know that the truth— if it exists—is out of reach. Everything stems from that knowledge. Yet you find it a mockery that men seek beautiful and loving names with which to beguile despair. Well, that is life. We cannot conquer death, so we use those deceptions to give shape to our lives, and this can be a marvelous shape so long as we remain aware and—don't laugh —keep our free will and are not content to be simply things before returning to nothing and darkness. You say that the solutions put forward by religion, philosophy, and science are inadequate. But you are wrong, Andrés, they are perfectly adequate if you can make use of them to give your life harmony and shape. The only reality, don't you see, is this seventy years of life during which matter takes on existence and the consciousness of existence? In itself, the truth is only of interest to professionals. Insofar as I am myself, I do without the truth altogether. It only interests me in relation to other people and to history, where it forces me to take up a position within time, not outside it. Your terror is insignificant, my poor Andrés, though I admit I don't envy you it. Long live religion, even the most absurd and atrabilious religion, if it can help us avoid this absurd agony you suffer from!"

"What if I were to kill myself?"

"Don't be silly, you won't, you aren't a hero. It is we, not you, we who have grown attached to things and created or accepted a life for ourselves, inadequately, poorly, it doesn't matter, it is we, as I said, who are the heroes. Why? Because we have learned to live with this terror, we've tamed it. We are ordinary human beings, not gods like you. When we feel cold, we wrap ourselves up warmly, we don't make the futile gesture of going out naked into the storm . . ."

Carlos lit a cigarette. There was a great deal more he could say, he had barely scratched the surface of what he could have said, of everything which, he now realized, he had worked out inside him already. But at the moment he was enjoying the satisfaction of having expressed his position toward life for the first time since adolescence. Was this his reality? Incomplete perhaps. He felt an immense melancholy rising inside him, as if in defining himself he had also limited himself. By means of self-deception, or whistling in the dark, or whatever it was, he seemed to have sealed off every road to himself except the one he had chosen. Andrés seemed meanwhile to have dwindled before him to a little shriveled-up demon, reduced to nothingness. After a long silence Carlos asked: "Well, what are you going to do?"

"I don't know. It's no good asking me now. Marry her off, I suppose, and make things a little easier for her . . ."

The doctor got to his feet and put a hand on Andrés's shoulder. This poor, impotent, absurd passion of his made him once more a touching, pitiful creature. He loved and was not loved in return. It was simple, after all, and understandable. Carlos wanted to show his affection for Andrés, but somehow the words and gestures eluded him.

"Since I can't have her love," Andrés said, "the best thing would be to help her be happy, as people are in novels. At least, that's how I feel now, at this particular moment. But don't forget—it's no use expecting me to be consistent and think the same thing tomorrow as today. Perhaps later on . . ."

"Later on?"

"What shall I do? I don't know, but it wouldn't surprise me if suddenly I felt the urge to murder her . . ."

They laughed and poured themselves another drink.

That night Carlos left Andrés's house feeling that he had reached his zenith as a human being, having managed to put his triumph—a small, possibly a lame triumph, but a triumph still—into words. Was it excitement or merely a touch of fever that made his heart beat so fast that his fingertips and his left ear tingled? As he went out, the pleasant chill of the street enveloped him. Everything around him, trees, transparent air, noises drawing near and then receding again into the distance, everything seemed to be measuring itself against his sharpened consciousness in search of its own reality. He diagnosed a state of hyper-esthesia in himself, delicious and disturbing as a poet's, a condition that made him powerfully receptive to the beauty and emotion in everything. The noise of the gate closing behind him reverberated with exquisite clarity in his ear-drums, and the cold metal of the doorhandle on his car revealed its precise shape to him as he enclosed it in the warmth of his plump hand. The movement with which he opened this door was economical and perfect.

Sitting inside the car, he stared out for a while at the house guarded by skeletal trees, still dripping from the afternoon's rain: it was a masterpiece of the non-functional, with its poorly executed decorations blurring the essential outline so that it was completely submerged under a pro-fusion of little turrets, unnecessary gables, terraces and balconies that did not open out of any room. The lights were on all over the first floor and filtered out to the garden through screening shrubs and bushes. Andrés's stooping silhouette was outlined briefly against a lighted square of window in the library, a hermetic being incapable of all emotion save the enjoyment of his own drama. "Later on . . ." he had said, but it was not a threat. Carlos was momentarily tempted to return and stay with Andrés till he had dispelled all the phantoms that bedeviled him. But Andrés was completely isolated now; his tragic posturing deprived him of the humility a man needs if he is to learn how to ask for, and accept, help.

Carlos started the car. The streets began to change, the lights were various, beautiful, pleasing. Everything was beautiful. But not to everyone. In a second-floor room Misiá Elisa continued to mock at death, and as her life dragged on, it was destroying valuable lives around her. Carlos did not want to have to think about those any more tonight. He had his own life to lead. He accelerated in order to reach home more quickly and find the warmth, deserved or not, that awaited him there because he himself had generated it. He intended to make the most of it tonight.

The light was on in the front hall as usual. But it was not a cruel light, as in Andrés's house; here the brightness complemented everything and added significance. That Tabriz rug, for instance, had been a terrible extravagance when they bought it in a sale a few months after they were married. Money had been scarce then, and to pay for it they had had to do without many things. Here was a photograph of his children when they were little, wearing the uniform of the English school they had been educated in, the best and most expensive school in Santiago. This was a photograph of Isabel in a ball gown. It was a pity that, being intelligent as well as pretty, she should be submerged in the vulgarity of adolescent social life, hiding her real value under a lot of stereotyped silliness. Still, Isabel was only seventeen; there was plenty of time to outgrow all that, and eventually, after many false starts and mistakes, no doubt, she would give expression to the real woman she had in her.

Carlos took off his hat and straightened his tie in front of the hall mirror. He listened to the muted noises of the house, the goings and comings of servants preparing dinner, a knife clattering to the floor, water gushing into a second-floor bath, the clock ticking on the stairs. They were pleasant sounds. Everything was functioning with quiet perfection. As he passed from the hall into the living room, he picked up the evening paper from the tooled-leather chest and unfolded it.

"Adriana!" he called.

As he said his wife's name, which ever since he had entered the house had been forming on his lips almost without his being aware of it, he felt a new glow of satisfaction at finding how warmly and easily the familiar syllables slipped off his tongue. To renew the experience, he repeated the name quietly to himself.

"Adriana."

As he heard himself say this familiar name, his love, also familiar, came to him again, refreshed after such a long time, because the love was there, and it was his, and it came easily. He sat down in an olive-colored plush chair and opened out the paper across his knees.

"Adriana!" he called again, more pressingly this time.

"Carlos? I'm coming, dear," his wife answered from upstairs. "Just a minute."

Carlos listened to his wife's light footsteps coming down the stairs. She appeared in the doorway wearing a pair of black slacks which she liked to put on at home but which he disliked. Yet in his present receptive mood he found himself well disposed toward them.

"It's incredible that she's over fifty," he thought.

Adriana was no beauty, and she hid her best features behind the banal mask of a woman who has given up trying to attract men and only wants to impress other women. But her husband's rediscovered love peeled away the bits and pieces of her purely feminine chicness, laying bare what he had once, long ago, admired so much: eyes not so much large as sparkling and expressive; a certain grace in her carriage and walk which she still had in spite of the rather haphazardly distributed extra pounds; a sumptuously transparent skin.

He gazed at her in silence somewhat longer than usual, but not exaggeratedly so. Adriana sensed at once that there was something strange about him, but she dismissed the thought. Carlos never varied, he was the same, always the same, so monotonously the same for such a long time now that if he suddenly changed, she thought, she would be embarrassed more than anything else. But why worry? She went confidently across to him, as she did every evening.

Blinded by the certainty that this love of his was the real thing, and had been waiting there, generously, to be taken up again whenever he chose, Carlos told himself that all the countless women he had loved and wearied of, the whole of his extramarital love life, were meaningless compared with Adriana. She went up to him and kissed him on the forehead. Carlos kept his self-control. This was not the moment for passionate demonstrations. But he could not help holding his wife's hand a couple of seconds longer than usual, clasped between both of his.

"Ugh, I'm so tired! Do you know, they took more than two thousand pesos off me at bridge? I was so mad! Rosa . . . Rosa! Put dinner on the table right away, don't wait for the children. Isabel has gone over to Pelusa's, and you know how long it takes her to budge, once she's over there."

"How are you?"

Adriana, cigarette in hand, was moving about the room, straightening an engraving here, moving a china figurine there. She was proud of her house. All her friends agreed that it was exactly right, not a trace of vulgarity or *eccentricity*—a word with terrible implications. This kind of pleasure made up for a different order of pleasures which she had given up long ago, which would be incongruous and irritating now, she thought, noting the sticky, plummy quality of her husband's voice as he spoke to her. Adriana asked, as if she had not heard him: "Do you want something, dear?"

Carlos repeated his question, suppressing the tone that had upset his wife. Adriana flopped on a sofa and began to flick through a magazine.

"You can imagine how furious I was with myself! Losing more than two thousand pesos like that . . ."

"Did you go to the charity tea?"

"No, I didn't. I suddenly couldn't face it. I'm sick of those awful charity teas. The only people you meet are social climbers or the wives of Central American diplomats, I can't think where they all come from. I fixed up one of the rooms here for bridge and asked Carmen Salas and Chepa over, and they both came, although one of Chepa's boys is down with scarlatina . . ."

"Which one?"

"Diego."

"The skinny little blond one?"

"Yes. And Alicia Amézaga. I hadn't seen her for ages."

"Who's she?"

"You remember. Carlos Bouchon's wife, the legal man for the Bank of Chile . . ."

"Can't place her."

"Oh, come on, Carlos. Of course you know the Amézagas! The two sisters who lived on Cienfuegos Street when we were courting . . . that time the procession went by . . ."

"Next to the Saldañas'?"

"No, the house just opposite, where Don Pastor Rodríguez lived when he was senator . . ."

"Oh yes. You mean the blondes with the stubby legs, nice-looking girls, though, used to go to the Plaza Brazil. Yes, of course. They were about your age . . ."

"My age? You must be mad. Alicia, the younger one, is about as old as my second sister . . ."

"Meche? No . . ."

"Yes, Meche. So you can figure out how much older she is than I. At least two years. Though she's very well preserved, I must say . . ."

Carlos read his paper.

They went into the dining room. There were white carnations on the table.

"Chepa brought them for me, they come from the farm. Huge, aren't they?"

"Mmm," Carlos said.

He stared hard at Adriana, who avoided his eyes. She rearranged some knives and forks and pushed a carnation more securely into place in the vase. Without looking at her husband, she asked: "Are you feeling all right? You look a little feverish . . ."

"Adriana!" Carlos cried.

She sensed that a scene of embarrassing intimacy was coming. It was one thing to call him "dear" and make sure he had good meals and was happy. But these dumbly romantic overtures, hopelessly belated as they were, struck her as, well . . . almost indecent. After her first, bitter disillusionment, and many secret frustrations, she had dedicated her life with professional zeal to being a thoroughly respectable, irreproachable woman. And it gratified her that people should know this, and how Carlos behaved too, without her ever complaining or acting the martyr. It was a triumph that allowed her to admire her own nobility of soul, forgetting that she was rather unemotional by nature. In any case, she was too old now for those . . . looks. At least as old as her first disillusionment.

"Adriana, my sweet! I don't know what . . ."

Just then Isabel burst into the dining room, humming. She kissed her mother and father and then sat down.

"All I want is salad and coffee," she said.

"Your face!" Carlos exclaimed. "You look like a painted doll! It's ghastly—you look like a servant girl on her day off!"

"We had a super time at Pelusa's, we laughed and laughed!"

"What were you doing?" Adriana asked, smiling. "You must have paint inches thick on your face. Why aren't you eating? There's stew . . ."

"You look awful," Carlos repeated. "Go and wash that paint off before you sit down."

"But, Daddy, some other girls and I were over at Pelusa's and we spent the afternoon trying out stage make-up. They bet me I wouldn't dare come back with all this paint on. I wish you'd seen the taxi driver's face! Ha, ha, ha!"

"Go and wash your face, I said. You look like a . . ."

"Carlos!"

Affronted, the doctor began to read the paper as he ate.

"It doesn't matter," Adriana said soothingly. "Why get so worked up about it? Let her finish her dinner."

Carlos did not answer. His wife and daughter started talking about clothes and gossiping, completely excluding him, as usual, from the closed feminine world which was Adriana's refuge.

Later, after wishing his wife and daughter good night, Carlos went up to his bedroom. As he listened to Adriana getting ready for bed next door, Carlos found his love welling up again, in spite of, or perhaps because of, everything, for this after all was her life: bridge, Alicia Amézaga's age, Isabel's make-up. Carlos paused for a moment and then opened the connecting door between their rooms.

Adriana was propped up in bed with a scarf knotted around her head to protect her curlers, a jar of cold cream in one hand and the fingers of the other covered with the ointment. As her husband came in, Adriana's movements froze in mid-air. She put the jar of cream down on the bedside table, hastily wiping her fingers on a sky-blue tissue. She felt neither fear nor repugnance. It was a duty, like any other, necessary from time to time, though she preferred the occasions to be widely spaced.

Much later, as they lay side by side in bed, Carlos felt the need to talk, explain, share his feelings with Adriana. But the words stuck in his throat. The day's emotions, or possibly a touch of fever, made him shed a few tears on his wife's cold shoulder. She lay there, pretending to be asleep, out of respect for Carlos, and she thought how, if this had happened ten years ago, she might be a different kind of woman now, leading a different kind of life. She didn't know whether the thought pleased or saddened her. What would her life have been like if Carlos had wept on her shoulder one night ten years ago? Possibly not as adequate to her needs as the life she led now. Her husband was generous and respected her. Adriana still loved him enough to surrender her body to him when he needed it, like tonight. But Carlos no longer had the right to expect her to share his feelings. Was this cold of her? Not really. It simply came of wanting a quiet life. There was nothing worse for a woman of her age than reviving old desires which had been buried away conveniently in a remote corner of her being, and nearly, nearly forgotten. No. Carlos had many rights over her, but her emotional participation was not one of them.

Lying there, tense, Adriana waited till her husband, believing her asleep, either went back to his own room or fell quietly asleep where he was.

PART THREE

 The Coronation

17 The early morning light grew slightly paler in the cracks in the walls. Lying with his eyes open and his hands clasped behind his head, Mario watched the cracks growing more and more distinct. Soon they were no longer just white stripes between the planks, and the light that streaked through them fished out of the gloom the dirty, torn bundle of blankets and mattresses on which René's children slept. René himself was snoring next door. Not his usual full-throated, self-satisfied snores, but short, irregular ones, like the snorts of a broken pump. Mario knew those snores too. He had had to listen to them through the long, uneasy nights the brothers had spent on the same mattress at the foot of one of the hills of Valparaíso. To Mario they had seemed like an eternity of identical, hopeless nights.

When he arrived in Valparaíso, he had immediately set out to look for the street mentioned in René's letter, Agravios Street. This proved no easy task; no one seemed to have heard of it. Or was it that they had heard of it but didn't want to direct him there so as not to get involved in the danger that René's presence there implied? For a day and a night and another day, Mario wandered over hill after hill, believing that every corner and cranny held a possible threat. He avoided the police, imagining that they would no sooner set eyes on him than cry out: "Off to prison with you, thief, brother of René!"

Meanwhile, since the police were the only ones who would know where Agravios Street was, he had to make do as best he could on his own. He wandered about the hills— Barón, Torpederas, Placeres, Polanco—catching a glimpse every now and then of the ships crowded together in the harbor's blue embrace under the miraculously clear skies of those interminable days. He went down to the port. "OSLO" said the letters on the prow of a ship which a line of sweating men was loading with sacks. One sack burst. There was rice in the puddles of the pier and on the tracks of the cranes. The name written in crude mauve lettering on the sacks was SANTA CAMILA FARMS, TALCA. So it was Talca rice for Oslo that the dockers were loading in such a hurry. Where was Oslo? Blond sailors leaned over the rails, and their shouts of laughter sounded foreign as they drifted to him down the salt wind. Their shouts rang with the impatience of other latitudes. A straggle of gulls appeared out of nowhere and swooped down on the stream of refuse oozing out of the ship, filling the air with their white clamoring. Oslo. Perhaps, after all, there was no such place as Oslo. Perhaps it was a mirage conjured from this transparent day to make him regret that he was here at all and forget René and the destiny marked out for him . . . a destiny which kept eluding him in this labyrinth of Valparaíso, so that he was left weary and lonely, with no Estela, no Fornino Emporium, unable even to find René, who would at least transform this vague menace into something concrete and actual.

He set off uphill again. His feet ached, and his shoes

were hot and clammy from so much walking. He had taken
so many creaking old buses in search of Agravios Street,
had gone up so many hills, down into so many valleys,
walking slowly, bemused by the bewildering profusion of
passageways, lanes, alleys, steps which led up and on,
twisting, turning, and losing themselves in this dirty huddle
of houses and hovels, that his footsteps had become mechanical and he let them lead him on so as not to have to stop
to think. In his weariness he had lost sight of his original
reason for coming here at all. Night fell. He was tired and
thirsty, and so, when he passed a cantina near the customs
house, he went in reluctantly. He sat down at a table. Under
the harsh lights, sailors were drinking, sitting next to their
sweating women; others were hawking contraband in a
corner. Some sat in silence, fuddled by the wine. Mario felt
a sudden urgent longing to become one of them, sign on
with some boat which would take him a long way from this
crushed existence of his. Oslo? Was there really a place
with a name like a furry toy? Go away forever. Mario
looked around him as the thought came to him that the
heavy hand of the law might even then be taking advantage
of his daydreaming to descend on him. Go away. Return
after years and years, with a different smile on his lips, his
memory full of other streets, shops, bars, friends, work,
winds—cleaned of all this. Return laden with gifts and
exotic cigarettes for Estela. No. Estela no longer figured in
his happy endings. Oslo? Estela? Every second he thought
fearfully that a heavy hand was about to fall on his shoulder,
branding him permanently. A policeman's hand? René's
hand? It was all the same. They represented the punishment
and disgrace from which there was no escape, because he
was a man now and had lost his job at the Emporium, because he had struck Estela in the face and called her a
thief. And Estela was pregnant and she wanted to get her

hands on him, just like the police. There was nothing he could do now. Just find René and stick to him.

Oslo? Estela? No. René.

He went out into the street again to tire himself out even more and so not to have to think about those names which were carving him up. A man stopped him under a street light and asked him for a match. The man's blanched face stared at him a little too insistently, as if trying to recognize him. This represented the most immediate danger. Mario said he had no matches and hurried off down the dark street. The stranger followed him for half a block, then went back and stood watching him from the corner. Before turning down the next street, Mario looked back. The man's finely drawn face might still be smiling under the blinking neon sign *Bilz*.

He walked all night. A brief, merciful sleep overtook him sprawled out on a pile of sacks . . . but then he walked all morning.

At last, at three in the afternoon, with his stomach burning with hunger and the back of his neck scorched by the sun's unerring rays, Mario found Agravios Street. Street? It wasn't really a street. On a hillside, at the point where the hill was no longer a hill and the city no longer a city but countryside, two houses stood leaning against each other: square, whitewashed houses crouched beside a gully. These two houses, to all appearances, constituted the whole of Agravios Street. The bigger house was No. 2678. A single square window, in the middle of a whitewashed face stained by salt and wind, was the house's only avenue of communication with the outside world. A short flight of steps led up from the ravine into the belly of the house, and a hen was dozing peacefully on one of the steps. After prowling around the house for a bit, Mario stood outside the window and shouted: "Señora, señora!"

Instantly, as if he had been expected, the window was thrown open. An old, black woman reeking of garlic poked her head, wrapped in a red scarf, out of the window. From that dark, furrowed face peered light-colored eyes, alarmingly young.

"Señora," Mario repeated, more softly.

"What do you want?"

Her toothless cavern of a mouth might have been a century old, but her voice, like the blue eyes, had refused to age. The head of a little blond boy of about eight appeared in the window next to the old woman's. He stared at Mario too.

"My brother René told me to look for him here."

"He isn't here!"

And the window slammed shut with such a bang that the entire house shook. The hen jumped up in alarm and ran off clucking till it vanished in the refuse of the gully below.

Not knowing what to do next, Mario stood for a moment with his hands in his pockets, staring out over the bay. The ship he had watched being loaded was steaming out of the harbor. Talca rice for Oslo. Hopelessly discouraged, he watched the boat for a long time, till it vanished over the horizon. The tugs plowed through the bay without leaving a visible mark on its smooth surface, and the smoke darkened the air for a second and then dispersed in that immense transparency. Goodbye Oslo!

He turned back and looked at the house.

A shadowy figure slipped out of sight behind the dirty windows. It was the only sign of life he saw in the house in the two hours he stood guard outside it. It was pointless to go on hoping. The best thing he could do now was go back. But where? He did not know. It hardly mattered anyway, it was all the same now.

He started off downhill again, feeling that before long other hopes would come crowding back. The vaguely criminal fate which had earmarked him simply because he was René's brother had now rejected him. He had done what he could to catch up with it, but it kept eluding him, slipping through his fingers. Should he go back now? Where? To Santiago? To Dora and Estela, both of them pregnant? No, no, he couldn't. He had cut himself off from that other, equally unpleasant fate. He had no right even to that. He was almost crying from exhaustion and confusion as he walked downhill. The street was very narrow, and the houses seemed so fragile that the slightest puff of wind, or the slightest noise—his own footsteps, for instance—might send them toppling like card houses.

He suddenly noticed a little barefoot boy trotting along beside him, wearing a man's jacket whose skirts brushed his grimy calves. The boy smiled at him sweetly. Mario's heart thumped with the realization that in that smile René had once more caught up with him. He hurried his steps a little, but the boy did not leave his side. Mario stopped on a street corner.

"What do you want?" he asked.

"I'm to take you where René is."

It was the little boy who had appeared at the window with the old woman. Mario nodded, obediently, and set off behind him. A little farther, the boy stopped to light a cigarette butt he took from a plastic purse full of such stubs. He offered one to Mario, who accepted it. They went up and down hills, streets, passageways, and alleys. Women called to each other from their balconies. In a basement, far below the level of the road, a shoemaker was mending shoes that looked as if they had been retrieved from a garbage dump. They walked along what appeared to be a mule or goat track, the houses below them clinging miraculously to the sides of the ravine—these houses were entered through the roof. Up above were clusters of houses on stilts which one reached up endless steps full of zigzags and sharp curves. Suddenly, at the end of a row of houses, there was the blue up-ended triangle of the sea.

They emerged on to a terrace from which one could see the whole of Valparaíso: from Concón to the Torpederas, all of it spacious, clear, celestial.

They reached a level spot. The boy turned to Mario.

"Tired?" he asked.

"No . . ."

"We're almost there."

Mario's only hope lay in following his guide—at least that meant going somewhere—and setting aside his suspicions and questions for the moment. At the first hint of skepticism, this boy, who looked as immaterial as the smoke he puffed out from time to time, would in all likelihood disappear, leaving him to start his search again all alone.

Near the Plaza de la Victoria they approached a solid-looking house, several stories high, adorned with crumbling caryatids hoary with the excrement of generations of pigeons. The splendor of the Valparaíso of transatlantic, mercantile opulence lay dying in the impersonal gloom of this street. Something impressive, though, like a corpse that will not stay buried, animated this grandiose husk of a street which had not managed to keep its former splendor.

They stopped in front of a door.

"There," said the boy, pointing to a second-floor balcony. Mario looked up, and when he turned back again, to ask for an explanation or for help, his heart gave a great thump of alarm: the boy had vanished.

The brass plate under the bell said: *Esteban Ríos Ferguson, milliner. Exclusive creations.*

Mario rang the bell.

After what seemed like a long time, he heard the bolt being drawn back. He pushed open the door, and his eyes traveled up the narrow white marble staircase in front of him to where a lean old man dressed in an immensely long coat, and with tartan flannel slippers on, stood looking at him, smiling behind his green spectacles.

"Come on up, young man, come on up."

Mario followed the man into a hall where huge mirrors seemed to chill the shadowy recesses. He stumbled against a screen on which a parrot was painted in rough-textured gold. Mario thought at first that the room was crowded with elegantly dressed ladies, but when the crack of an opening door let in some light he saw that they were not real women at all but wicker heads without faces, stiffly upright on their wooden stands, silent beneath magnificent showy hats, drooping feathers, or swathed in sequinned veils which glittered like thousands of cat's eyes in the gloom.

"You must be one of the . . ." The old man did not finish his caressing question, but took Mario gently by the arm and led him toward a brightly lit doorway.

Through the door Mario could see a room where three or four women sat drinking with some men around a table. A tall, bearded sailor was wrestling playfully with a woman in green who was trying to make him put on a hat covered with bows and flowers. They were all laughing. But it was as if they were only pretending to laugh: their laughs were featureless, like the bald wicker heads of which there were dozens in this room too. The woman won in the end and crowned the bearded sailor with the hat. He smirked coquettishly, and some of the wicker dummies let out roars of laughter. Then they all seemed to merge with the wicker heads, and Mario no longer knew which were real and which were not.

"No . . . no, I'm not," Mario answered.

In one of the inner rooms a child was screaming. Mario smelled that familiar odor of food and damp clothes drying over a stove which one finds in poor homes, and what had at first struck him as luxurious lost its glamour. Everything here was wretchedly poor; it had been lent a deceptively rich appearance by the shadowy gloom and his own fear. The old man squeezed his arm affectionately, as if urging him on. His amiable smile hung suspended, as if he awaited a word from Mario to deepen it still further. The woman in green came up. Her face was bright red, as though she had just scrubbed it with a rough cloth.

"Is this one for me?" she asked.

The old man shrugged, and his voice and gestures became meltingly gentle. He pointed to the room the woman had just left.

"In there, young man, don't be nervous . . ."

"He's got sweet little light eyes . . ." the woman murmured.

"No . . ." Mario said.

At this refusal, the door to the lighted room swung to with a bang. The baby screamed as if it were being torn limb from limb.

"Well then," the woman said impatiently, "what do you want?"

"Is René here? I'm his brother, and I . . ."

The old man let go of Mario's arm abruptly. His gentleness had vanished, shattered. The gleam in his eye seemed to pierce the green lenses of his spectacles.

"René? That scoundrel? You're his brother, are you? You don't think he'd still be here, do you? I'll have that shit kicked out of the place if he ever shows up here again! You know what the bastard did? Screwed up the best piece of business I ever had in my life! Couldn't keep his mouth shut.

Two months wasted because of him. They nabbed him and threw him in jail and I'm only sorry they didn't catch him with the goods on him so they could keep him on ice for a good long time. He's coming out tonight. And if he talks I'll kill him. I'll kill him! He knows what I'm like—you tell him what I said. I'll kill him!"

So Mario found René in jail. They hadn't been able to pin anything on him because he had had nothing on him when they took him in, no weapons or anything else, so they let him cool his heels in a cell a couple of nights and then released him, like any tramp.

The two brothers walked in silence toward Agravios Street, climbing up and down the hills in the dark with the wind full in their faces. René hung his head, defeated. As they approached the house, all the questions that had been accumulating inside Mario all these months suddenly burst out and swept over René like an avalanche. What were they going to do now? What had René done, why did René send for him, how did they catch him? What if Dora and the children died of hunger? Was there any danger still? What were they going to do now? He had given up his job at the Emporium and they wouldn't give it back to him now. He had dropped everything when René sent for him. They must do something, anything.

"Anything?" René asked, looking at him suddenly like someone who has just pounced on an insect off guard.

"Yes . . ." Mario's voice trembled as he said this small syllable which sealed a definite bargain.

"Promise?"

"Promise."

Mario and René shared the same lumpy mattress at the house in Agravios Street. René's loud snoring, his restless tossing and turning in bed, effectively kept Mario from sleeping. He lay there with his thoughts whirling through his mind, like a dog chasing its tail.

They stayed in that house for what seemed like an eternity. René would leave in the morning, saying: "Wait here."

In the evening he always came back looking so haggard that it was hard to ask him just what one was supposed to be waiting for, or make him instantly produce some risky job which would allow Mario to share his guilt. René grew more and more haggard with every day that passed, and refused to answer Mario's questions. "Wait," was all he would say. Everything had become meaningless. Oslo? Estela? René? Everything was abject, deflated, the same, just names, devoid of meaning.

"Wait."

Mario waited because he didn't know what else to do.

He never left the house in Agravios Street but amused himself playing marbles with the fair-haired boy, who won his few remaining pesos between puffs at the eternal cigarette stub. In the evening, when the wind forced the little boy to wind himself in his voluminous jacket like a chrysalis, Mario would sit on the steps in the front of the house and look at the lights on the hills, and the boy huddled up against him. The hen, which was tame, though a little hysterical, would doze on his lap.

This went on till one day René returned a little earlier than usual, more crestfallen than ever.

"I'm screwed," he mumbled. Nothing else, but defeat had matched the opaque color of his odd eyes.

The next day he said: "We're going back to Santiago . . ."

And they caught the night train.

Wisely, Dora greeted them as if they had just been away on a weekend spree. She abandoned herself to her joy at having René back, saving the recriminations for later. She thought he looked thin and ill and scolded him like a child for having let his clothes get so dirty. She helped him into bed. Defeated, he let her do what she liked. Somehow, using the Lord knows what lies and promises to the storekeepers, Dora managed to produce some meat and bread and at once set to work preparing a meal. Later, when both brothers were asleep, she sat for hours sewing feverishly at her colored-cloth toys.

Now Mario could hear René snoring next door just as he had all the nights he could remember. Then he heard him stir, wake, and then start a whispered conversation with Dora before getting up.

"A gentleman came by, looking for Mario the other day," Dora said.

"A gentleman?"

René's voice went sharp, knife-edged.

"Yes, a gentleman."

"What did he want?"

"He said the girl who worked in his house was pregnant . . ."

"And?"

"He said Mario was the father."

"Did he come by car?"

"I don't know."

"How was he dressed?"

Mario realized that the other end of the thread of his life had now come into René's hands, the thread that would lead back to Estela and the big house standing among the trees in its decaying garden. No, Estela needn't think she was going to catch him now, gentleman or no gentleman. René was there to help him defend himself and show him how to make the most of his opportunities. Estela could look after her baby herself! René's voice was clear and positive as he questioned Dora about the gentleman, and the questions were leading him straight to Misiá Elisa's house. Mario squeezed his eyes shut to see stars and colored spots but only succeeded in seeing the word *thief*. Only, this time it didn't frighten him.

René said nothing to Mario about the gentleman's visit.

That evening the two brothers, whom the disaster in Valparaíso and all other disasters had brought closer together than they had ever been, sat smoking on the doorstep. The street bubbled with life: children playing ball, lighted windows, girls giggling in little groups under the street lights, people going or coming or passing by. Dora's recriminations had finally caught up with them. When she asked for money to buy food, it turned out that neither René nor Mario had a cent. And at that she had begun her moaning again, only louder than ever. She called them thieves, bums, good-for-nothings. To punish René, she told him she was pregnant.

But, sitting in the street with his brother, René chatted about pleasanter things. For the first time he let Mario in on some of the details of his past life, a risk he could take quite calmly now that the same destiny had marked them.

"... we lived in Iquique. You don't know Iquique. It's a great place, pretty, really pretty. My father had a little store near the harbor. I keep thinking about that little store, I don't know why. There were always some sacks outside the door, with dried peas and lentils and beans, and the tops of the sacks were left open, like this. We sold fresh vegetables too, when we could get them, they don't grow there much ... and there were hanks of rope hanging from the ceiling, and large spoons and white enameled pots and pans—what I liked most was when they let me write the price on them with a black wax pencil. And there were twig brooms on the shelves, and laundry soap, the stinking, blue kind, and combs and sometimes even calicos and woolens, and jars with candies or marbles. Some kids once made me swallow a marble by telling me it was a candy. And you know, there wasn't much difference!"

René laughed easily, and Mario, guessing what turn the story was about to take, knew that he was going to be questioned about the gentleman, the house, and Estela . . .

"Sometimes, on Saturdays, when there was no school, we would pinch some cakes and candies and off we would go to the beach to swim and get the sun. We bathed stark naked. I'd like to see the sea again—the real sea, not the sea of Valparaíso. Valparaíso's a shit-hole, a real shit-hole!"

He spat disgustedly.

"My father had only one eye, but he was a great talker and as lively as anything. In the afternoons he would take a wicker chair outside the store, to the mud road—just like this one—and sit there smoking some filthy-smelling cigarettes in yellow paper, Yutard I think they were called, yes, Yutard. And his white moustache went all yellow like the cigarette paper. Well, the old devil used to sit by the side of the road, calling out to all the women who went by, and sometimes, if they were neighbors or friends, he gave them a good pinch on the backside. That's where I got my way with women! And you too . . . come to think of it! I've heard a couple of things lately . . . Sometimes the old man would beat me and leave me black and blue for a week. I can't remember what it was all about now, but it happened whenever he got drunk. He was a great one for red wine. The *camanchaca* fog caught him when he was drunk, coming home late one night, and he got pneumonia. He was very old by then. Then he died, but I don't remember much about that. And mama, she was your mama too, married your father after that, and they kept up the store but it started losing money then because she began to fight with the customers."

René was flying higher and higher, like a kite, and almost

seemed to have forgotten Mario. But suddenly he turned on him.

"See? That's why I want to get my hands on some cash. Not to throw around, believe me. I want to settle down somewhere on my own. I've been thinking of going back to Iquique, as a matter of fact. But how? I'm flat broke. And how can I go on living with Dora? I've had just about all I can take of her, I tell you—and now she has to go and get herself pregnant again. No, I've got to get away—I can't stick around much longer. But it's no use sitting here with my arms crossed. No one's going to give me any business now, not even the crap I used to get, because they don't trust me any more. Where am I going to get the cash, then? I haven't even got enough to make a blind man sing. I'd do anything to get my hands on some cash and leave this place, *anything*! What about you?"

"Me? Sure, me too . . ."

"Why don't you join up with me, kid? Go up north together, to Iquique, say? We could open up a bar, a little bar near the port, where the sailors take their contraband, and then you pass it on to the big boys and soon you're rolling in money. The thing is—how do we start? We need money, first of all, they don't give bars away. A nice little bar, not too large, then with a little luck and the right word here and there . . . if there's one thing I'm good at, it's talking them up and pouring out drinks. God, it would be great—that's the way to enjoy life. And I want to enjoy life. All I'm doing here is rotting away, little by little."

"So what? Where's this cash coming from? We don't know anyone with cash . . . no one at all . . ."

"No one? What about the rich gentleman Dora was going on about, who came here asking for you the other day? Is he a friend of yours?"

Mario shivered. It had started. As in a dream, trying to

stop himself at first but gradually letting his words and hidden motives carry him along, he began talking about Estela, and the baby, and the gentleman, and the big house where he lived. René pretended not to know anything about Estela. But when Mario said he was thinking of marrying her, he lost his temper.

"Marry her? You're crazy. Don't give me that soppy stuff, you aren't twenty-one yet, and I won't let you . . . no, you've got to help out here with Dora and me. You can't get married, you owe me something for all the sacrifices I've made for you. No . . . no . . ."

His anger gradually subsided to a tone of friendly advice.

"You're still young, kid, and you've got your whole life ahead of you to have a good time in. Look at the mistake I made, shacking up with Dora . . . I'm screwed now, really screwed. You want to get screwed too? You want to be like me? Eh?"

This did the trick, not that Mario needed much convincing. Bewitched by this magnetism of his brother's which made him talk about the things René wanted to hear instead of the things he wanted to talk about, Mario told him all about the big gloomy house among the trees. It had some nice things inside! Lamps, ornaments, carpets . . . René listened in silence. He was letting his brother work up to the idea that was already flourishing in his own mind, the idea that could prove their salvation. Almost at once, as though he had decided to let this idea mature in its own good time and at the same time win Mario's confidence completely, he talked about other things.

"These rich people! . . . and here we are without a cent. And we never had a cent either. But you can't complain, I've always done what I could for you. You owe everything to me, as you know, so . . . You weren't in Santiago yet when I was out of work and had to go around begging for food on a little plate . . . there were plenty of us unemployed in those days, let me tell you! That was sometime ago . . . I remember the long lines, we were a pretty ragged bunch by then, around the porch of the Church of the Sacramentinos . . . behind the steps were big kitchens that used to let out smoke. That was the nearest we got to a meal. Soon after that, I met Dora, who had a job in a factory, and I never looked back! Look back! Here it is twenty years later, and I'm just where I was then, minus my little plate! It must have been about then that your father died and my mother was a widow again—half nuts, they say he was, a Yugoslav or something. Then she died and you were left an orphan and I sent you money so you could come and live with me in Santiago. You owe everything to me, you see, Dora and I have brought you up and everything, you can't say you ever lacked for anything . . ."

18   As the days passed, Misiá Elisa's condition seemed to become stable.

"It's her saint's day soon and she wants to be well for the party," Lourdes explained.

"Perhaps there will be more people than there were for her birthday."

"I doubt it. Do you think Don Andresito will want us to serve that delicious stuff he's been drinking lately? Have you tried it, Rosario?"

"Don't be silly. I never touch wine."

"This isn't wine. And anyway wine is bad for you. You don't suppose Don Andresito would drink it if it was bad for you. We've never known him to be any the worse for it."

"He's been behaving a little strangely, though . . ."

"That's something else. You know, he's getting just like the señora, poor thing. It must be old age."

"Why doesn't it happen to us then?"

"We're different. Look. Just try some. Just a drop, it's wonderful for the chest."

"Mmmmmmm. It's very sweet . . ."   ຂບ້

"Yes, isn't it. I think it's very good. And if Don Andrés drinks it, there can't be anything wrong with it, the way he looks after himself. I'm going to give the señora a little and see how she likes it."

"The señora's been very well lately."

"I know. And we thought she was dying only a week ago! You know what I think cured her? Estela! And I'm not saying that just because she's my niece. But I'm sure it's her influence, she's such a good girl. I'm so glad they gave her to me. Have you noticed how she's filling out? She looks like a real lady now that she's had a permanent and puts some make-up on. And you know, she never leaves the señora's bedside. There they are, praying together all day long. That's the only thing I don't quite like. What could have happened to a young thing like that to make her pray so much?"

Andrés, too, was astonished at his grandmother's return to health. And his own spirit, as if in answer to his grandmother's signal for calm, likewise observed a period of melancholy poise. But from time to time, as he sat at the foot of his grandmother's bed listening to her reminiscences or soothing her incessant suspicions, he would find himself drawn—quite involuntarily—to examine the confused depths within himself, and there in the center of the chaos he would see his passion for Estela, hooked to him like a hawk draining blood. In an attempt to give his feelings for the girl a little dignity, to commit himself to some heroic course of action, he had gone to look for the famous Mario. They told him that Mario was not in Santiago. He left his name and address and went away, feeling ill. The squalor and poverty of the house, the ugliness of the woman he spoke to, the odor of food and unmade beds and dirty children mortified him with the thought that Estela had not only reduced him to inward cha⌐ but had also brought him within reach of this intolerably poverty-stricken existence in which anything shady or sinister—crime, vice, theft, anything—was possible . . . understandable even, Andrés reflected. Anything would be better than accepting such wretchedness. He felt a fierce pleasure, as in the most exquisite revenge, in the thought that Estela would be dragged down by this life till she resembled that appalling woman who had been so suspicious of him. He would no longer desire her then.

When he saw how the girl's face brightened as he told her of his visit, he felt like beating her for being such a fool and welcoming such poverty and misery rather than give herself to him and the beautiful life he could offer her. He felt like hitting her till those soft cheeks and eyes— which a gleam of hope had set fluttering open again—were bruised and spoiled. He wanted to break, to crush those rosy-palmed hands which in her agitation she did not seem to know what to do with.

"When is he coming back?"

"Soon," Andrés repeated.

The girl went back to her place by the old woman's bed. She sat there, rosary in hand, listening while Misiá Elisa called on the almighty to punish all sinners and cast them into the flames of hell. Then Estela fell on her knees and wept, and her head was bowed in contrition. She swore to Misiá Elisa that if it were not for the baby she would never see Mario again, because he and everything to do with him was dirty and loathsome.

"You repent now, but that does not make you any less a sinner—you gave yourself gladly, and took pleasure in it. You won't go to hell, but you will certainly spend a long, long time in purgatory, burning in the flames. Only fire can remove the stain of your sin. It is only we who have never sinned who can go straight to heaven . . ."

As Estela knelt there in the semi-darkness, she cursed her misfortune in ever having met Mario.

The moment she left the old woman's room, an altogether different emotion possessed her.

When she noticed that Andrés was in one of the rooms nearby—hearing him cough or light a cigarette—she would steal closer to him unawares, as if she wanted to place herself in his protection. Then the stain Misiá Elisa talked about seemed to vanish and the nearness of Andrés filled her with a passionate longing to be with Mario again, to touch him, live with him, however dirty it might turn out to be, even though he had hit her and might well hit her again thousands of times, even though he had called her a thief.

One evening while Andrés was resting in his bedroom, Lourdes announced that there was a gentleman downstairs who wanted to see him.

"A gentleman? What gentleman?"

"Well . . . I don't know, maybe he isn't a gentleman really. He's just a man. He says it's urgent."

"Do you know him?"

"No, he's never been here before."

"Who can it be?"

"He's waiting for you downstairs. I expect he wants to try and borrow some money. I'll go down and keep an eye on him, shall I? You know what people are like these days."

Andrés went down to the vestibule, where René appeared to be making an envious inventory of its entire contents. His shiny suit hopelessly belied the air of smiling confidence he had assumed to put himself on a level with such luxury.

"Good afternoon. You wanted to see me?"

"Ah, Señor Abalos. Delighted to meet you. Please forgive me for disturbing you," said René.

"What do you want?"

"Well, Señor Abalos, I don't like to intrude on a busy gentleman like yourself, but it seems you came to my home a few days ago and left your address, so I thought I would drop in and see what it was you wanted. My wife isn't too bright, you know, and didn't explain it very clearly to me. I'm sorry I wasn't there to receive you myself, but I was detained in Valparaíso on urgent business."

"Why have you come and not Mario?"

"Well, you see, he is under age and I am acting for him in this matter."

"What matter?"

This poor wretch was too feeble, Andrés thought, too ridiculously vulnerable. Surely there wasn't a threat or vice in the world which this pathetically downtrodden creature, with his ineffectual strutting, could possibly represent. This was poverty and nothing more.

". . . the matter of the girl."

"Estela?"

"Yes, I believe that's what she's called. He's in no position to get married just yet, you know, a young man like that, without a job . . ."

"I could get them to give him his job back."

"Ah . . . !"

This was out of the question. Getting his job back would mean many things to Mario, independence, security, a return to a bright, easy, normal way of life; marriage, children, even financial independence if they gave him another counter job at the Emporium.

And he, René, would be shut out from all this, without hope of salvation, his ambitions all bottled up inside him, suffocating him. No, he could not permit this offensively confident gentleman to help Mario. He didn't want to go back to a life of querulous complaints from Dora, smelly second-hand clothes, and a beer now and then as a great treat. He wanted other things, and to realize them he needed Mario's help.

"Tell your brother to come and see me."

Hearing the gentleman pronounce what amounted to a life sentence on him with such composure, René was swept by a great surge of hatred, and he lost his head.

"Come to think of it, how do we know the baby *is* Mario's? You seem very eager to get Estela married off all of a sudden . . ." he said, one eye on Lourdes, just visible next door, spreading out what looked like a veritable treasury of silver on the dark tabletop. This sight had an instantly calming effect on him.

It was a second or two before the full force of René's insinuation that he, not Mario, was the father of Estela's child, sank in. But when it did, he was overwhelmed by abhorrence for this world of vile innuendo, extortion, and vice which he had allowed to brush against his own. How dare this broken creature overstep the limits which had been so scrupulously upheld by generations of Abalos?

"Get out of this house at once! And if you know what's good for you, you won't come back," Andrés said, dismissing René instantly.

Andrés went up to his room. He opened the little door in his bedside table and took out a bottle. Life was becoming increasingly hard to face without the help of this bottle. He sat down on the bed and took a long swig. And another.

And another. But however much he drank, he knew he would never succeed in breaking out of this carapace of inhibition which kept him from carrying out his one consuming desire—to fling himself hungrily on Estela.

René left the house with silver objects in profusion dancing before his eyes, a sight that was deliciously restorative to jaded pupils. A treasure of silver it was, and he could almost have reached out and touched it. He had gone to the Abalos house with a swarm of vague ideas buzzing in his mind, confident that he would find salvation there but uncertain as to the form it would take. Stealing something, a piece of jewelry, for instance? Exploiting some weakness of Don Andrés's, a penchant for Estela, or Mario perhaps? Suggesting himself as pander to the caballero's vices—whatever they might be—and gradually assuming control of him and his possessions? But by the time he left, it was all perfectly clear. And quite simple. All he had to do was break into Don Andrés's house one night, pile all the silver into a sack, and leave. That was all.

As the plan took shape in his mind, René's old toughness, which the Valparaíso fiasco seemed to have shattered, returned to him. Nothing presented any difficulties, nothing was too dangerous, or uncertain. His left eyebrow arched in his old expression of tough cynicism, and a cruel resolve tightened the thick lips outlined by a thin moustache. He felt his moustache. It was untidy and unkempt, like his hair. After making sure that he still had a few pesos left which Dora had managed to earn with the sale of a couple of cloth toys, he decided to pay a visit to a barber shop near where he lived. Nothing was more suited to agreeable meditation than a barber's chair.

"Not too short at the back, Juanito," he said as he sat down.

"Where have you just come from?"

"I had some business outside Santiago to take care of. No, shave me first, please . . ."

"How did it go?"

René did not answer. He allowed his head to drop back on the head rest and closed his purplish eyelids. The solid contours of his face were softened by the white foam, which lent his cheeks a look of greenish transparency. Eyes closed, the white cloth masking the shabbiness of his clothes, the barber's ineffably gentle hands massaging his face and throat and stretching the skin near his ears, the scent of soap and cologne—all this helped relax his mind and open dazzling new vistas to it. He felt as if he had only just stumbled on his real self. The future was clear and beautiful, probably up north somewhere, but in any case a long way from the bed he shared with Dora and the humiliation of having to beg her for the few pesos she made sewing cloth toys.

He half opened his eyes. He looked at Juanito concentrating on his degrading task, his cheeks sagging with the fatigue of existence, like the cheeks of some disillusioned, good-natured bulldog. Reflected in the mirror, he saw the razor gleam near his Adam's apple, and with a slight hiss a patch of foam was cleared away.

This gleam in the hands of an insignificant person constituted a threat.

Estela!

The important thing was to make sure that Estela was not involved in the plan, to convince Mario of the necessity of leaving her out of it. If Mario insisted on taking Estela with him after the burglary, everything would be ruined. The girl's disappearance would start a line of inquiry which would lead directly to Mario and to him. While he was talking to Señor Abalos, he had caught sight of a collection of silver pheasants, some fighting, some pecking at the polished mahogany. René knew the man he could sell them to and what he could expect to get for them too. It was no use lying to himself, though—Estela was the only one who could let them into the house and show them the way to the dining room. But suppose they thought of a way to keep the actual plan a secret from her? The best thing would be for her to let Mario in to make love, and then it would be simple for the boy to let him in without Estela noticing. Yes. That was it.

Later on, sitting at the Condor drinking beer just before closing time, a clean, revitalized René with glossy cheeks and well-groomed hair discussed his plan with Mario.

"Don't you see that she got herself pregnant just to get her hooks into you? That kind of trick doesn't fool me. Women are all the same, kid, all they want is a man to kick them around and give them money so they don't have to work. And don't give me that line about love and romance. You marry her because she tells you she's pregnant, and the next thing you know, she'll be confessing she missed one. It was a lie. She never was pregnant. She just wanted to get herself married . . . but now you're hooked, and it's too late. No. Love them and leave them . . . that's what a real man does. Look at Dora. If it wasn't for Dora, would I be in the shit state I'm in now?"

René's excitement mounted as the words poured out of him. Listening to his plan unfold in the darkened bar just before closing time, Mario felt his defenses crumbling, everything loosening up inside him. The boy's wary grin gradually changed to a smile of complete surrender, and his raised eyebrow exactly mimicked René's.

"When?" Mario asked, letting his body sprawl out comfortably, one arm draped over the back of a chair.

"Tomorrow. No, the day after would be better," René said.

He had not planned it like that, but Mario's unconditional surrender made it all the more urgent to get moving. He could already feel the wad of notes in the bottom of his trouser pocket. His gold fillings sparkled as he talked, excitedly waving his pudgy hands adorned with their ring.

They drank beer after beer.

René's euphoria communicated itself to Mario. Thief? What did it matter? The main thing was to have a ball. He wanted women, suits, ties, and people around him to treat him with respect tinged with awe. Tightening the young, taut muscles in his forearm, he thought how silly he'd been never to put his strength to proper use. His fists ached with the urge to slam someone till they drew blood, knock someone out with one stunning blow so that everyone said: "Look, that Mario over there, you don't want to mix with him."

Estela? She was nothing, just one in a myriad of women he had promised himself in the future. He wasn't going to let any woman get the better of him. As for the kid, well, it wouldn't be the first bastard the world had ever seen. And Estela wouldn't be able to make trouble because she was nothing but a thief herself when all was said and done. Yes, a thief. Like him. René let fall an encouraging hand on his brother's shoulder.

". . . you'll have to go there tomorrow night and make up with her. And tell her to let you in the night after so you can do it properly. See? Then you can let me in without anyone knowing, and we'll grab all that stuff that's lying around on the dining-room table. Then you can take the stuff to Don Saladino Páez, who doesn't know you from Adam, and I'll tell you how to make sure he pays you a good price. Then we'll leave early the next morning, just the two of us, with all the money . . ."

Mario went to Estela the following night.

When he felt her arms around him, and her silent weeping, the boy's obduracy melted away. Standing in that dark doorway which had witnessed so much of their love, and its scant rhetoric, he was stirred by Estela's beauty all over again, and by her warm lips beneath his in the cold night. She was so pretty! So completely his! When she cried, the boy found himself weeping a little too. His tears seemed to well up out of the farthest, deepest corners of himself and travel right through him. Estela neither blamed nor questioned him; she clung to him, glorying in the joy of having him back. A renewed burning faith cancelled out all the doubts Misiá Elisa had sown, and she just stood there, without speaking, for a long time, warm with love and contentment, clinging to this body which gave her life all its meaning.

"Would you like to go with us to Iquique?" Mario asked, and felt her lashes fluttering affirmatively as they brushed against his neck.

Yes. He would take her with him wherever he went, no matter what happened. René's stipulations vanished from his mind. René could count him out unless it was agreed that he would take Estela. They arranged to spend the next night together in one of the downstairs rooms, and Mario decided not to let her in on the plan till then.

"All right then," she said. "I'd better go in now. Tomorrow's the señora's birthday and I still haven't finished everything I'm supposed to do. They're giving a party . . ."

"Party? How can we sleep together then?"

"They'll all be gone by nine o'clock, silly, and everyone in the house will be so tired they won't hear a thing. So it will be better for us . . ."

"Why are you in such a hurry to go in now? What have you got to do?"

"Oh, dozens of things. I've got to put all the silver in

the dining room away by tomorrow. The *patrón* says we can't leave it out on the table. Listen . . . do you know, the old man's getting just like the señora. He said he won't take it out of the cupboard again till the señora dies, and heaven knows how long that may be . . ."

"He's going to lock it up? Where?"

"In the dining-room cupboard. Why?"

"Oh, nothing. I just wondered. Who keeps the key?"

"My aunt Lourdes. But why? Come on, tell me . . ."

They said good night.

Things were going better than Mario could have hoped. The fact that the silver was being put away for an indefinite period meant that the theft would not be discovered till after the old lady's death, and the fact that Lourdes had the key meant they would need Estela's help in getting it. René would be forced to include Estela in his plan for escape.

Mario had to wait more than an hour on the corner near the park for a streetcar. The bell of a church nearby had tolled midnight by the time it arrived. The conductor who took Mario's fare was so sleepy that the driver started the streetcar without waiting for his signal.

There was only one other person, a woman, in the car. Mario sat down behind her, next to the window. He closed his eyes, intending to doze during the streetcar's long circumambulation before it reached his part of town. There was nothing to look at in this streetcar, with its yellowish light trembling overhead, except the advertisements, and Mario knew them by heart. He settled back comfortably in his seat and crossed his arms. As he did so, he was suddenly reminded of the roundness of Estela's waist. He hugged his arms closer as though she were still there.

"Where's Iquique?" the girl had asked him.

She was so ignorant, and little, and silly, and so completely his! Mario had laughed at her ignorance without being able to tell her much more himself than that Iquique was up north somewhere. Tonight without fail he would tell René that unless Estela was in on the plan and came with them afterwards, he could count him out.

The woman sitting in front of Mario had long, lank hair. She looked out of the window, revealing a profile netted with wrinkles. The tired flesh was already sagging over the cheekbones and jawline. She wasn't an old woman . . . she was just a woman, like . . . like Dora.

The woman stood up. Her stomach was monstrously swollen and her shabby dress rose up a little in front, exposing pathetic, slightly grubby knees. She staggered slightly with the movement of the streetcar. Her hollow eyes silently appealed for help, and Mario helped her regain her balance.

"Please, help me off . . ."

Appalled, Mario got to his feet and helped the woman down the aisle toward the door.

"I'm on my way to the hospital, just one block," she whispered.

Mario got off the car with her.

The woman seemed scarcely able to move. A cat which had been scavenging in a garbage can scampered off as it heard them coming, and the garbage-can lid was sent clattering to the ground. The cat streaked off, miaowing with terror, into the night.

"Just the next block," the woman whispered feebly, apologetically.

As her steps grew more and more shaky, she gritted her teeth to stifle the howl of pain which Mario had been expecting. He was supporting almost her entire weight now. The angry thought occurred to him that these muscles of his were cut out for nobler tasks than supporting women

like Dora along in the throes of childbirth. As he would have
to help Estela along in a few months' time. The woman's
pain-twisted face was very close to his. A second later the
face collapsed on his shoulder, like Estela's. They couldn't
go on walking.

"Wait here. I'll go and get help, it's only half a block
from here," Mario said.

"No, no, don't leave me, please don't leave me," the
woman moaned. Mario helped her sit down on a stoop.

"No, no . . ." she moaned while Mario tried to pry her
hands off his sleeve.

"They'll come for you in a minute."

"No, no, no . . ." the woman shrieked, and her shrieks
rang out louder and louder in the deserted street as Mario
ran toward the hospital.

No! No! He wasn't going to be trapped into this, not for
anyone . . .

He rushed into the hospital, woke the dozing attendant
and told him what had happened, and then ran away. It
was Estela he was running from, for good this time; horror
and repugnance had completely blotted out the tenderness
of an hour before. It was Estela's long-drawn-out cries that
pierced his ears as he ran, and again at home, as he tossed
and turned in bed, unable to shut out the groans that stabbed
the silence of the night, or to find sleep until dawn.

19 ⚘⚘ The old woman awoke that morning feeling so well, so strong and lively that she decided, for the
first time in three bed-ridden years, to get up and receive

her saint's day visitors sitting in one of the bedroom chairs near the balcony. Lourdes and Rosario, overcome by this turn of events, went up early, weeping with happiness, to help the señora dress.

"How pleased Don Andresito will be when he comes down and finds you out of bed!" Lourdes cried.

"He gets up later and later these days. Have you noticed how he stays up till all hours reading in his room?" Rosario added.

"That boy is going to ruin his eyesight," Misiá Elisa observed.

"He reads all night long," Rosario said disapprovingly, "and drinks liquor . . ."

"What liquor?" the old woman asked. "So he's become a drunk as well as a dirty old lecher now? Well, I suppose it was the only thing left . . ."

"Don't say that, señora," Lourdes murmured. "What's wrong in a gentleman on his own indulging himself a little? It's not as if he were drinking wine like drunks do."

"And why a dirty old lecher?" Rosario asked.

"Why? Haven't you seen how he follows her around with his tongue hanging out?" said Misiá Elisa, pointing at Estela, while the two maids shook their heads sadly, in disapproval.

Estela heard this remark from the corner where she had gone to get the señora's clothes from the chest of drawers.

But she was so full of happiness and contentment that the old woman's words did not touch her. Besides, she thought, innocently trustful, the señora did not know how kind Don Andresito had been, finding Mario for her like that.

"But Estela doesn't love him," the old woman went on. "Of course she doesn't. Why should a young girl love an old man like that? If he had been young now, who knows what might have happened? He, he, he! You might have found it a little harder to keep your virtue then, eh? If you want to get yourself an old goat of an admirer, child, find one with lots of money, like a sensible girl. You may as well make the most of this life since you're already damned in the next. I know a little secret, don't I, a dear, sweet little secret, and I'm not going to whisper it to a soul . . . isn't that right, Estela?"

It had been so long since Misiá Elisa had got up last that dressing her was a complicated operation. Lourdes opened a huge cupboard of solid oak in the room next door and spread out a sea of boots and shoes on the floor around her, from which she finally selected a pair of black kid boots, almost new. None of the buttons was missing, and the soles had barely been scratched by the señora's passage across the carpeted floors of the house. Lourdes took out a cloth and sat with her legs crossed in front of her, looking like some creole household deity, shining the boots till they sparkled like mirrors.

Rosario, meanwhile, summoning every ounce of strength from arms as hard as seasoned wood, lifted Misiá Elisa bodily out of her bed. Then, clutching the handle of her stick, with her nightgown trailing on the floor, the old lady let herself be helped across to the armchair which had been placed by the window. There she proposed to remain for the rest of the day.

"I want to wear purple bloomers," she said.

While they helped her put them on, under her nightgown, she asked for other things: a pair of black lisle stockings; a knitted petticoat for warmth; gloves, just in case.

Lourdes put her stockings on for her. But first Misiá Elisa pulled the petticoat back above her knees and shook her head sadly as she contemplated what was left of her legs.

"It makes me feel quite sad to see them!" she explained. "So white they're almost blue, look, and thin, so thin! And knees so stiff and rusty they're no good for anything, even walking. Once . . ."

Kneeling at her feet, the two maids helped her put on her boots, Lourdes one foot and Rosario the other. Then, insulated by the woolly petticoat and stockings, Misiá Elisa Grey de Abalos was ready to tackle the most important part of her toilette.

"Which dress shall I wear?"

"The black silk one with the lace fichu," Rosario begged.

"For heaven's sake, señora," Lourdes cried, "you don't want to wear anything somber like that! You need a festive dress . . ."

"Which one do you suggest then?"

"The pretty one with the white taffeta bodice," Lourdes urged.

"Ah, yes, that one then. I'd forgotten I had it."

Armed with combs, brushes, pins, and elastic bands, Estela gathered up the señora's hair, white and transparent as spun glass, and twisted it into a little knot on top of her head. Then she finished off the coiffure with a pale velvet ribbon. The old lady gazed at herself in a hand mirror.

"I look pale," she complained.

Without being asked, Lourdes went and got the little jar of rouge kept for the occasions when the old woman felt she looked pale. Misiá Elisa closed her eyes so as not to have to look while her lips and cheeks were anointed with the red paste. She had never approved of women painting themselves. But hard as she rubbed those nonagenarian cheeks, Lourdes could not make the spots of rouge merge with the natural coloring of her face and lips; they remained smudged and crudely unnatural, like the face of a weird puppet that has been left out in the rain. With a black pencil Lourdes darkened Misiá Elisa's eyebrows slightly and colored her eyelids.

Not till then, with her feet propped up on a stool and a shawl around her knees, did Misiá Elisa open her eyes and stare out through the window into the garden. The light profiled her superbly aquiline nose, as solid as ever, the one solid feature salvaged from that wreck of a face with its pitiful, flaccid patches, a mask of stray sinuousities which age had bleached and time had shriveled. A flabby double chin hung down on her white collar, and helped conceal some whiskers near her ears. The hand resting on her stick kept her body in a grotesque parody of the graceful posture of former days—shoulders thrown back, bosom swelling like a pigeon's—when she drove with her husband in their victoria through the shady avenues of the park.

Lourdes and Rosario were whispering together.

"No, no, Rosario," Lourdes said. "Not till this evening, so it can be a surprise . . ."

"But wouldn't it be better right away? She would love to receive her friends wearing her spangled dress and her boa and little crown, like a princess."

"No, you don't understand. It's an evening dress, not an afternoon one."

"But, Lourdes . . ."

"No, no, I don't want to now. It's much better to wait till nighttime, when everyone's gone."

"Much better *now*!"

"Look, Rosario, stop pestering me, will you. It was my idea, wasn't it? And it was me Don Andresito gave the dress to, and the silver flowers, not you. So?"

"Oh, have it your own way then. So conceited you've become since Estela came here. I can't think what's come over you—you're so pleased with yourself."

"Now, now, Rosario! God punishes the envious, you know."

"Who'd envy a fat old servant like you, I'd like to know?"

Rosario had been in a bad mood all day because it was Lourdes who had the most spectacular present for Misiá Elisa this year. They had had a little quarrel only that morning over a few centimeters of liquor that had mysteriously vanished from a certain bottle. Each blamed the other, which led to the first difference between them in years. As the morning wore on, though, and they went about putting the house in order, locking up the silver, arranging flowers in vases and jars, their old amity returned. They opened another bottle and took tiny swigs from it as a sign that peace was restored.

"Why hasn't Andrés come down yet?" Misiá Elisita inquired.

"He must be asleep still."

"This isn't the time for a young man to get up! He'll get fat and soft, and we women like our men hard, don't we, Estela? Go and wake him, child, and tell him to come down and talk to me, I'm bored with all this domestic chitchat. Tell him to bring me a nice present."

Estela went upstairs quite confidently. Her misgivings over Don Andrés had all vanished when she saw him taking such a keen interest in Mario's return. But when she opened the bedroom door the male smell of the place, a smell of masculine flesh, warm bed, chamber pot, half-smoked cigarettes, and above all alcohol, struck her with disturbing force, and made her blush.

"Don Andrés . . ."

"Who's that?"

"Don Andrés, the señora wants you to go down to see her."

"What time is it?"

"A quarter after eleven."

"Open the curtains," Andrés told her, yawning.

Estela noticed that he spoke in a slurred manner, as if he

had something sticky in his mouth. She raised her arm to draw back the curtains.

Drowsily lying there, Andrés noticed how the light caressed the line of her arm as she raised it to pull the curtains back. Desire surged up in him so violent, urgent, and naked that he could no longer hide it.

"Come here, Estela . . ."

Estela went over to the bed and bent down to pick up a glass which had been overturned on the carpet.

"The señora said you were to take her a present," she said. Andrés was staring at her out of dazed, sunken eyes. He suddenly reached out to seize this fresh young body, so close to his own.

Terrified, Estela dodged away from his outstretched arms and Andrés flopped over the edge of the bed like a clown. The girl fled from the room.

As the afternoon wore on, it became obvious that no one was coming to see Don Ramón Abalos's widow on her saint's day.

Lourdes and Rosario had been busy all afternoon, putting the finishing touches to the preparations for the party. Lourdes kept tasting the punch. She also arranged some tiny lace-edged napkins on the trays around the glasses. On another set of trays Rosario made sugary mosaics of ginger-snaps, eclairs, cookies, and candied egg yolks. From time to time one of them would peer out of the kitchen window and exclaim, looking at the gate: "Bah, I thought I heard someone!"

The sun sank behind thick belts of cloud, but still no one rang the front bell of Misiá Elisa's house. All the lights were on, and the brass and the waxed steps shone. The flowers spilling out of vases in all the rooms gave off that silky, nostalgic fragrance which flowers exude in heated rooms that have been prepared for visitors for a special occasion.

"Was that someone ringing?"

"I don't think so."

"Why don't you go and make sure."

There was no one there.

The branches of acacias and sponge trees swayed mockingly to and fro in the huge neglected garden. The crests of the palms on either side of the front porch were invisible, swathed in low mist.

"It looks as though it's going to rain," Lourdes said. "Listen, do you know what Don Andresito did this afternoon?"

"No. Wasn't he asleep?"

"No. At about three in the afternoon, after the señora had asked for him hundreds of times, he finally came downstairs. And what do you think happened?"

"What?"

"Well, he was in an awful mood apparently. And when the señora said: 'Why haven't you been down before to congratulate me?' what do you think he said?"

"What?"

"The poor man *was* in a terrible mood of course. Heaven knows why, but what he actually said was: 'Do you think I'm in a fit state to bother with such stupidities? It's high time you died anyway,' or something like that. Did you ever?"

"Stupidities? High time she died? Poor lady. I can't believe Don Andrés would be so cruel."

"I tell you he was!"

"Mother of God!"

"Then she let him have it, you know how she gets. She called him a dirty drunken good-for-nothing, and a dirty old lecher, and sinner, and Lord knows what else. You should have heard them going at each other, shouting and screaming. And the señora got so angry! It left her very weak, and I thought she was going to go and die on me right there. Do you think Don Andresito is such a sinner? I don't believe it, it must be one of the señora's ideas, he's such a good boy! Though sometimes . . . well, it must be old age creeping up on him. Guess what he said when she called him an old lecher!"

"What, tell me."

"He said: 'Filthy old bitch . . . you know what I'm suffering now, and it's all your fault!' "

"Goodness, Lourdes, you mustn't use words like that, an unmarried woman like you. You'll go straight to hell . . ."

"Why should I? The rich people say them, so why shouldn't the rest of us repeat them? Anyway, you see now what a funny mood the boy's in. And the way he was going on at the señora! Dreadful! He never used to be like that. The next thing, he'll be accusing us of stealing, like the señora does. Listen . . . have you tasted my punch?"

"Some time ago."

"Ah, but you ought to taste it now that it's matured for a while. And I've put a little more fruit in. Have another taste, just a little one, now that the fruit's blended in. No, not too much, I think it may be a little strong for the liver. What do you think?"

Rosario rolled her eyes.

"Mmmm, it's delicious."

"In a minute I'm going to put the ice in and a drop more liquor and then it'll be better still. I've got a knack for making punch . . . Don Ramón showed me how to do it himself before he and the señora quarreled. He told me the secret was to make it very slowly and keep tasting it as you go."

At eight, when they had given up hope of any visitors, Dr. Gros phoned. He said Adriana was in bed with a migrane and wouldn't be able to come and see Misiá Elisa. But she sent her her warmest greetings and said to tell her that she would come to see her one of these days without fail. He wasn't sure whether he would be able to come or not—he had had an urgent call at the clinic which might keep him late. Andrés came to the phone to speak to him.

"You must come, please," Andrés said. "I've got to talk to you. Please come, you mustn't leave me alone. No, no, it doesn't matter when. I'll wait. I'm frightened of spending another night in this house, yes frightened. No, no, I'd rather wait up. It doesn't matter what time it is, I can't sleep anyway."

He sat down in the library to wait.

At about nine that evening Lourdes went to ask him if he wanted anything. There was all that food they had made for the party, she explained, which no one had touched. They ought to phone the Sisters of Mercy the next day to arrange for them to take all the leftovers; in other words, everything. It would be a sin to let such a feast go to waste.

"No," Andrés said." I don't want to eat. The dead don't eat."

"What makes you think you're dead?" Lourdes asked, with such a raucous scream of laughter that Andrés gave a startled jump.

"I just know I am. And you're dead too . . ."

"You're mad, that's all that's wrong with you, Don Andresito. What nonsense! Who ever heard of dead men talking? Ha, ha, ha! Listen, will you need me for anything? Because Rosario and I thought we'd give the señora a little party, just the two of us . . ."

"Go ahead, go ahead."

"We thought it would cheer her up, you see. Imagine— people being so ungrateful, not remembering to come and see her today! Even Don Carlitos, who would have thought it!"

"He is coming later. I shall wait for him here."

Estela had been invited, but she excused herself from

coming to the little party. She felt a little feverish, she said, and asked her aunt if she could sleep downstairs in Rosario's room while the party was going on.

"They've got no energy, these young people nowadays," Rosario murmured, wrapping herself in the long white boa. She picked up the punch bowl and went up to Misiá Elisa's room behind Lourdes, who had already gone up with the spangled dress and the crown of silver flowers, an extraordinary floral diadem.

They found the old woman asleep, with her head lolling back on a cushion, but her eyes were half open.

"Poor thing, she's asleep. Don Andrés must have worn her out saying all those horrible things to her," Lourdes exclaimed.

They put all the things they were carrying down on the dressing table. Then, while the old lady slept on, they rushed about making the room look suitable for a coronation. They ranged the vases of flowers around Misiá Elisa and scattered some white petals at her feet. Then Lourdes concealed some lamps among the flowers so that they lit up Misiá Elisa's face. Rosario tied bows and streamers to her walking stick. From time to time they would each take a sip of the punch to make sure the ice had not watered it down too much as it melted. It really was delicious. The lighting made Misiá Elisa look unearthly, isolating her in an illuminated niche of flowers in the midst of the darkened room. She was still asleep. Her sleep was punctuated by a rhythmical little snoring sound at the back of her throat. She was alive.

"How pretty! She looks like a little girl with those painted cheeks!" Rosario cried.

"Now?" Lourdes asked excitedly. "Shall we start now?"

"Wait, we have to have music."

"Turn on the radio."

"No, the señora doesn't like modern music. What happened to that nice gramophone of Don Ramón's which the señora liked so much?"

"I know. It's kept in the bottom of the cupbard in Estela's room, right here."

Lourdes got the gramophone, one of those models with an enormous trumpet decorated with multi-colored flowers. After a lot of inexpert fumbling, they managed to get the machine going and the music started up, a frail thread of melody almost swamped by scratching and chirruping noises.

"How lovely!" the two maids exclaimed.

Lourdes woke the señora.

"Happy saint's day! Happy saint's day!"

"What's the matter, my dear, what's the matter? And the guests? Where are all the guests?"

"What do you want guests for? They're nasty and ungrateful, all of them. Rosario and I are going to crown you queen because you're the loveliest, noblest, best person there is . . ."

"Crown me queen?"

"Yes, and have a party to celebrate too."

"Oh, how nice! Just as I was feeling so sad too, because no one brought me any presents, not even Andrés . . ."

Like the legendary merchants of the East, the maids laid their magnificent gifts at the queen's feet: a dress covered with glittering stars; a long, long, white plumed serpent; a scepter decked with ribbons and streamers; and a crown from which sprang a multitude of silver flowers.

"What lovely things! A dress for a queen! And a crown . . ."

With considerable difficulty, because the señora seemed to have grown much weaker during the day and could no longer control her movements, they dressed her in the spangled gown. The frail silk gauze tore here and there while they were putting it on, and a shower of spangles fell among the petals on the floor, like a shower of stars. The old woman seemed unaware of what was happening. Her eyes were so dim and weak, and her body so enfeebled that Rosario had to close her fingers around the scepter for her.

"I want to wear the boa," Lourdes said.

"*I* want it," Rosario insisted.

The argument rapidly developed into a brawl. They exchanged shouts and blows and chased each other around the furniture, shrieking insults, until at length, after a lot of struggling and tugging, the feather boa snapped in two, leaving each maid with half a boa to wind around herself. A cloud of tiny white feathers hung suspended for a long time in the transfigured atmosphere of the room.

"Now it's all ready for the crowning," Lourdes said.

"She seems a little tired to me, Lourdes. Why don't we give her a drop of punch to revive her?"

"Good idea," said Lourdes, filling up a glass.

"Don't put any fruit in it, it might not agree with her."

"No, of course not. Just plain punch, because she's been having a little trouble with her digestion."

The object of these ministrations refused to open her mouth. Only by inserting a finger into her mouth and forcing it open could Rosario manage to tip a good part of the contents of the glass down the old lady's throat, while she struggled and whimpered like a child. Instead of reviving, though, she passed out.

"Now's the time . . ."

They started up the gramophone again. They stuck flowers in their hair and wrapped themselves in the white feathers. Then the two maids, the one tiny and rotund, the other tall and square, picked up the silver crown and went up to the old woman.

"Long live the queen!" they cried as they placed the crown on her bowed head.

"Long live the nicest, prettiest little queen in the world!"

With repeated curtsies and salaams they backed away from the throne. Lourdes's glasses fell off and Rosario, with a shriek of laughter, kicked them under the dressing table. Lourdes did not bother to look for them.

Then both the maids, light, winged, and weightless as air, began to dance. They strutted about, screaming with laughter, gave little hops, waving, bowing, and genuflecting to each other, waving their hands and arms about, undulating their bodies like nautch-girls and childishly chanting the tune on the gramophone. In their excitement they forgot all about Misiá Elisa, who sat with her head slumped forward and her silver crown askew above her painted face, apparently unconscious.

A little later the two maids flung themselves breathless and sweating on the bed, their hair hanging loose and their feathered decorations in shreds. They chatted and laughed for a moment or two and then fell asleep. The gramophone came to the end of its tune but it went on squeaking and squeaking for a long time. Then the only sound to be heard in the silent room was the breathing of the two old women as they slept. One last tiny white feather fluttered down on Misiá Elisa's hand, through whose bluish veins a little blood still flowed.

20   From where they were standing in the dark street, Mario and René peered through the trees, watching the lighted windows of the house. Bizarre figures, dancing

and bowing to each other, appeared in silhouette against the blinds of one of the second-floor windows. They could also hear music.

"Hell of a party they're having up there!" René exclaimed in a nervous, irritable voice.

They had had to change their plans at the last minute.

"We'll just have to kid the girl along. We'll tell her you love her and we're only doing it for her, and that we're going up north till the fuss dies down and we'll send her money later so she can come and join us. But not right away, it will have to be some months later, when the fuss has died down. Otherwise we'll be in the shit. That way she gives us the key without a word, and then you don't send her a cent so you can have a good time on your own. I'll show you how to live, don't you worry. And she won't be able to say anything when the old girl kicks the bucket and they find out about the robbery, because if she says it was us they'll take her in as an accomplice anyway, and it won't be so easy to get hold of us by then because with any luck we'll be in Buenos Aires. Then it'll be into the clink with her, as an accomplice."

When they got off the bus, René threw the tickets away with an impatient gesture and his hand closed around Mario's elbow like a vice as he led him toward Misiá Elisa's house. They had arrived early for their rendezvous with Estela. Prowling like caged beasts up and down the sidewalk outside the house, they went over and over the details of their unsavory plans. René asked Mario for the time so often that Mario ended by losing his temper.

"What do you keep asking me the time for, you big shit?" he shouted. "Didn't you know I sold the watch to go and get you out of jail?"

Estela came a little late. She listened, calm and withdrawn, to the two men as they stammered in their eagerness to explain their plan to her. She closed her eyes to block out every sensation except the pressure of Mario's warm hand on hers. When the brothers had finished, she looked up serenely at Mario and said: "But you do love me?"

René's fingers crushed his brother's elbow. Mario was frightened.

"Yeah, of course," he said.

Estela sighed, then said: "All right . . . then."

And she went back into the house to find the key to the cupboard, which was kept in her aunt's apron pocket.

"The silly bitch swallowed that all right," René said, laughing.

Mario laughed too, and repeated the word *bitch* over and over with gloating deliberation. He hoped it would help dissolve the last ties that bound him to Estela and suppress the tremor in his belly and all along his nerves and muscles, as if everything inside him were floating about, weightless. He gritted his teeth, trying to fight back the trembling. He had to do something quick, something that would stiffen his resolution. It was too late to back out now—anyway, this wasn't the moment to quit. After all, it wasn't as though any of this were really his or René's fault. It was Estela who was to blame for everything, and Dora and the kids, and this poverty, which meant he had had to give up a good job at the Emporium to go and find René, and the lost watch, and this urgent, suffocating need to run away from it all before he could even hope to aspire to the good things of life, things which the people in that house in front of him had in overflowing abundance; all this was to blame, not him. Anyway, even if he and René were at fault, what did it matter? Or the police, and his self-respect slowly rotting away during the years in a stinking cell—that didn't matter either, not a damn! He had to take a chance and prove himself, now or never. Besides, this was hardly the moment

for thinking things over, because this was the only way left
for him.

It did not take long for Estela to come out this time. She
gave Mario the key, and he felt a redoubled sense of urgency
as his hand closed over the cold metal.

"But it may not be possible . . ." Estela whispered.

Mario and René, who had been about to start for the
house, froze in their tracks.

"Don Andrés is downstairs, and he isn't going to bed till
much later," she explained.

"You'll have to take him to some room with you and keep
him there so he doesn't hear anything," Mario said quickly.

He ground his teeth in the effort to forget everything,
everything but his poverty and the woman giving birth in
the street while he ran away. He had to be strong enough for
anything, even making Estela do what he had just suggested, so he could keep on running, blindly running and
running . . .

"But how?"

"Come on! The old fool likes you, doesn't he? Well, all
you have to do is get him into some room with you and keep
him busy there till we've done the job."

"No."

When she refused, René seized her so roughly by the
shoulders that it hurt. The two brothers backed her against
the wall. She could feel their labored breathing and the
throbbing pulse in the hand with which René was bruising
her shoulder.

"No," Estela repeated, more firmly.

At this, they thrust up closer, and the silence generated
by the warm bodies deepened and shaped itself into a threat.
Estela moaned, almost too faintly for them to catch what
she was saying:

"He makes me . . . feel sick."

"You'll have to choke it down then," Mario exclaimed in a voice that sounded like a shout, it held so much suppressed savagery, but was in fact hardly louder than a whisper. "So he makes you feel sick? Well, how do you think *I* feel, having to steal? Eh? And I'm only doing it for you, you silly bitch, so we can be happy. Don't give me that line about feeling sick. You've got to do something to help if you want to come with me. Otherwise I'll just leave you alone to look after the kid. What sort of a lady do you take yourself for, anyway? Makes her sick, she says! So we have to do all the dirty work while she stands around doing nothing because helping might make her sick! Well, I'm not buying that, do you hear? All you have to do is lead the old guy on a little and get him to go into another room with you till we've finished, even if he does make you sick!"

He could hardly breathe. Estela was looking at the ground. Her love, as great as it had ever been, hung from a thread, and this thread could snap: it was not very strong and the weight it bore was very heavy.

"Tell me you love me," she asked Mario.

The simplicity with which she put this request left Mario speechless. He felt like taking the soft round neck in his fingers and throttling it till the bones cracked and his hands were steeped in warm blood. Just then he felt René's ring bite warningly into the arm which René was holding.

"Yes," he said, but the syllable seemed to stick in his throat.

Estela had them follow her into the garden and hide among some shrubs outside one of the lighted windows. They saw Andrés walk from the hall into the library, sit down for a moment or two and take a drink, then another longer one, get up again and start pacing to and fro between the hall and library, passing through the drawing room and

the anteroom, and finally return and fling himself down on
one of the sofas. As Mario watched these comings and
goings, the flutter in his belly spread so that he was trembling all over when Estela told them they must watch
through that window to see when she took the master off
with her, and only then enter the house. When she had gone,
Mario turned and was sick into some dried-up lobelias, from
sheer fright.

A moment later Mario saw Estela going into the library,
where Andrés had just sat down with a book. She picked
up a magazine from the floor and rearranged the flowers in
one of the vases as though trying to put off the evil moment
as long as possible. The man's eyes fastened on her at once,
hungrily, and his formerly irresolute manner crystallized
into an attitude of desire.

"No!" Mario exclaimed, very low.

He was frightened. He had not reckoned with the lust in
the man's eyes as they slid over Estela's body, or the suppressed longing in those thin, hairy fingers gripping the
arms of his chair. Then the girl turned and faced Don
Andrés, who said something to her. Then he touched her
hand. The relationship established between these two
seemed so obscene to Mario that once again he muttered:
"No . . . no."

And he jumped up, not even stopping to think that he
could be seen through the library window. Estela fell back
a step, and Don Andrés, still staring at her and talking to
her, bent toward her.

"No . . . no . . . !"

René pulled Mario down in a fury. The boy seemed on
the point of rushing in to rescue Estela. Mario struggled
and struggled to escape from René's steely grip. Then a
sudden, unexpected blow stunned him and after that he just
sat on the ground, his head in his hands, weeping. The

memory of that first evening with Estela on the hillside
came back to him, and how they had lain together side by
side, counting the birds wheeling overhead in the sunset
glow. And the quiet miracle of the time he had worked
at the Emporium, when the simplest things, like the feel
of the watch on his wrist, or the prospect of an hour or
two with Estela in a doorway or under a street light,
meant happiness. Mario groaned as he crouched there on
the ground, confused, afraid, repentant. He did not see
his brother avidly watching what was going on in the library.

"What's the bitch waiting for? We haven't got all night."

The man inside was standing now, facing Estela. He
did not take hold of her but stood very close, so that their
bodies almost touched, and murmured something to her
very seriously and with an air of considerable agitation.

"Dirty old bastard," René remarked.

Estela left the room, followed by Don Andrés.

"Now," said René.

Mario stood up and looked through the window.

"Where is she? Where did they go?" he asked, still tearful.

"Stop that crying, will you! If you ask me, there's only
one man around here and that's me! Now look, if you don't
do exactly what I tell you from now on, I'll kill you, do you
hear? I'll kill you! What are you crying about, anyway,
didn't you see how the girl was eyeing the old man? Now
shut up. And follow me."

Mario had turned to wax in René's hands. The chaos
inside him as emotions dissolved only to re-form and dissolve all over again was such as to numb his brain and
prevent him from knowing his true feelings. He allowed himself to be led toward the back door. The kitchen smelled of
liquor and sweets.

"The party," René whispered.

As instructed, they passed through the doors Estela had left ajar and found themselves in a little passage leading into the dining room, where the cupboard could be seen gleaming dully. A great feeling of peace, as if he were at last to be relieved of a suffocating weight, spread through René. In twenty minutes, perhaps less, the job would be done, and he would be able to step out of the shadows into the sun, a free man and master of his own fate, a long long way from Dora, a conqueror who has only shed his burdens at the cost of countless sacrifices to enable himself at length to expand, grow, live the full life. His fears vanished. The calm economy of his movements was dedicated to a marvelously precise, definite end. If anyone were to get between him and the contents of that cupboard now, he thought, he would be able to kill that person quite coolly.

Meanwhile in the library, Estela, coming a little closer than usual, had asked Don Andrés if there was anything he required. If not, she would like permission to go to bed. He stood up as if to read the invitation which the girl, in her embarrassment, was trying to keep hidden, imprisoned within herself. When Estela went into the Turkish smoking room which led off the library, a dark place in which mother-of-pearl inlaid tables and glass narghilehs shone faintly, Andrés followed her.

Here was this being who haunted every corner of his shabby thoughts, actually offering herself to him! Oh, it didn't matter that she did so in a coarse, brazen way which deprived the offer of the last vestiges of the poetry for which he had once hungered! Once his throat was no longer parched with thirst, he would find some way of changing all this ugliness into tenderness, the tenderness he carried within him intact and virgin, ready to be given away. But not now. There was something more pressing, more urgent, to be done first. As she stood beside the tooled-leather divan, the girl's body seemed to incline toward him across the little space which separated them. Withdrawn but resigned, like an animal which knows it can no longer defend itself, she was still, nonetheless, offering herself to him. In a moment he would be stroking those moist, pink, crumpled palms and those palms would be caressing him, yielding up their secrets and their mysterious power to him. He needed them and was determined to have them, those palms of hers. He realized now that it is only the incomplete being, the one who wants and desires, who is alive. The self-sufficient are stone, objects incapable of growth or death or increase in any but the most mechanical sense, because to need is of the very essence of life. Then Andrés Abalos uttered the question in which he conjugated his entire self, all his years of solitude and self-sufficiency, all his years of being a stone. The answer would be his sentence.

"Do you love me, Estela?"

Estela said nothing.

As if in revenge for this silence, which left him with nothing but animal lust, Andrés flung himself on Estela, pulling her against his sweating, shaking body and covering her lips with his burning ones.

A dolorous void of revulsion opened up within her. She wanted to thrust off this withered body, which smelled rankly of alcohol and desire, but it held her so that she could not get free. She pushed with open palms against the flaccid muscles of his chest just where the dressing gown had fallen open, baring his nipples. He made her sick, as she had told Mario.

"Do you love me?" Andrés asked again.

"No, no!" Estela cried, unable to restrain herself.

Andrés's mouth devoured the girl's lips. In the darkness of this kiss something blazed, suddenly, like a flash of lightning within her. She felt disgust, but not at Don Andrés's poor body, or his pathetic famished kiss. She was disgusted by other, more important things. By the lack of respect, the human dignities defiled, and above all by the way Mario was using her, exploiting the love she had so trustingly given him, without a thought for her feelings, exposing her, sullying her. The wounded pride of the human being betrayed flamed up suddenly in her belly as if to destroy this child which was growing there. The black hand of evil had touched them all, they were all lost and bewildered in their despairing solitude, and evil had taken advantage of this to approach each one of them by a different path.

But she wasn't going to put up with this disgust a moment longer!

The feeling of nausea which burst up in her was so overpowering that she bit savagely at the lips pressed over hers. Her courage had suffused her with light which made everything clear, and as she saw the look of astonishment, mortification, and pain with which Andrés raised a hand to his mouth, a tremor of pity led her to touch the man's hand for a moment as if to try and relieve the pain in some way. What difference did it make that he was a gentleman and she was nothing but a peasant girl whose mother had given her away? She had to save herself, save Mario by getting him away from René, and punish René.

"Señor," she cried unhesitatingly, "you are being robbed. They are stealing all the silver from the cupboard."

Dazed, Andrés covered the shame of his mouth with his hand, unable to take in anything but his own pain. When Estela ran out of the Turkish room, he fell back on the divan, giddy and bewildered, laughing wildly, his eyes blurred by tears.

Estela threw open the hallway door. The two stooping

figures dropped all the silver objects they were carrying and began a terrified flight in the direction of the kitchen. When Mario saw that it was Estela, he stepped forward, not knowing whether to embrace her or punish her for the alarm her appearance had thrown them into.

"They're coming," Estela said, quite calmly. "I told them you were stealing Misiá Elisa's things."

René, who had begun picking up the silver, dropped it once more in a mixture of rage and panic and struck Estela hard in the face. The brothers dragged her through the kitchen and out into the garden. Estela struggled, crying out: "No, no . . . don't do anything to me, please . . . no, Mario, no . . ."

Outside, René took her by the throat and forced her back against the wall. The sound of his furious gasping breath and the pressure of his hands on her throat drove every sensation but panic out of the girl. René started to bang her head against the wall.

"Bitch! What's your game, you fucking bitch? Take that, you bitch!" he shouted. "Take that! You thought you'd fuck us up? Now take that! But you'll find you're going to end up in a much worse mess than any of us, you wait! Bitch, bitch!"

He banged and banged her head against the wall. In his hate he forgot the danger of being discovered, and he wept as he went on punishing and destroying this creature who had dared to topple his hopes. He had to hit her and hit her. Unleash the vengeful wrath of his heavy limbs upon her while his incandescent, odd-colored eyes glittered with tears in the darkness. He kept repeating, like a groan: "What did you do it for? Why did you do it, bitch? Take that . . ."

Mario was struggling too, not quite clear whether he wanted to free the girl, hit her himself, or hit his brother. Finally René released her as the awareness of danger made him freeze, and Estela dropped to the ground, unconscious.

"Come on, we'd better go before I kill her," René said.

Mario stared at Estela's bloody face and wide-open, perhaps already sightless, eyes.

"Come on, stupid," René repeated, taking Mario's arm.

Brusquely, Mario shook off René's grip. Like someone kicking an animal to make sure it's dead, he kicked Estela, who moaned.

"Come on, shit, they'll catch us," René repeated.

Mario had bent over to shake Estela, and didn't hear. At this point René realized what his brother did not yet know. Finding himself abandoned, alone, he struck savagely at Mario.

"You'll have to answer for this too, you bastard!" he said thickly.

And he turned and fled from the shower which had begun to fall.

Mario lifted Estela, not sure whether he was going to punish her some more or what. He made her stand up and started to push and propel her across the garden made murky by the rain. She staggered forward like a sleep-walker, with a blood-smeared face, not hearing the boy's insults. Her legs threatened to collapse under her. But deep down in this dark night of physical pain there was a spark that might suddenly be kindled into light, the proud knowledge of her victory. They went out into the street. Mario took one last look at the house, its outline smudged by the rain. There was a light burning on the ground floor, and another, fainter one on the floor above. He had to get away quickly, far away! He gave Estela a push to make her walk in front of him, and then another and another, because if she lagged behind, she might fall and he wouldn't be able to go back for her. They crossed several streets under a

pall of rain which gradually began to wear thinner. A little
farther on, Mario wiped Estela's face with a rag.

The pair lost themselves in the city, looking for shelter,
for a place somewhere, they didn't know where, in which
to find refuge.

21   Andrés went on laughing for a while, then
suddenly fell silent. He sat up on the divan.

How did Estela know that it was precisely the silver in
the cupboard which was being stolen? She must be an accomplice. Knowing his weakness for her, she had made use
of it to get him out of the way and conceal the robbery. Of
course. It was not passion, even of the basest kind, nor
curiosity, nor the tedium of this great house full of old
people which had led her to provoke him into seducing her.
She had been making use of him, nothing more.

Suddenly a ray of panic tore through the darkness which
shrouded Andrés's mind, piercing to his very depths, as
though the maid servant's sharp teeth biting his lips had
finally severed the infinitely frail artery of his life. He was
no longer a living person, or a man. He was just a thing,
matter poised before its return to the void, where there is
neither time nor duration. In a few years he must die, and
the cessation of this individual consciousness which clearly
isolated him from other objects would also be the end of
what some people know as the soul. Then in a little time
the worms would have reduced his body, locked in its cold
coffin, and with it all the material signs of his individuality,
to dust, leaving only a little heap of rubbish and a few

yellowing bones. Years and centuries. After that his coffin, tired of preserving the unity of these poor remains of his, would rot too and mingle its substance with the indifferent earth. Years, centuries, millennia, millennia without end.

The city where his remains were buried would be wiped from the face of the earth, and much later, when all was inanimate matter and no trace of the human race could be found, the planet itself would probably explode and return to the dust of chaos.

No, it was too horrible! Anything rather than stare at the black horror of such a future without the defenses of a living past to strengthen oneself with!

When Estela bit him, she thereby denied him the right to live even a little, even artificially and belatedly. For him now the years to come would be a gradual drawing near to the terrifying void, the slow, step-by-step approach as each minute, each hour, each year came to an end, of the atrocious sentence of extinction.

Or had he merely imagined that Estela bit him? What a wonderful relief it would be if all these horrors were simply hallucinations, like those his grandmother experienced! Estela and that mad planet whirling through time and refusing to make room for him . . .

Suddenly he heard the noise of countless metal objects clattering to the ground. He began to laugh again and stood up.

"They're stealing . . ." he told himself.

He set off toward the dining room. As he opened the hallway door, he caught sight of all the silver Mario and René had abandoned in the terror of their flight.

"Thieves!" he exclaimed.

He knelt down to pick up the silver, replacing each piece with meticulous care in the cupboard. As he examined them one by one, the memories they evoked gradually replaced his painful thoughts. The silver pheasants which the Brazilian ambassador had presented to his grandfather. His mother's dinner service. The twin platters which, according to the family legend, had been part of the plate of a president of the Republic in the previous century. Quietly and lovingly he put every piece back in its proper place and checked that none were missing.

In that case, there couldn't have been a robbery. What had put this idea of a robbery into his head then? What and why?

"Ah, yes, that was what she said after she bit me. But what kind of thieves are these who don't steal anything? Ah, I have it! The robbery was a hallucination on my part. There hasn't been a robbery at all. Lourdes didn't shut the cupboard door very well and it opened under the weight of the stuff inside and the silver fell out on the floor. I imagined the whole thing, just as my grandmother imagines that people are stealing her tortoise-shell combs and her gloves. Although it's possible they took something from one of the other rooms . . ."

He made a thorough inspection of all the rooms, and when he had satisfied himself that nothing was missing, he flung himself down on the red plush ottoman in the hall.

"Of course," he said to himself, "I'm going mad like my grandma. What about Estela?"

He answered himself: "She'll be asleep in her room, as she is every night. She must have been quietly asleep for two or three hours now. I haven't seen her all evening. And there I was, imagining that I held her in my arms and that she kissed me and told me she loved me!"

As he reached this conclusion, he was invaded by a feeling of great peace. At last, in admitting and accepting his madness, he was able to escape from all responsibility, even from having to distinguish between the real and the unreal.

Perhaps death itself would finally prove to be nothing but a horrifying fiction. Madness then was a liberation, the great escape! He had always been mad, nothing but a shadow. He smiled placidly.

He was still smiling and sitting on the ottoman when Lourdes and Rosario came tiptoeing down from Misiá Elisa's room, leaning on each other, the tattered boas still wrapped around them and flowers and bows in their hair.

"Why are you so cheerful, Don Andresito?" Lourdes asked.

"Why? Why not? As you see, I couldn't be happier. But you seem to have been enjoying yourselves too . . ."

"Yes, we've been throwing a little party for Misiá Elisita. You should have seen how pretty it all looked. We crowned her with a little crown of silver flowers and dressed her in a spangled dress, and we danced and everything, I wish you could have seen it! But then it got a little late and we went to sleep for a little while."

"Lord, what a pair of lunatics! But why didn't you invite me? I could have worn my top hat and Spanish cape. And I've been so bored, nothing's happened all evening."

"But you said you wanted to wait down here for Don Carlitos. Hasn't he come yet? What a time to go visiting respectable houses! Well, I'm going to bed, I'm worn out and I've got a splitting headache. Come on, Rosario. See? She's half asleep. Good night, Don Andresito."

"Good night, Lourdes. Good night, Rosario."

"Good night, señor."

As Andrés watched them weaving and staggering and finally disappearing through the door to the servants' quarters, he pondered: "Is this another hallucination? It must be. The things I keep imagining! What, Lourdes drunk and wrapped in my grandmother's white boa . . . ha, ha, ha!"

The arrival of Carlos Gros interrupted his laughter.

"What's the matter?" the doctor asked.

"With me? Nothing. Why should there be? There's just been a robbery."

"A robbery? Is that why you're laughing? I should call the police if I were you . . ."

Andrés got up from the ottoman and shouted angrily: "You don't believe me? You think I'm mad, do you? You think I'm imagining robberies, like my grandmother? If you don't believe me, go and look in the cupboard where the silver is kept, in the hallway beside the dining room. They took everything, the pheasants, everything, everything. They didn't leave a thing. Go and see if you don't believe me . . ."

Carlos went and found everything in perfect order. When he got back, he said: "But it all seems to be there . . ."

"What?" Andrés shrieked. "What do you think then, that I'm imagining things, seeing visions? I suppose you think I'm stark staring mad . . ."

As he said this, he felt a distinct pleasure in cutting his last ties with reality. If he could succeed in persuading everyone, and particularly a doctor like Carlos, that he was mad, well then he would be mad, and none of those horrors could touch him and nothing which had happened that night was real.

"Don't you believe me, idiot? Don't you believe me? You think I'm mad, don't you, that I've gone out of my mind? Tell me, don't be afraid to tell me . . ."

"No, of course I don't, of course not. Calm down, Andrés. Sit down. Of course they took all the silver . . ."

"And I suppose you won't believe me either when I tell you that Estela gave herself to me tonight and told me she loved me? I can see you don't. Very well then. Go into the Turkish room and see if I'm not telling the truth. Go and see Estela, she's sleeping right there on the divan where we made love. Why don't you go? Do you think it's another lie, a figment of my imagination? Or have you got such a low opinion of me that you don't believe even a maid servant would look at me? Eh? Answer me . . ."

Andrés, his eyes streaming with tears and his lips frothing a little, advanced threateningly toward Carlos.

"Wait, sit here," the doctor murmured placatingly. "I'm going to look."

If Carlos claimed, on his return, that Estela was asleep on the divan in the Turkish room, it would be a sign that the doctor accepted his insanity, because it would be a lie. Estela wasn't there. It would be a lie, the sort of lie one tells the seriously ill or those condemned to death.

"Well? Are you convinced?"

"Yes, she was sleeping on the divan . . ."

This was his sentence, the proof that was needed. The matter was settled and there was no need to suffer any more. Estela had given herself to him and she loved him. Death was just a fable, a bogeyman to frighten naughty children with, and his life would go on forever. Then, quite calmly, he began to talk to Carlos.

"And do you know? Rosario and Lourdes and I gave my grandmother a marvelous party, she was so sad because no one came to see her on her saint's day, poor thing. Not even you, or Adriana. You didn't come because she's an old woman and her life is of no importance. She might as well have died thirty years ago, when she started to go mad. But you know quite well she's not mad, she's the one person who knows the truth. She's the saintliest, meekest woman alive. Don't you find her meek, Carlos?"

"Yes, indeed . . ."

"And do you know what we did?"

"No . . ."

"We crowned her because, well, you know how she's always saying she's a princess, and she wouldn't lie! We danced all night. And we dressed up as magicians and fairies and dragonflies and young people. I put on my Spanish cape and with the help of a little trick I know I produced a live rabbit out of Grandfather Ramón's hat. A live rabbit covered with green spots. Look, look, there he is, over there, running to his hiding place under the buhl table! And you know something? It was that magic spell of mine which won over Estela. Don't you believe me? Don't be afraid to say so if you don't. You know I won't mind . . ."

"Yes, yes, I believe you . . ."

Hearing these words, Andrés sank back against the arm of the ottoman, breathing a sigh of relief and peace. Carlos's words had severed his last obligations toward the world of the living. Everything was rearranging itself into a new bright, clean universe, with its own benevolent laws whose disposition was known to himself alone, and these laws excluded everything painful, humiliating, or ugly.

"It was a charming party, Carlos," he went on. "You should have been there. But I suppose you were busy with one of your love affairs and so you didn't come. There was everything you could imagine, wine, cakes, and lots and lots of people, all beautiful and young . . . and we behaved so well we weren't punished at all . . ."

The description of the party went on for some time. Carlos was thinking that tomorrow, first thing, he would have to call in a panel of doctors to examine this pathetic parody of a human being who had once been his best friend. Perhaps he was mad, perhaps it was no more than a passing crisis. In any event, Andrés had gone into a corner of life from which it was not easy to come out again. Assuming he did come out, sick or not, his life would be very different from now on, the life of an irresponsible being who must be looked after and treated like a delicate child.

Carlos's heart was wrenched by a spasm of pity. This was a farewell to Andrés Abalos the man. Carlos might continue to love him henceforth but no longer as an equal. Because his own life as a man, a doctor, and a father still had a long way to go to reach its fulfillment. Now he must order Andrés to bed, to rest. Tomorrow the specialists would indicate what treatment must be followed, if any.

"Well, Andrés, old man, it's getting late. Time for bed. You look as if you could do with some sleep . . ."

"Yes, yes, I'm just going," Andrés lied. "Lourdes is making up my bed upstairs. She's going to help me to bed tonight because—you know something?—I really am tired, I don't know why . . ."

"Good, well, I should go straight to bed then. Oh, one thing—what was it you wanted to speak to me so urgently about when we were talking on the phone this afternoon?"

"When we talked on the phone? I don't remember telling you to come . . ."

Carlos was about to protest, but recollected himself just in time.

"Ah . . ."

He found it hard to keep back the tears when he thought that outside, in his car, the most beautiful woman he had ever had was waiting for him. He was about to start what promised to be the most wonderful of all his mistakes.

"Good night, Andrés. Go up and get some rest."

"Good night. Love to Adriana and the children. Oh, look, is that the evening paper you've got there? Would you leave it, if you've already read it?"

When Carlos had gone, Andrés put on his glasses and unfolded the paper. Then he laid it aside and went into the library in search of a pair of scissors. He cut the paper into neat squares and made the squares into paper birds like the

ones his grandmother had shown him how to make one cold
rainy winter when he had had to stay in bed with measles,
when he was very, very young.

22   After the storm, the sky over the city
cleared, leaving the air transparently suave. The constellations smiled down in sparkling profusion as if making a gift
of their abundance to the few people looking up at this hour
from streets, balconies, hills, parks, and windows.

In the forlornness of the neighborhood slums, the breeze
found endless distractions. It sent stray sounds—the chink
of a falling coin or some casual conversation—weaving from
block to block to block. And where a dog had passed it
sent the stars hurtling into the depths of an ecstatic puddle
on the sidewalk. Despite the cold, it was pleasant standing
on a corner with one's coat collar turned up, watching the
way the breeze toyed with a sheet of newspaper in the empty
street, wrapping it round a tree trunk, a gutter or a garbage
can, or flattening it against a wall or a dripping wrought-
iron grille.

A great handful of livid lights hung suspended above the
center of the city. Northward, southward, westward the
houses straggled out, becoming poorer and poorer, smaller
and smaller, till at length they were scarcely distinguishable
from the hillside fields. A few people perhaps—a couple in
search of shelter, for instance—might find the gift of a
cloudless sky there.

In a quiet street, in her big ornate house standing in its
moribund garden, Misiá Elisa Grey de Abalos, still wearing

her flowering silver crown, had awakened in her armchair next to the window. But wakefulness and sleep were barely distinguishable in her weakened state. It had not occurred to either Lourdes or Rosario to adjust the pace of the evening's festivities to the strength of a being whom time had rendered infinitely frail. There was barely a flicker of life left in the old woman now, and only the dimmest spark of consciousness. However, she could see the stars through the rain-streaked windows, and having lost the power to distinguish between near and far and seeing nothing but sparkling lights all the way up from the showers of spangles on the floor to the brilliants on her coronation gown, she thought that these were stars too and that she was surrounded by them. Then she supposed that she must already be dead and that she was ascending very gently through the firmament straight to heaven.

She closed her eyes.

She was too exhausted to notice that it was then she died and not before, when she thought she saw herself surrounded by constellations.

A NOTE ON THE TYPE

THE TEXT of this book is set in *Monticello*, a Linotype revival of the original Binny & Ronaldson Roman No. 1, cut by Archibald Binny and cast in 1796 by that Philadelphia type foundry. The face was named Monticello in honor of its use in the monumental fifty-volume *Papers of Thomas Jefferson*, published by Princeton University Press. Monticello is a transitional type design, embodying certain features of Bulmer and Baskerville, but it is a distinguished face in its own right.

Composed, printed, and bound by
The Haddon Craftsmen, Scranton, Pennsylvania
Typography and binding design by
GEORGE SALTER